I0604520

Make No Mistake

The Novel

Julie Wise

Library of Congress Cataloging-in-Publication Data has been applied for.

ISBN 978-1-0695255-0-5 (Paperback)
ISBN 978-1-0695255-1-2 (eBook)

For all women, past, present and future.
I see you.
I hear you.
I stand with you.

One day, an army of grey-haired old women may quietly
take over the world.
~ Gloria Steinem

Chapter One

Maggie's world shattered on a quiet Saturday in June when she stepped onto her front porch. As she pulled the morning newspaper from the mailbox, a headline caught her eye.

"Oh…my…God," she said, sinking down on the top step. "It's begun."

BREAKING NEWS. In a late-night session, the Supreme Court voted to strike down Roe v. Wade. According to a statement released by newly appointed Chief Justice Daniel Power, the ruling gives state legislatures the ability to restrict or eliminate access to abortion. In states with existing trigger bans, abortion is illegal effective immediately, overturning nearly fifty years of women's rights. Details to follow.

Maggie dropped the paper. Hundreds of women's faces paraded through her mind, women she had helped, women who had helped her. All that work. All those years. Gone, like dust in the wind, because of a few white men in black robes.

She headed back into the house, tossed the paper on the kitchen counter and called her best friend.

"Ali, drop everything. Did you see the paper?"

"Yes, Maggie."

"Since when does the Supreme Court meet on a Friday night? I mean, we saw the signs, but I never thought they'd go through with it."

Silence.

"Al? You know what this means, right? It's a declaration of war. Against women. We have to do something."

"We, Mags? Count me out this time. Jerry's starting chemo next week, my dad's being assessed for Alzheimer's this aft, and I'm run off my feet trying to help Abby with the twins."

"I know but…"

"There's no 'but' here, Maggie. We aren't twenty years old anymore. I don't have the energy to take a stand. Heck, I can barely keep myself upright most days. And you, have you forgotten what it was like? The death threats? Being afraid to walk past your kitchen window for fear someone would take a shot at you? I can't believe we're even having this conversation."

"Ali, this could affect your granddaughters. They'll be teenagers in just a few years. It's about their future. Their rights, as young women. Somebody needs to do something."

Maggie slammed a pot on the stove, sloshed in some water and oatmeal, and flipped on a burner.

She heard Alicia sigh.

"Okay, Maggie," Alicia said, "maybe somebody does need to do something, but does it have to be you? You're retired now. And you've got some serious health issues. Are you willing to put your life on the line again?"

Maggie stirred the pot.

"Yes, I am. If we all stand back and say, 'Somebody else will take care of it', it's game over. We've been here before, Al. This is just the beginning and it's a slippery slope. If they get away with this, there'll be no stopping them."

"Aren't you being a tad dramatic?"

Maggie banged the spoon down, splattering oatmeal across the stove.

"This isn't just about women, Ali. Don't you get it? If men like Daniel Power are allowed to twist and bend the rules of our society to meet their needs, we all suffer."

"Maggie, I've gotta go. Promise me you won't do anything foolish. You sound like your old self, full of spit and vinegar. I love that about you, but times have changed. Let the next generation deal with this."

Maggie opened the drawer of her night table and pulled out a worn notebook with a black leather cover. She sat on the edge of the bed, leafing through the pages until she found what she was looking for.

She tapped her fingers on the open page, staring at words she had written during nights of rage, days of hesitation. Smatterings of ideas scattered across pages and years of her life.

The phone rang.

"Hey," Maggie said.

"Okay, listen," Ali said, "because I'm only going to say this once."

"Right," Maggie said.

"And after this phone call, I'm not going to speak of this ever again. Got that?" Alicia paused and added, "I have two words for you. Book club."

Maggie was silent.

Alicia groaned. "Plan B, Maggie. Remember?"

"Of course, I remember. It was my idea."

"Well, just thinking maybe the time has come to use it. I know you, and you're not going to let this go. So that's my contribution. You're welcome, by the way."

The phone clicked.

Maggie smiled.

A few hours later, Maggie sat back and studied the email she was about to send. Blind copied to a network of over five hundred people in the United States and around the world. From an anonymous email address she had hoped she would never need to use.

Book Club.

Just two words.

Enough to launch a revolution.

She clenched her jaw and gazed out the window. In the golden glow of the midday sun, kids ran back and forth in a game of street hockey. A roar echoed off houses whenever one team scored; arms and sticks held high as the players surrounded the one who had made the winning shot. Solidarity, she thought. It's the only way.

She pressed Send.

Chapter Two

Daniel Power was having a rough day. His assistant had erased the notes for his acceptance speech. He was stuck at the side of the road while his driver replaced a flat tire on the limousine. And his mother was on the phone.

He settled into the seat cushions and calmed his voice.

"Hello, Mother."

"Yes, Mother."

"No, Mother."

"Of course, I remember it's your birthday this weekend, Mother. You'll be 100 years old. That's something to celebrate, isn't it?"

He listened for a while.

"Yes, the Mayor will be there. Yes, the President is sending a special proclamation, and I will do my best to drop by after my meetings."

He glanced at his watch and peered out the window. The driver gave a thumbs-up and scrambled to his feet, wiping his forehead.

"Yes, Mother. Whatever you wish. Your happiness means everything to me. If you want a larger suite, I will arrange it. No, don't worry about the cost. I can handle it."

He waited.

"Yes, I know, Father always took good care of you. I do try my best, Mother. Have a good evening. I have to go now."

Daniel tossed the phone on the leather seat. He rolled down the window and yelled at his driver.

"Get a move on. I don't have much time."

As soon as the limousine pulled up in front of his house, Daniel dashed in the front door and up the stairs, pausing at the top to catch his breath.

"Car's waiting," he shouted.

He tossed his keys on the hall table and strode into his bedroom, pulling off his tie and jacket and tossing them on the floor. His tuxedo was not hanging on the hook in his walk-in closet. He rifled through his suit rack, searching. In no time, rumpled shirts covered the carpet, ties lay scattered, and several jackets hung precariously over a chair.

"Madeline! Where the hell is my tux?"

"Everything's on your bed," his wife called from across the hall.

Daniel grumbled as he stomped back into the bedroom to dress. By the time he attached the cummerbund, he was breathing hard. He sat on the edge of the bed and reached for his Italian leather shoes.

"Everything to your satisfaction?" Madeline asked from the doorway, her slight figure backlit by the hall chandelier.

Daniel glanced up. Madeline sported tight black jeans and a dark long-sleeved shirt. Her blonde hair was tied back in a short ponytail.

"You're not even dressed yet? The car's out front. What are you waiting for?"

She smiled and turned away.

"I'm not going with you."

Daniel leaped to his feet and ran after her, shoelaces flying. He grabbed her right arm and twisted her around, shoving her against the wall.

"You good-for-nothing bitch! This is my big night and you're not going to spoil it."

He shook her shoulders, sending her head backward with a thud.

"It's not like you actually have a choice. You are my wife, and you will do as I say."

He could feel his heart tapdancing in his left temple as he watched her face. Damn woman didn't even blink. He cursed and shoved her away.

"Go get dressed."

He watched her steady herself against the wall and walk into her bedroom. The door closed sharply.

"You have two minutes," he yelled. "Be downstairs or there'll be hell to pay."

Madeline slipped her phone out of her back pocket.

Chinatown station in 5, she texted.

What???
Be there
K

She grabbed her backpack and a duffel bag and dropped them to the ground through the open window. Pulling a black wig and a ball cap over her hair, she stepped out onto the ledge. She inched her way toward the trellis and climbed down, clutching the woody branches of wisteria, hoping they would hold her weight.

When she reached the ground, Madeline grabbed the bags and headed out the back gate into the alley. It started to rain. She picked up her pace and followed the lane to the main road.

Melting into the crowd, she disappeared down the stairs into the metro station.

Daniel rapped his knuckles on the door a couple of times.

"Time to go."

No response.

He tried the door handle. It was locked.

He pounded on the door.

"Let me in, damn it. Or you'll be sorry."

Silence.

He grabbed his key chain from the hall table. His hand shook as he shoved a key into the lock. The door opened with a click. He stormed into the room.

Empty.

Rage scorched his face. She would pay for this.

He checked the bathroom, flinging back the shower curtain. In her walk-in closet, he yanked all the dresses off hangers to see if she was hiding in behind. He struggled down to his hands and knees and looked under the bed. Just boxes and dust.

Then he saw the open window.

He ran over and leaned out, expecting to see her broken body in the garden below. He raced down the stairs and out the back door, eyes darting in all directions.

Nothing.

He ran his fingers through his thinning hair and checked his watch. He could still make it.

On his way through the house, he stopped in front of the large gold mirror in the foyer.

"Forget her," he said, sucking in his belly and adjusting the cummerbund. "You're a fine-looking man. Powerful too. And tonight, that's all that matters."

Nodding to his reflection, he turned and strode out the front door to the waiting limousine.

As the driver pulled away, Daniel banged on the glass partition.

"Can't you go any faster? I'm gonna be late."

He pulled some money out of his wallet and shoved it through the opening in the glass, scattering the bills across the front seat. He sat back and crossed his arms.

"There's more where that came from. Just get me there on time."

The limousine picked up speed.

As they approached the Capitol buildings, Daniel could see all the lights blazing. He gestured at the vibrant glow.

"See that? That's all for me."

The President strolled down the Grand Staircase at precisely eight o'clock. His wife and daughters followed at pre-arranged distance. When he reached the Entrance Hall, he paused, smiling and nodding at the crowd, careful to make eye contact in order of influence.

He beckoned to his wife and daughters to join him. He wrapped his arm around his wife and smiled at his daughters. Cameras clicked and whirred.

"Can we get one of you with Judge Power, Mr. President?"

"Certainly, Jeremy. I'll ask my secretary to locate him."

He heard Ryan's quiet voice in his ear.

"He's not here yet, sir. As soon as he is, I'll bring him over."

Not here? That seemed unusual given that the night was in his honor.

"Just let me know when he arrives," he said.

He turned back to his wife and, sliding his hand down her back, gave her hip a quick squeeze.

"Why don't you and the girls mingle with the guests?" he suggested.

"Of course, Andrew. Whatever you wish."

She gave him a peck on the cheek, and sauntered away, hips swaying. Her red designer gown clung and rippled as she moved.

Third time's a charm, he thought, watching her leave. Too bad she couldn't give him a son. Nothing but miscarriages. Might be time for a change. He made a mental note to discuss his options with Daniel and Frank.

"Sir? Judge Power has arrived," Ryan whispered.

The President turned back to the photographer and smiled.

"Jeremy, I think we can give you that photo now."

The President greeted Daniel with a firm handshake and a clap on the back.

"Danny boy, good to see you. Where's the little woman?"

"Oh, she sends her apologies. Said she wasn't feeling well, female stuff, you know," Daniel said with a wink. "Women – can't live with 'em, can't live without 'em."

They both laughed and turned to face the photographer.

"Just one more, gentlemen. Thank you."

After the final photo, the President took two champagne flutes from a passing tray. He handed one to Daniel and they clinked glasses.

"Here's to the future," the President said.

"Our future," Daniel replied. He dropped his voice and added, "Everything set for Mother's big birthday this weekend?"

The President nodded and murmured, "One hundred years, can't believe the old biddy has lasted this long. Certificate framed; delivery arranged. Anything else?"

"She wants a bigger suite."

"I'll give you cash."

"Sir?" Ryan was back. "It's time to go in for dinner."

"Righto, let's do this."

The President led the way into the State Dining Room. Daniel followed closely behind, nodding at business leaders, attorneys, and statesmen as he passed.

In the doorway, he stopped to savor the view.

At the far end of the vast room, a string quartet played music Daniel didn't recognize. White and gold cloths covered tables encircled by cushioned chairs draped in gold brocade. Crystal wine glasses sparkled in the glow of the massive chandeliers. Daniel straightened his bow tie and stood taller.

The President gestured for him to stand to his right at the head table. Too bad Madeline wasn't here to see it, Daniel thought. His belly clenched in anger. Then he noticed how many women were in attendance. All easier to impress than his wife.

Once everyone was seated, the State Governor walked over to the microphone.

"Thank you for coming," he said. "For the few of you who may not know me, I am Governor Wainsworth. It gives me great pleasure this evening to welcome you to a very special State dinner, hosted by our illustrious President. Tonight, we honor Judge Daniel Power on the occasion of his appointment as Chief Justice of the United States of America. You will be hearing more from him after dinner, and for many years to come."

Chapter Three

Lena slumped against the wall of the Chinatown station; backpack slung over her right shoulder. She had been waiting for twenty minutes. It was rush hour, and she was tired of being jostled.

"Lena, there you are."

"Mom? You said five minutes. And what's with the ball cap and all the black? You goin' Goth?"

"Walk with me, Lena," Madeline said. "We need to take the train on the other side."

"No, wait, you need to tell me what's going on. And what are you doing with my bag?"

Lena grabbed the duffle bag from her mother and planted her feet firmly on the concrete.

"I'm not going anywhere until you explain," she said, arms crossed.

"Not here," Madeline said, glancing around. "C'mon. We have to go."

Lena groaned, picked up her bag and scuffed along behind her mother to the opposite tracks. Three stops later, they climbed the stained concrete stairs in silence to the street. It was pouring rain. Lena sprinted to the entrance of a closed hotel and waited in the one dry spot under the rusty awning. Water cascaded all around, drowning out honking horns and conversations as people dashed by.

"Cut the cloak and dagger routine, Mom. What the hell is going on?"

"Please keep your voice down," Madeline said. "Here's the deal. You can't go home for a while. I packed some clothes in your bag. I know the term is over, so you need to find a way to stay in town until I work something out. Your Dad is…not safe for you to be around right now."

"I don't understand."

"He's involved in something that will change your life, and not in a good way," Madeline said. "He needs you, and me – his happy family – to show up and support his twisted plans. Not happening. Not if I can help it."

Lena studied her mother's face.

"I don't get it," she said.

"You have to trust me on this," Madeline said. "The best thing for you to do is carry on as if we haven't talked. Just go about your life as usual. And if you have to go back home to get anything, go during the day when your father's at work. And take Brad along. Your father won't try anything if Brad's there. I'm serious, Lena. He will stop at nothing to get what he wants."

Lena hesitated and then remembered her father's broken promises. The countless times he'd let her down.

"Okay, whatever," Lena said.

"One more thing," Madeline added. "My cell phone won't work within the hour, so don't try and call me. I will get in touch with you. Just promise me that you will not go back to the house alone for any reason."

Lena rolled her eyes.

"Fine," she grumbled. "I never saw you, we didn't talk, and I'll get Brad to go with me if I go back home. Happy now?"

She let her mother hug her.

"I love you," Madeline whispered. "Remember that. I will be in touch as soon as I can. Oh, and delete those last few texts from me, okay?"

"Will do," said Lena, pulling out her phone. "Love you too, Mom."

She watched her mother step out into the downpour and vanish into the night.

At the corner, Madeline stopped to tug her black rain jacket out of the backpack. She put it on and zipped it up, pulling the hood over her ball cap. She hoisted the backpack onto her shoulder and continued along the sidewalk, dodging puddles as she headed back to the metro station. Four stops later, she got off the train and headed toward the river.

There were fewer people around because of the rain. She passed a fast-food restaurant packed with customers trying to stay dry. A man with a briefcase and a black umbrella hurried toward her, head down. She stepped out of his way and continued on.

The boardwalk along the river was soaked, trees dripping, branches hanging low. She found a bench and set the backpack down. Unzipping the front pocket, she pulled out her cell phone. She checked the messages one more time, turned it off and tossed it as far as she could into the river.

She felt around in her jacket pocket for her new cell phone. No turning back now. She left the river and headed to the bus station.

As the bus rumbled along country roads, Madeline glanced at the nearby passengers. Most had fallen asleep. The woman across the aisle lay with her feet tucked up on the empty seat beside her. In the row behind, a teenager hunched forward, resting his head on his arms. Madeline yawned and dug inside her backpack for a granola bar. It would have to do for now.

She peered through the rain-stained windows. The crescent moon highlighted the silhouette of a silo. She stretched, tugged her cap lower on her forehead and checked her watch. Twenty minutes to go.

She smiled in anticipation.

She skipped down the steps of the bus into the cool night air and waved down a taxi. Ten minutes later, the car pulled up outside a two-story brownstone building. Madeline paid the driver, grabbed her bag and raced up the stairs to her sister's apartment. Daniel would never find her here. He didn't even know she had a sister.

She chuckled as she dropped her backpack in the kitchen and picked up a photo on her way to the bathroom. She pulled the box of gray hair dye out from under the sink and set all her tools on the counter – scissors, hair razor, two old towels, latex gloves, Vaseline, dye brush. She opened the timer on her phone so she could press start when she was ready.

As she brushed her shoulder-length blonde hair, she studied the photo. Max, her twin sister, was in Italy now. All part of the plan.

"Thanks, sis," Madeline said, giving the photo a kiss.

She moved everything off the white tile floor and wrapped a towel around her shoulders, fastening the edges together with a red plastic clothespin. She picked up the scissors and began to cut one side of her hair. When she was finished, she stepped back, glancing between the photo and the mirror. She nodded her approval and shaved the other side of her head.

She applied the toner evenly and set the timer. While she waited, she put the laptop on the kitchen table and started it up. She checked the balance in her new bank account and was delighted to see the amount had increased. Substantially.

"Oh, Danny boy," she crooned, "your money, money's m-i-s-s-ing."

She typed his name into a private search engine and scrolled through the news items. Apparently, he had gone to the event without her. No surprise there. After twenty years of marriage, she knew him well. He had probably stayed overnight at the White House after a few too many drinks. Scanning the internet for her own name, she held her breath. No missing person report. She still had time.

One more item left on the to-do list. The timer sounded. She headed back to the bathroom to apply the dye. After resetting the timer, she returned to the laptop.

Logging in to the bank account she shared with Daniel, she set up donation to the World Organization for Women, an organization she had lobbied for years ago. Long before she met Daniel. Those women had stood by her through some tough times. And now she had the chance to give back, thanks to Daniel's decision to set up a joint account and two others in her name to hide his assets from the tax department.

"That was your first mistake, sweetheart," she said, grinning. "No, actually your first mistake was to underestimate me."

With a few clicks of the mouse, she donated $1 million to the World Organization for Women in the name of Daniel Power, Chief Justice of the United States of America.

Email was next. She had deleted her old account before she tossed her phone into the river. She logged in to the anonymous account she had created two years ago. She typed in a few high-profile media addresses from memory and attached the press release she had written about the donation. It included a few quotes from newly appointed Chief Justice Daniel Power about "the truly admirable work of the women's organization on the occasion of their fiftieth anniversary". She pressed Send.

"Try and worm your way out of this one, Daniel."

Her phone pinged as a new email arrived. Madeline smiled when she saw the subject line: *Book Club*. This is going to be fun, she thought. She shut off the computer and went back to the bathroom.

"I am woman, hear me roar," she sang, fist-pumping the air.

The sun was shining brightly as Madeline headed out to run some errands. She started down the sidewalk, stopped and turned back to the apartment. Once inside, she went straight to the bathroom. She plucked out her contact lenses and tossed them in the garbage. On the night table beside the bed, she found an old pair of her twin sister's red-framed glasses. She put them on and checked herself in the mirror.

Thank goodness our prescriptions are close, she thought. I look just like Max now, gray hair and all.

She locked the apartment door behind her and walked briskly into town. First stop – post office. She selected a padded envelope and slid a new cell phone inside with a brief note. She quickly addressed it and handed it to the postal clerk.

"I want it sent priority mail," she said. "Can I get a tracking number?"

"Yes, of course, ma'am," the young woman said. "One-day, two-day or overnight service?"

"Overnight, please. Thank you very much."

"My pleasure."

As she left the building, Madeline checked one more item off her mental list. Now for groceries.

Browsing through the vegetable bins, Madeline heard a familiar voice behind her.

"Max, when did you get back from Italy?"

Madeline stopped the grocery cart, adjusted her glasses, and pasted a smile on her face as she turned around and saw Lori, an old friend of her sister's. She hoped she could pull this off.

"Just returned a few days ago," she said. "It's good to see you, Lori."

She let herself be wrapped in Lori's bear hug. So far, so good, she thought.

"I almost didn't recognize you, all dressed in black like that. You usually wear such vibrant colors, like a living breathing watercolor painting."

Madeline glanced down at her outfit, silently cursing her sister's fashion sense.

"Yes, well, the airline lost my luggage," she said, thinking quickly "So, I'm down to yoga pants and t-shirts."

"That happened to us last winter when we went away. We did get our bags eventually. The airline even delivered to our door. Hopefully, you'll get your things back soon. Is your lovely niece going to be visiting this summer? I've forgotten her name…Leah, Lena?"

"Lena," Madeline said. "Not sure what her plans are yet. You know what it's like being away at college. Suddenly there are more important things to do than hang out with Auntie Max."

They both laughed.

"You must come by for dinner one night," Lori said. "I'd love to catch up."

"Definitely. I might be heading to the cottage for a bit, but I'll give you a shout when I get back. How's that sound?"

"Looking forward to it!"

Madeline finished her shopping and walked back to the apartment, stopping to look in the window of Judy's Dress Shop. That embroidered denim dress was not as flashy as her sister's usual style, but it would be a good start.

When Lena arrives, she thought, I'll have a lot of explaining to do.

Chapter Four

Daniel snored, waking himself up. Pushing up on one arm, he glanced around and realized he wasn't at home.

"Oh," he groaned, holding his head, and sliding back onto the pillow.

Scenes from the previous night ricocheted through his mind. Champagne and wine during dinner. Lots of it. Speeches. More champagne. After dinner, the President invited a select group of politicians and businessmen to a private party in the Blue Room. Everyone wanted to toast Daniel's new position. He was not one to say no to a drink.

A vague memory of saying goodnight to everyone in the doorway of the Executive Residence; the President insisting that he spend the night.

There was a girl, although he couldn't recall her face. But she made him feel like he was seventeen again.

"You've still got what it takes, you old fox," he muttered.

And somewhere he had a wife.

He sat up abruptly. A lightning bolt of pain whipped through his head.

"Jeezus!" he cried, clutching his forehead.

Where the hell *was* Madeline?

He shuffled his legs to the edge of the bed and began pulling on his clothes. He had to find Madeline. But first, he needed a strong drink. And maybe some coffee.

The President was already in the Family Dining Room, reading the newspaper. He glanced up as Daniel walked in.

"Did you have a good night?" he asked, winking. "I left you a little something on the pillow. I trust you enjoyed…her."

"Like old times," Daniel smirked.

"Let's get down to business then, shall we? Could you close the door? Thank you."

The President poured a cup of coffee and handed it to Daniel.

"Look," he said, "I've been thinking. About Mother."

Daniel sat up, blinking like a confused owl.

"What does Mother have to do with anything?" he asked.

"Danny, she's kept quiet about our family connection for many years. But she's a hundred now. Her mind is going to go one of these days and then she'll be blabbing to anyone who will listen about who you and I really are. We've come so far. We can't risk that. So, here's what I propose. Let her celebrate her big birthday and then she'll pass peacefully in her sleep. No questions asked because of her age."

Daniel slammed his hands on the table.

"What? No. Is this about the money for the suite? I'll take care of it. She's always been good to you, even if she's only your stepmother."

The President raised his hands in mock surrender.

"Okay then, we'll let her be. For now. But if she speaks out, Danny, she's your mother, your problem. Got that?"

Daniel glared at him and gulped down some coffee. The President sat back in his chair and watched him closely.

"We've always been a good team, haven't we?" the President said quietly. "You, me. And Frank."

He smiled as Daniel squirmed in his chair.

"And now we've got it all. Absolute power, where it counts – government, courts, police. Who's the man with the plan, Danny boy?"

Daniel raised his cup and gestured at his stepbrother.

"So, on to other business," the President said. "This new legislation you're working on. I know I should have asked my staff to do the draft but the less they know, the better. Someone's been leaking word to the press, so I've given my aides separate projects to work on and told all of them it's top secret. That frees us up to get this legislation ready to go."

Daniel reached for a bagel.

"I know it's not going to be popular in some sectors," the President continued, "so I'm counting on you to make sure there are no legal loopholes. You already got the decision through the Supreme Court. We control most of the House and Senate. California could be a bit of a problem, but Frank's looking for something good on the governor there. It's a slam dunk."

He mimicked the perfect shot before picking up the coffee carafe. "Refill?"

Daniel held out his cup.

"Of course, it helps that Vice-President Charlton is…indisposed," the President said. "For the foreseeable future. The timing is unfortunate. For him."

Daniel grinned.

"Dan, we have to act quickly, or we'll lose control of our own country," the President added. "I saw stats yesterday that were terrifying. Did you know there's a population explosion happening with Blacks, Hispanics and Asians? Within twenty years, *we'll* be the minority. Can you imagine? We can't let that happen.

"It's white men who've made this country great. Why, if it weren't for us, people would still be living in shacks and shanties. Our forefathers built this country from nothing, and we have to maintain their legacy. That's what this legislation will do – it will protect our people, keep our jobs and communities safe, and uphold strong family values. Am I right?"

Daniel nodded; mouth full of bagel.

"I expect to see the final draft of the legislation on my desk by tomorrow morning. Can you handle it?"

Daniel swallowed quickly. "Of course."

"Okay then, my driver will take you home once you finish eating. It's a pleasure doing business with you, Danny boy."

The President stood, clapped Daniel on the back and strode out of the dining room. He stopped in the doorway and turned back.

"One more thing, could you take a look at the prenup I signed? If I were looking to make a … change, what are my best options?"

The limousine dropped Daniel off in front of his red brick mansion in Kalorama about a mile from the White House. He unlocked the front door and stepped inside.

"Honey, I'm home," he called. His voice echoed through the foyer and along the upper hallway.

"Madeline?"

A cat bounded toward him and rubbed up against his leg.

"Well, Kat, at least you know how to welcome me."

He bent down and rubbed the animal's ears. The cat purred and settled in at his feet.

"Who's a good kitty? Bet she didn't feed you, did she? Typical. Always thinking about herself."

Daniel rummaged around the kitchen, dug out a can of cat food and dumped it into a bowl. He tossed the empty can in the sink and filled another dish with water.

"There you go. Dig in."

He brushed tawny hair off his black pants and headed upstairs to do a quick search.

Everything was the same as the night before. The window in her bedroom was wide open; dresses lay crumpled on the floor, and the edge of the floral duvet was halfway across the mattress where he had tossed it.

He sat down on the edge of her bed, resting his throbbing head in his hands.

"Okay, whatever," he said, pushing himself back onto his feet. "I'll deal with you later. I've got more important things to do."

He went into his bathroom and fumbled in the medicine cabinet. He popped a couple of pain pills into his mouth and washed them down with a shot of bourbon from his stash in the closet.

He pulled off his jacket, bow tie and shirt and dropped them on the floor. She could look after that when she got back. He wasn't going to lift a finger around the house from now on. That was her job.

He grinned as he pulled on jeans and a t-shirt, thinking about the legislation he was writing. *They won't know what hit them, those stupid bitches. We'll show them.*

Humming softly, he headed into his office to get to work.

Chapter Five

Maggie sat up, clutching her throat, tears streaming down her face. She struggled to catch her breath, eyes frantic, heart pounding. Her mind scrambled, surged and fell into a deep pit. C'mon, c'mon, she muttered as she wrapped the blanket around her shaking body.

She rocked back and forth, gulping air as splintered images collided in her mind.

Turning on the light, she forced herself to check under the bed and in the closet. The bedroom window was locked. Drapes closed. She was safe.

She pulled her robe from the end of the bed, threw it on and plodded out to the kitchen barefoot. As she waited for the kettle to boil, she spooned nettle tea into the teapot, and swayed back and forth, watching the moon slice the sky.

She glanced at the clock – 3 a.m. She carried her mug into the living room and set it on the coffee table. Tucking a frayed patchwork quilt around her legs, she leaned back, her eyes focused on the middle of the table. Happiness in a bottle, she thought, reaching for the pale-yellow tablets. Her hand swerved to the side, landing on a book. *Anne of Green Gables*.

"Hello, old friend," she whispered, as she picked it up.

Opening the brittle cover, she stroked the faded inscription with her fingers.

To my "Anne-girl" from her "Diana"

Mags and Ali, bosom friends forever! Christmas 1962

Maggie set the book in her lap and sighed. Maybe Ali was right. Maybe she was too old for another battle. Then she remembered the email she'd sent. The wheels were in motion. She'd have to deal with the nightmares somehow.

Maggie shuffled into her therapist's office, shoulders hunched, eyes on the floor. She dropped her bag beside the couch and sat down, wedging a pillow behind her back.

"I'm losing my mind," she told Sharon. "The nightmare is back. Every night for the past week. I'm getting no sleep."

"What can you tell me?" Sharon asked.

"I'm running from someone. A man. And he wants to kill me."

"Is there any reason someone would want to kill you, Maggie?"

Maggie shrugged.

"Was there ever a time in the past, Maggie, when you felt afraid? Threatened?"

Maggie frowned.

Sharon waited.

"Sure, but that was a long time ago," Maggie said. "I was heavily into the women's movement. And there were a lot of people, men in particular, who wanted me to shut up. So many death threats. But I wasn't worried. I knew what I was doing."

"What were you doing, Maggie?"

"I was standing up for what I believed in. For justice. For women's rights. And we made one helluva a difference. But now, the government's changing all that. I can't sit back and say nothing."

"What is it you want to say, Maggie?"

Maggie stood, eyes blazing, arms flying.

"I want to tell the government to f…, I mean, to take a flying leap. After all these years, they have no right to do this to us. Who the hell do they think they are?"

"I can see this is very important to you, Maggie. Can you tell me why?"

Maggie shook her head sat down slowly. Her eyes dropped to the carpet.

"I've never told anyone," she said in a low voice.

She glanced at Sharon and turned away.

"I can't."

"Maggie, you know that everything we talk about is confidential, right?"

Maggie nodded.

"When we first began to meet, I told you I would not judge you for anything you might say, think or do. That still holds true today.

So, if this is something that you want to share with me, I will listen. And if you're not ready, that is fine too."

Maggie sat for a moment, then grabbed her purse and rushed out of the office. She sped past her car, her feet barely keeping up with her pounding heart. Thoughts and images tumbled and swirled through her mind. She reached for her pills and couldn't find them. They must be at home, she thought, picking up the pace.

Blackness began to creep into her vision like an ink blot seeping across paper. No, not here, not now. As she turned toward her street, she grabbed a neighbor's rail fence, holding on while she tried to slow her breathing. She crossed the street and leaned against the oak that sheltered the corner. The ink blot started to recede. She stepped carefully along the sidewalk counting the cracks to calm her mind.

"Outta the way, ol' lady!" a skateboarder shouted, shoving her as he raced by.

"Old lady, my ass!" Maggie yelled, stumbling off the sidewalk, scratching her leg on a fire hydrant.

When she reached her front gate, her feet led her along the curved path to the porch. She sat down on the steps, trembling. She watched the sun dance through the leaves and the breeze tousle the blossoms in the garden. Her heart settled, and she rested her chin on her hands. After a few moments, she pulled out her phone.

"Need a favor, Ali" Maggie said. "My car's at the mall. Could you give me a ride to pick it up?"

"What happened?" Alicia asked. "Did you have one of your spells?"

"No, no," Maggie said. "I just left the therapist's in a bit of a hurry, that's all."

"I'll only come if you make a follow-up appointment," Alicia said.

"Fine," Maggie said, rolling her eyes. "I will make a new appointment. Are you coming to get me or not?"

Chapter Six

Daniel read through the draft legislation for the fifth time. It was all there, ready for Congress to approve. A brilliant piece of legal craftsmanship that would supersede all state legislatures and enforce a total ban on abortion across the country. He was particularly proud of the limitations paragraphs he'd added. Just what the President ordered. He stretched, yawned, and clicked the Save button.

As he opened the side drawer of the desk and noticed his stash of George T. Stagg was getting low. He picked up his phone and sent a text to his assistant.

Mark, case of G. T. pronto

He took out the bottle, poured a glass and raised it to his nose, inhaling the aroma. Nothing like a silky bourbon to settle the mind, he thought.

His phone buzzed. Unknown caller. He rejected the call and turned back to the laptop.

The phone vibrated again. Another number he didn't recognize. He turned the phone over and nearly dropped it as it buzzed in his hand.

"What the hell?"

He looked at the number. Jack Winthrup, *The Nation Today*. Better take it, he thought, clearing his throat.

"Jack, my boy, it's been a while. How are you? And the new baby?"

"Good evening, Daniel. Just fine, thanks. Do you have a few minutes?"

Daniel forced a smile into his voice.

"Anything for you and *The Nation Today*. You know that."

"Great. First, congratulations on your new appointment. How does it feel to be the most powerful man in the country, second only to the President?"

This is going to be easy, Daniel thought.

"I'm honored, truly honored," he replied revving up his interview voice. "I highly value the respect of the President. Our country is blessed to have him as our new leader. I am humbled by his appreciation for my many years of hard work on behalf of the people of our fine nation. I look forward to helping him implement policies that will safeguard and protect the values we all hold dear."

He could hear Jack typing over the phone. He must have him on speaker phone.

"Excellent," Jack said. "Just a couple of things and then I'll let you go. Is it true that the rumored national anti-abortion legislation will be reviewed by Congress this week?

"Now, Jack," Daniel said, closing his laptop quickly, "I can't comment on rumors. If the Congress is looking at new ideas, that's for them to determine. Not me."

"But I understand that, in your new role, you will be responsible for approving any drafts from a legal perspective. Is that not true?"

"I do have the legal authority to review new legislation, yes, but only after approval by Congress. Let's not put the cart before the horse. I don't think members of the House and Senate would be impressed if I suggested otherwise, would they?"

Jack typed for a minute.

"Just one more question. What prompted you to make such a generous donation today to the World Organization for Women? Was this decision made before your appointment as Chief Justice? It seems out of alignment with proposed government policy."

Daniel was silent.

"I don't know what you're talking about, Jack. You must be mistaken. I'm not even aware of that organization. Perhaps you should check your facts."

"I have the media release from your assistant right in front of me, Daniel. No mistake."

"Could you email me a copy, Jack? I need to investigate this further. Don't print anything about this until I get back to you. I don't want false information circulating. I'm sure you understand."

"We go to press in less than an hour, so I look forward to hearing from you, Daniel."

Jack hung up the phone. He tapped his fingers on the desk. There was definitely a story here. He picked up the phone again and made another call.

"Joanna? It's Jack. I hear you received a hefty donation today from an unlikely source. Can we talk?"

Daniel called his assistant as soon as he got off the phone.

"Mark, what the hell is this about a donation? The World Organization for Women? What the fuck is that?"

He listened for a moment and shouted, "What do you mean you don't know anything about it?"

He clicked on the email attachment from Jack and scanned the press release.

"No shit! I've got a press release right here that was sent to *The Nation Today,* and it came from you. Your name is at the top, along with your contact info. I found out about it just now when that asshole, Jack Winthrup, called and asked me about it. A million dollars? To some women's group? If you don't know what's going on, you'd better find out fast. And get back to me. I've got to stop this from going public."

Daniel slammed the phone on his desk and pushed his chair back. He paced around the room and stopped, a grin on his face. He called his bank manager.

"Brian, it's Dan. I've got a bit of a problem, and I need you to do something right away. What? Ya, I know it's late, but I'll owe you big time, buddy. Here's what's happened. A donation has gone out from my account to the wrong organization. Not sure how it happened but my assistant is a useless piece of shit. Anyway, I need to put a stop on it immediately so I can clear up the mess before it goes public. Can you do that?"

"Thanks, bud. I owe you."

Daniel set the phone down. Now all he had to do was issue a media release explaining the mix-up. He was halfway through writing it when his phone rang.

"Brian, what's up?"

Daniel felt heat rising from his neck and spreading across his face.

"Just a sec, I need to put you on speakerphone."

He set up his phone to record the conversation and then switched the call to speakerphone.

"Okay, tell me again. There was noise in the background here so I couldn't hear you clearly."

"Dan, the amount you are speaking of was transferred earlier today from your bank account to the organization you mentioned. It was a direct donation so there is nothing I can do from the bank's perspective."

Daniel felt like a gorilla was sitting on his chest. His head throbbed. He opened his eyes and noticed the words on the laptop were blurry.

"Dan? You still there?"

He pressed his palms on the cool surface of the red mahogany desk and counted to ten.

"Is there anything I can do about this?" he asked through gritted teeth.

"You could contact the organization, explain the situation and ask them to refund you the money. However, keep in mind that the money came directly from your account, so it does appear it was your decision."

"Which account did it come from?"

"Let me see." He heard Brian's fingers dancing across the keyboard.

"Your joint account," he said.

"Brian," his voice came out as a squeak, "can anyone else access my accounts?"

"Only someone who has signing privileges. Let me check."

As he waited, Daniel realized he knew the answer.

"Okay, so it looks like your wife is the only other name on that account."

Daniel's heart was pounding so hard, he was sure Brian could hear it through the phone.

"Actually, Dan, I think you should take a look at all your accounts. The balances seem unusually low."

Daniel roared and thumped the desk, sending the phone scuttering off the edge. He picked up the whiskey glass and threw it against the wall. Amber drops stained the white couch and the beige tile. He kicked the desk drawer closed.

"Dan?" His bank manager's voice called from the phone on the floor.

He picked up the phone, ended the call and hit a number on speed dial.

"Frank, it's Daniel. Got a job for you. Get over here. Now."

Chapter Seven

Frank checked the voice message from Daniel and turned his phone face down. This had better be good, he thought, pulling me away on my poker night.

"Duty calls. Gotta wrap this up, guys."

"Just as well," Marty said, tossing his cards on the table, "you're wiping us out."

"Luck of the draw. Some nights are like that," Frank said as he gathered up his winnings.

"Next week my house," Pete said. "The wife's taking the kids to the parents', so we'll have the place to ourselves."

"Grab your booze on the way out," Frank said. "You won't feel like you're leaving empty-handed that way."

His friends clapped him on the back and headed out the door.

Frank took one more swig of beer and grabbed his keys.

Twenty minutes later he pulled his red Corvette up to the gate at the Power residence. He pressed in the key code and revved the engine while he waited for the gate to open. Putting his foot to the floor, he took the curved driveway at full speed, braking hard as he reached the front stairs.

Daniel met him at the door.

"What took you?" he growled.

"Good to see you too, Dan. Believe it or not, I have a life, and a day job. It's midnight. You're lucky I wasn't in bed. This better be good."

Daniel shook his head. "It's Madeline. She's vanished. I need to find her, or a major deal is screwed. Important enough to take up some of your valuable time, Chief Inspector?"

Frank raised his eyebrows. "Missing since when?"

"Last night. She didn't go to my inaugural dinner. She said she wasn't feeling well. When I got home, she was nowhere to be found. The window in her bedroom was open. I looked everywhere. I don't know what's happened."

Frank took a pen and notebook out of his pocket.

"Did you try calling her?"

"No answer."

"Did she seem distressed?"

"No more than usual. She's not an easy woman to deal with. You're a lucky man. No wife, no bullshit."

"What was she wearing?"

"I dunno. Black, I think. Not the dress I bought her."

"Can I take a look at her room?"

Daniel shrugged. "Sure, but you won't find anything. Nothing's missing. I did a thorough search."

Daniel showed him upstairs to Madeline's bedroom.

Frank noted the clothes on the floor in the closet and the messy bedspread.

"Is this how you found the room?"

"No, I told you, I searched everywhere for her. The dresses are where I dropped them when I checked the closet. I tossed the bedspread so I could see under the bed. The window was wide open but I closed it when I got home this morning."

"Why did you wait until now to call me? You shouldn't have touched anything. Finding prints is going to be tough now."

"What, too much for you to handle, Fancy Francey?"

Frank grabbed Daniel by the neck and shoved him up against the wall, his feet dangling. Daniel gurgled and squirmed as Frank slowly lowered him to the floor.

"Don't call me that," Frank hissed. "Do it again and you're a dead man."

Daniel scuttled to the far side of the bed, clutching his throat and wheezing.

Frank stared at him; fists clenched. He cracked his knuckles, widened his stance and took a deep breath.

"Now, where were we?" Frank said, his voice as rough as sandpaper. "Oh, your dear wife, Madeline. If you want my help, you'll do as I say."

Daniel nodded.

"For starters, I need her cell number and a list of friends and phone numbers. Does she have any family apart from your daughter? Siblings, parents?"

"No friends that I know of," Daniel croaked and cleared his throat a couple of times. "She spends all her time here or at the country house. Her parents died before we got married, and if she has any other family, I've never met them."

Frank glanced up from his notes. "I'll need your daughter's contact info including address. She may have heard from her."

Daniel pulled out his cell phone. "I'll send you their info. Lena's almost done her year at Georgetown, but I don't know what she's doing for the summer. She lives in a house with a bunch of guys. That's all I know. Look, this is not about Lena. Madeline's the one I need. And by tomorrow morning. You have to keep this quiet. Just between you and me. There's a hefty bonus in it for you."

Frank shook his head. "You're not giving me much to go on. I'll be in touch as soon as I know something."

He strode out of the house and drove off, tires squealing.

Parked in the shadows behind a coffee shop, Frank dialed Madeline's cell number. Daniel had asked him to install a tracking device on his wife's and daughter's phones a year ago. Frank hadn't asked why. None of his business.

The phone didn't even ring. He checked the location tracking history. Madeline had been down by The Yards near the Anacostia River. The last ping was from the riverbank. Frank started the car and raced through downtown, braking hard near the waterfront where the phone had last signaled.

He jumped out of the car and looked up and down the river. Nothing. He followed the bank east and west briefly and then returned to the bench. Bending down, he checked for prints in the mud, but the heavy rain had washed away any signs. He debated calling in the local search and rescue to drag that section of the river but remembered Daniel had asked him to keep it quiet.

He returned to his car and called Lena's phone. It went directly to voicemail. The tracking showed she was at her apartment. He checked his watch: 1 a.m. She was probably sleeping. He decided to head home and come back in the morning. Daniel could wait.

Chapter Eight

Jack leaned back in his armchair. The house was silent. Hannah and their month-old baby, Evelyn, were sleeping. He read over his notes from the interview with Joanna Price, CEO of the World Organization for Women. She had sounded surprised about the $1 million donation, particularly that it had come from Chief Justice Power.

"I don't know what to tell you, Jack," she said. "I just started my holidays. If you want an official quote, then I'd say that the World Organization for Women is very appreciative of the generous donation in recognition of the fiftieth anniversary of the founding of our organization. The money will be put directly toward supporting women in crisis and empowering women around the world to achieve equality in relationships, the workplace and in society as a whole. I'd be happy to do a longer interview with you once I have more information."

There's something missing from this story, he thought. The donor claimed to know nothing about it; the recipient was not aware of it. It was a substantial amount of money for no one to know anything.

He got up and grabbed a coffee. He typed World Organization for Women into his search engine.

An hour later, Jack pushed back his chair with a low whistle. The World Organization for Women was impressive. It had been founded in 1975 by five women: three in their early twenties; the other two in their fifties. According to the history page on their website, the founders saw a need to bring women's issues out into the open for discussion. Margaret Carpenter, long-time director, was quoted as saying,

"It's time for all of us, regardless of gender, age or race, to recognize and acknowledge the vital role women have in society, and to honor and respect that role by ensuring full equality at home, in the workplace and in society, here in this country and around the world."

The initial group had grown to three million members representing nearly every country across the globe. Although their focus had expanded over the years, the goal remained consistent: inspiring, informing, and empowering people to take action in support of equal rights for girls and women.

Down the hall, Evelyn whimpered briefly. Jack sat up and listened. He heard Hannah talking softly to her, followed by silence. He returned to his reading.

The World Organization for Women had led the abortion fight in the seventies: marching, carrying placards, staging sit-ins and hunger strikes. In more recent years, they had advocated, successfully, for girls' education and the abolition of child marriages. From awareness campaigns about HIV/AIDS, genital mutilation of girls, and abuse of women, the organization had done it all on a global scale.

Nationally, they focused on human rights issues involving Indigenous Peoples, the LGBTQ2S+ community as well as immigrants and refugees. Other issues included access to employment, housing, and affordable daycare.

"Whoa," he whispered, jotting down some notes. "This is not a group you want to mess with. I wonder what Daniel Power is up to."

Jack awoke to the clang of a pan on the stove and the smell of bacon frying. He rolled over and checked the clock. It was 7 a.m. He groaned and threw back the covers. He had a lot of work to do to be ready for the print deadline but first he wanted breakfast with his girls.

"What time did you come to bed?" Hannah asked as she poured two cups of coffee.

"Oh around 2 or 2:30," Jack said. "I couldn't keep my eyes open any longer. If Evy woke up, I'm sorry I didn't hear her."

"That's okay, it was a pretty good night. Best one so far. She fed around midnight and then slept until 4 a.m. And so did I. I feel like a new woman this morning."

Jack wandered over to the bassinet. Evelyn was sleeping soundly. He stroked her face gently with a finger and she turned her head, making sucking motions with her mouth.

"Don't you wake her, Jack," Hannah said. "I want to have a quiet breakfast with you for a change."

He smiled and walked back toward the stove.

"What can I do to help?" he said.

"Just sit down and drink your coffee," she said. "I'm about to serve up. Bacon, eggs, and toast. We haven't had a cooked breakfast since Evy was born."

As they ate, he noticed Hannah was watching him closely.

"What gives?" he asked.

She took another bite of egg, wiped her mouth with a cloth napkin and rested her arms on the table.

"You haven't stayed up late like that in a long time. Not since you were working on that investigative piece about the police services. So, are you going to fill me in, or do I have to wait to see it in print?"

He took a sip of coffee, holding her gaze over the rim of the cup.

"You don't miss much, do you? Even when you're living on a three-hour sleep schedule."

Hannah raised her eyebrows and waited.

"Okay, there's something going on that I can't quite figure out. It's going to be a big story, and I want to be the one to break it."

"Naturally," she grinned as she poked his shoulder.

He gave her a summary of what he knew so far.

"Let me see if I've got this straight," Hannah said. "A million-dollar donation to an international women's rights organization from a guy who believes women are to be kept barefoot, pregnant and in the kitchen. A man who is in the President's pocket; the same president who has plans to ban abortion on pain of death. You're right, it doesn't make sense."

Jack nodded.

"The current CEO knew nothing about the donation," he said, "although she just started holidays so maybe that's why. She said the organization focuses on women's rights, equality in the workplace, and women's self-determination. This is not an organization that Power, or the President, would want to support. I have more phone calls to make today. I talked to Ed last night, and he said he would save space for a feature on the World Organization for Women this weekend."

Hannah closed her eyes and sat back in her chair, deep in thought. She twirled a thick strand of hair with a finger.

"I'm guessing you spoke to Judge Power, right?" she asked.

"As soon as I got the press release. He seemed stunned and said he'd get back to me before we went to press last night, but he didn't. I called his assistant close to press time, and he wouldn't answer any questions."

Evelyn began to squawk. Hannah drank the rest of her coffee and stood up. She pressed a hand into her husband's shoulder.

"If anyone can figure this out, you can, Jack."

As she walked away, she paused and turned.

"*Cherchez la femme*, Jack. They say that behind every powerful man is a powerful woman. What do you know about Mrs. Power?"

Jack stacked the dishes on the counter. As he let the water run, he leaned back against the kitchen island. Hannah had a point. Although he had done some quick searching last night into Madeline Power, very little information surfaced.

She had been married to the judge for twenty years and they had a daughter at college. She was younger than her husband by at least fifteen years and had a college education but that was all he could find. It was odd for a high-profile person to have a blank past.

He finished washing the dishes and dried his hands on the towel. He headed down the hall to his office and called Joanna back.

"Sorry to bother you on your holidays, but we're going to run an in-depth feature of the World Organization for Women this weekend, and I need some contacts. Can you help me out?

Chapter Nine

Lena was sprawled out on her bed after breakfast, scrolling through her phone, when Brad tapped on her door. He tossed her a package.

"What's that?" Lena asked.

"Dunno," he said. "Delivered just now. It was addressed to me, but the note inside says it's for you. Surprise package, I guess."

He walked back to the kitchen, whistling.

Lena sat up and grabbed the package. She looked at the address and recognized the handwriting. She dumped the contents on the comforter. A cell phone, and an envelope that said, 'For Lena'.

Curious now, she turned on the cell phone. A text message popped up from a number she didn't know.

Summer cottage. Bus leaves at noon. Don't be late. Leave old cell under mattress. Tell no one.

She opened the envelope. A one-way bus ticket.

She sighed. More mysteries, Mom?

She checked her watch. It was 11 a.m. She jumped out of bed and threw her laptop into her backpack along with her new cell phone and her wallet. She buried the old phone under the mattress and picked up her duffel bag.

"Hey Brad?" she called as she headed to the kitchen.

"Yeppers."

He handed her half the jelly sandwich he was making.

"Thanks. I'm heading out for a bit. Not sure when I'll be back, so can you lock up when you leave?"

"Sure thing. Have fun!"

Lena went out the back door and through the neighbor's yard. It was a shortcut to the subway station. She ran down the steps and hopped on the train as soon as it pulled in. Six stops later, she was at the bus station. Her bus was waiting so she joined the line and climbed on board.

The bus pulled into the village station late afternoon. Lena yawned and stretched and grabbed her bags. She joined the slow-moving line of passengers preparing to disembark. Through the window she saw a familiar face.

She bounced down the stairs and ran toward the gray-haired woman, her arms outstretched.

"Auntie Max!" she cried. "What are you doing here? I thought you'd still be in Italy."

They wrapped their arms around each other in a big hug.

As Lena pulled away, she stopped and looked at the woman more closely.

"Mom?"

The woman smiled and whispered, "Just pretend I'm your auntie for now, okay? I will explain when we get somewhere quiet."

Lena shook her head. "What's with all the drama? Honestly, I'm beginning to feel like I'm in a spy movie."

Madeline laughed and wrapped her left arm around her daughter's shoulders.

"Believe me, I know exactly how you feel. First things first, shall we pick up a pizza on our way home?"

"Now you're talkin'!"

Bolstered by coffee, toast, and a few hours of sleep, Frank drove back to Lena's house. He watched the house from the car for a few minutes.

It was almost noon. He got out of the car, climbed the front stairs, and rang the bell. No response. He tried the door handle. The door was locked. He glanced up and down the street and then strolled through the side gate to the back door. No response there either. The door was concealed by a wide trellis, so he knew he could jimmy the lock without the neighbors noticing.

He stepped inside the back hall, closed the door quietly, and called out, "Hello? Anyone home?"

The house was silent.

He walked quickly through the kitchen and living room, noticing dishes in the sink and an empty glass on the table. Someone had been here recently.

As he climbed the stairs, he paused and listened. No sounds from the bedrooms.

In the bathroom, there were towels on the floor. He opened a door in the hallway and peeked inside. Lena's room. Pretty obvious from the hand-painted sign on the windowsill. The bed was made; the desk was tidy. He tried calling her phone. No sound, but the locator showed it was in the room. He opened the drawers in the desk, dresser, and night table, checked the bookshelf and under the bed. Finally, he looked under the pillow. Nothing.

"It has to be here," he muttered.

He bent down and reached between the mattresses. As he swept his hand back and forth, the tip of his index finger brushed against something hard. He shoved the mattress off the bed.

He swore when he saw the phone. He grabbed it and checked the messages. Just a few from friends but no indication of where she might be. Or why she'd hidden the phone. He pushed the mattress back on the bed and rearranged the covers. Picking up the brown teddy bear, he set it on the pillow as she had left it.

Before leaving, he looked for a laptop. The desk was full of school notes but nothing else.

As he started back down the stairs, the front door opened.

"Who the hell are you?" Brad said.

Frank straightened up and pulled his shoulders back. He forced himself to walk slowly and confidently down the stairs.

"I'm a friend of Lena's parents. And who are you?" Frank asked.

Brad set his coffee on a chair in the entry and stood still, arms crossed, deliberately blocking the doorway. He knew he could take this guy on height and weight, but he held back. Something in the man's eyes. He was either a thief or a cop.

He pulled out his phone and started to dial 911.

"I wouldn't do that if I were you," Frank said in a low voice. Brad looked up and noticed he was holding his jacket out from his body. A gun. Definitely a cop.

"Where's your warrant?" Brad asked. "If you're here on police business, you need a warrant."

"Relax," said Frank, opening his arms wide and dropping them at his side. "I'm here because Lena's Dad asked me to stop by. He hasn't heard from her in a while, I was in the area, and so I stopped in. The back door was unlocked. She's not here, so I'll be on my way. But when you see her, can you ask her to call her father?"

Brad raised his phone and snapped a photo. Before Frank could grab him, he was out the door, over the fence and out of sight.

"Fuckin' kid."

Frank slammed the front door shut and ran to his car. Tires squealing, he pulled a U-turn, cutting off a truck and sped off in the direction Brad had gone. He spent a half hour crisscrossing side streets. The kid had vanished.

His phone rang. He groaned when he saw the number.

"Frank here."

"Well?" Daniel asked. "Have you found Madeline?"

"Still working on it. I know she was down by the river last night based on her phone locator."

"What happened?"

"I'm ruling out possibilities," Frank said. "I could dredge the river, but I suspect the most we will find is her phone."

"No, I said no involvement from anyone else. Or didn't you hear me?"

"Loud and clear. I was just at Lena's," Frank added. "Her phone was hidden under the mattress, but she wasn't there. I'm wondering if they're together."

"I don't give a shit about Lena. I need to know where Madeline is. I have a major deal underway, and it could destroy me if she doesn't show up. What do I have to do? More money? You've got it. Just find her!"

Frank heard a loud click as Daniel hung up.

Daniel slammed the phone down on his desk. Suddenly he remembered that he had not called the reporter back last night.

"Shit! The media!"

He grabbed his phone but before he could dial Jack's number, another call came through.

"Danny boy."

Daniel swallowed and forced a light tone into his voice.

"I was just about to call you," he said. "The draft legislation is ready. I can deliver it within 30 minutes if that suits you," he said.

"Excellent," the President replied. "I look forward to seeing what you have."

Daniel hung up and poured a glass of bourbon. If Madeline were here, she'd say it was too early in the day for a drink.

"Here's to you, bitch." he said, raising his glass.

He picked up his phone again and called his assistant.

"Mark, get over here. You need to come up with a way to spin this donation, so it looks good. Got it? I expect a solution by the time you walk into my office."

Fifteen minutes later, Daniel dismissed Mark and called his limousine driver.

"White House," he ordered. He grabbed his briefcase and waited by the front door. He was soon climbing the wide stairs of the North Portico. He was surprised to see the President waiting for him in the doorway.

"Well, hello," he said. "To what do I owe this honor?"

He noticed that four bodyguards were stationed nearby, two inside the door and one on each side of the President.

"Come into my office, Dan," the President said. "We need to talk."

They strode down the long hallway. The President glanced at his watch. When they arrived at the office, the door was wide open. The President gestured for Daniel to go in first. Security moved into position outside the door.

"First things first," Daniel said. He set his briefcase on a small side table and unlocked it. He pulled out a blue file folder and handed it to the President. Without glancing at it, the President placed the folder on his ornate oak desk.

Daniel remained standing. His racing heart echoed like gunshot in his ears. He couldn't swallow. His tongue felt like coarse sandpaper.

"Dan, I understand you've made a donation. Without consulting me. Care to explain?"

Daniel tried to read the President's body language – hands folded on the desk; eyes blank. The President wasn't smiling. But he wasn't frowning either.

"An unusual step, I'll admit," Daniel said, "but a necessary one. You see, I knew our legislation was in the works and I decided to confuse the enemy, so to speak. This way, that World of Women or Women's World or whatever it's called, won't anticipate what we are about to do. Their guard will be down because they will think we're on their side. First, we pamper them, and then we nail them to the wall. And they won't have time to do anything about it. It's a perfect ploy, don't you think?"

The President stared at him. As the silence grew, Dan wondered if he had overplayed his hand. After a few minutes, the President stood up extending his right hand across the desk.

"Well done, Danny boy, well done. I never knew you had a crafty side to you. It just might work."

Daniel sat down in a nearby armchair. His legs were shaking. He pulled out a tissue and dabbed his forehead.

"Thank you. I know I should have run it by you, but time was of the essence. I had to do it while Madeline is away. The money is from our joint account and it's easier to explain it to her after the fact. Not that it's any of her business, of course. But it's a sizable sum and it's best if she doesn't ask questions."

"She's away? For how long?"

"Not sure. She was gone when I got home from the inaugural dinner. Just left a note saying she was heading to our country house for a while."

The President raised his eyebrows.

"You know it's essential for us to appear with our wives and children to promote family values, right? That will be a key part of selling this legislation. Get her home and prepped before next week."

He opened the blue folder and began to read.

The President closed the folder and leaned back in his chair, resting his hands behind his head. He rocked back and forth; eyes shut.

He stood, looked at Daniel and smiled.

"Well done, Dan. This is exactly what we need. And here's how it's going to play out."

He straightened a pen on the desk.

"I'm going to give this to Ryan so he can pull together the media release and talking points. I'll call an emergency joint session of Congress next weekend. We may need to lean on a few senators, call in a few favors, but it'll pass, no problem. There will be a reaction from the public and certain interest groups, but we'll nip it in the bud. And thanks to your donation, the most vocal of the groups won't see it coming so we won't have any trouble from them."

He pressed a button on his desk.

"The boys will show you out. We'll talk again next week. Pleasure working with you."

He picked up the blue folder and paused, mid-stride.

"What did you find out about the prenup?" he asked quietly.

Daniel cleared his throat.

"It's air-tight," he said. "You can't divorce her."

The President frowned.

"No wiggle room?"

"Well, there is one possibility," Daniel dropped his voice. "If she dies before you …"

"Let me talk to Frank," the President said and hurried out of the room.

Chapter Ten

Brad sighed with relief. The cop's car had not been down the street for an hour. He looked out the garage windows and glanced quickly in both directions. He opened the back door and crept along the fence, keeping his head down. When he reached the corner, he peeked into the laneway. No cars. He sprinted across the lane and vaulted over his brother's back fence, landing in the dirt under the apple tree.

He stood up slowly and brushed off his shirt and jeans. He hopped over some tall plants, dashed to the house, and tapped on the side door.

Jack opened the door.

"What the heck?"

Brad raised a finger to his lips. "Just let me in and I'll explain."

Jack stepped back and let him pass, locking the door behind him. They stepped into the kitchen.

"Hannah and the baby sleeping?" Brad asked.

"They just went into the bedroom for a feed," Jack said. "So probably best to keep our voices down."

"No problem."

The brothers sat in silence for a few moments.

"Okay, so what's up, kid?" Jack asked. "It's not often you show up on my doorstep."

Brad shook his head.

"Something really weird just happened."

He pulled out his phone and scrolled through the photos.

"Recognize this dude?"

Jack took the phone and looked at the photo. He whistled softly and handed the phone back to his brother.

"He was in my house," Brad said. "This morning. I'd popped out to pick up a coffee and when I came back, he was walking down the stairs like he owned the place.

"Do you know who it is?" Jack asked.

"No idea. And he wouldn't tell me. But he made a point of showing me his big ass gun, so I figured it was a cop. He told me to let Lena know her Dad's looking for her. I took the photo and split."

Brad leaned forward, dropping his voice.

"He chased me with his car, a red Corvette. I made it to Curry's garage and ducked inside. When it looked like the coast was clear, I came here. I didn't know what else to do."

Jack pulled his chair closer to his brother.

"Look, Brad, that's no cop. That's Frank Westholt."

"The Chief Inspector?"

"Yes, at least that's his day job. It's just a cover really. He's actually head of Secret Service for the President, and he does not play by the rules. In fact, in his world, there are no rules. He's totally in the pocket of Daniel Power as well as the President. I know Lena is Power's daughter, and your roommate, but it seems odd that Westholt would show up at your house looking for her."

Brad stared at his older brother.

"What do I do now?"

"Chances are he's watching your house. For Lena, not you. Do you know where she is?"

"No. She headed out before I did."

"Why don't you head to the parents' place for a few days? Lay low. Not a great move on your part to take his photo, by the way. He's probably gunning for you now. But if you stay put, I'll see what I can find out. Do you want a ride over to Mum and Dad's?"

"Sure, thanks. But first, what I could really use is some food. Got anything?"

Jack dropped his brother off at their parents' house on the outskirts of the city. They invited him in for a coffee, but he waved them off, saying he had a deadline. Before driving away, he typed an address into the GPS on his phone. Jack eased his motorcycle onto the highway behind a line of transport trucks. The engine hummed and sang as he geared up. Nothing but the best – Kawasaki Ninja

1000SX. He grinned, feeling the bike's eagerness to break out – a stallion eyeing the open field.

"Okay big boy, let 'er rip!" he whispered.

With a roar, he blew past buses, cars and trucks, a blur of green and black weaving in and out, leaning hard into curves, conquering the straightaways. He felt the surge of adrenalin as trees whipped by. The pressure of deadlines vanished in a cloud of dust along the shoulder of the road. Almost as thrilling as whitewater rafting, he thought. Or free climbing. That inexplicable high of flirting with disaster, knowing that the next move could be your last…or your best.

He began to gear down. His exit was coming up.

He pulled his motorcycle into a driveway in a quiet neighborhood. The white clapboard house was a story and a half with well-tended gardens along the path leading to the turquoise front door. Jack walked slowly along the meandering path, surprised by the number of perennials he recognized: green and white hosta, blood-red poppies, yellow day lilies, and lupine in rainbow colors. Hannah's green thumb must be rubbing off, he thought.

He lifted the brass door knocker and gently tapped three times. Through the open window, he heard a woman's voice, "Bloody hell!" followed by a rustling and slamming as if she was gathering up papers and putting them out of sight.

As he waited, he glanced around. On the covered veranda, there was an old rocking chair with a well-worn gingham cushion, and three mismatched wicker chairs around a glass table. Two books sat on the table: *No Is Not Enough; Anne of Green Gables.* Odd pairing, he thought, as he heard footsteps approaching.

The door opened. A short woman with curly shoulder-length grey hair glared at him.

"And you are?" she asked.

"Jack Winthrup, *The Nation Today*," he said, smiling and holding out his right hand.

The woman scowled and crossed her arms over her blue t-shirt, emblazoned with three capital letters in bold font – **WTF**.

Noticing he was staring at the shirt, she said slowly and clearly, "Wednesday, Thursday, Friday. Not what you might think."

She waited a moment and asked, "So what do you want?"

"I'm looking for Margaret Carpenter. *The Nation Today* is doing a feature on the World Organization for Women and I want to interview her as the founder of the organization."

"One of the founding members," she corrected him. "And what if she doesn't wish to be interviewed?"

"Well then, I guess I walk away and do my best to write the story without her insight," he said. "But you and I both know that your input would make it a much more solid feature."

She studied him.

"Okay, you have 30 minutes," she said. "I have things to do."

She opened the door and led him into the living room.

He sat down on the couch and pulled out a notepad and pen.

"What? You don't use a laptop?"

He smiled. "I guess I'm old-fashioned. I like the feel of a pen in my hand when I do interviews. It frees me up to focus on the person."

"Want a coffee?"

"Sure," he said. "Just cream if you have it."

Maggie came back from the kitchen and set two mugs of coffee on the table. She sat down in the blue armchair and stretched her legs out, crossing her ankles.

"What do you want to know?"

Jack studied Maggie as she talked. When she spoke of the early days of the women's movement, her gruff exterior softened, and her eyes sparkled as her hands fluttered through the air. He guessed she was in her early seventies. But she had the energy of a much younger woman.

"You have to understand the context," she said. "The sixties and seventies weren't just about hippies and free love. It was about women finding their voices. Women who had been silent for too long. Sure, we had the right to vote, but our hands were tied in so many ways. Marriage and children? That was the only acceptable path. If we had children without being married, we were sinners. If we chose not to have children or not get married, something was wrong with us. And heaven help women who wanted marriage, a career and children too."

She shook her head.

"You're too young to understand, but it felt like we were damned no matter what we did. We had no real choices. Not like men. And that's where the women's movement started. We wanted to make our own choices, instead of having our lives dictated to us."

She stared into space for a moment. Jack waited; pen poised over his pad.

"Where was I?" she asked.

"Choices," he said.

"Ah yes. It all started with the abortion issue for me. I knew far too many girls who had been forced to carry pregnancies to term and then give up their babies for adoption because abortion was illegal. A few refused to go through with it and had hatchet jobs in shady clinics. One girl I knew bled to death. The town hushed it up.

"Some of my friends got married right out of high school because a baby was on the way. Most of those marriages ended in divorce a few years later. A close friend was raped, and her parents sent her to live with a cousin until after the baby was born. People shunned you if you were unwed and pregnant. As if having a man in your life made everything peachy keen."

Jack noted the warning glitter in her eyes.

"So, I decided to do something about it," she said. "The vision for the organization was mine, but I couldn't have done it alone. Each of the founding members brought key skills to the table."

"What are the names of the other four?" Jack interrupted.

"I'm sure you can find that out," she snapped.

Jack smiled. He already had the names.

"Sorry for interrupting," he said. "Please continue."

Maggie leaned forward and rested her forearms on her knees.

"We didn't set out to change the world, but I guess that's what happened in the end. The World Organization for Women was about making our local communities more accepting and welcoming for women and children. Sure, it started with the abortion issue but, over the years, it evolved into something much bigger – a global organization focused on empowering not just women and girls, but people in general. We raised funds to support education and build healthy communities. Hard to believe it all started fifty years ago with our little group of five."

"Did you ever marry?" Jack asked.

"I was married once. He died. End of story."

"I'm sorry. Any children?"

"I think we're done here," she said, standing up, hands on hips.

"I'm sorry. I just have one more question. Please sit down."

Maggie snorted, crossed her arms, and remained standing.

"Looking back, did you accomplish what you set out to do?"

Maggie sat down slowly, tucking her legs underneath her. She rested her right elbow on the arm of the chair and leaned her head against her hand. She took a deep breath and let it out softly.

"We definitely accomplished a lot," she said. "So many people joined the marches and protests. The media jumped all over it. And eventually legislation was passed. Women had more choice."

She sat in silence for a few minutes.

"Given the current political climate, I do wonder if it was all in vain."

She stood up abruptly.

"Time for you to go," she said.

Jack tucked his pen and pad into his briefcase.

"Is there anyone else you think I should talk to?"

"The current CEO," she said quickly, opening the front door. "She can provide you with more up-to-date information."

She closed the door behind him and leaned against the wall, her body shaking. I don't know if I can do this, she thought.

Before starting up the bike, Jack picked up his phone and called a friend at the police station.

"Robbie? It's Jack. Got a favor to ask. Can you find out why Frank Westholt was at my brother's house this morning? I'll text you the address. Thanks."

Chapter Eleven

Maggie got out of her car and stood facing her therapist's office. She forced her shoulders down, away from her ears, and took a deep breath. It was now or never.

She muttered a greeting to Sharon and sat down on the edge of the couch, tearing a tissue apart between her fingers.

"Whenever you're ready, Maggie," Sharon said. "No rush."

Maggie clasped her hands together and looked up at Sharon.

"At one of our first sessions, you compared therapy to peeling away the layers of an onion. Do you remember?" she asked.

Sharon nodded.

"And you said that each time I worked through a layer, another one would surface. Well, I think what I'm about to tell you is at the core of the onion."

"How do you feel right now?"

"Terrified. But fuckin' determined."

"Okay, then. Let's jump in and see where we land."

Maggie stared into space. She could feel the terror building, like a dam about to burst. The walls of the office disappeared. She was 17 years old.

"It was June 20. The whole gang had gone over to Tom's house after graduation. There were seven of us. We'd been friends for years. Some of us met in elementary school, the rest in high school. It was our last night together, so we wanted it to be special."

She pictured each of her friends, the way they were that night, excited about being done with school, and a bit nervous about the future.

"I was on top of the world. I'd won three awards plus a scholarship to a college journalism program. My parents were over the moon. Especially Mom."

Maggie smiled and glanced sideways at Sharon. "I was so into writing. I couldn't wait to make my mark on the world."

Her eyes drifted off again.

"We were good kids," she said. "We didn't drink or do drugs, although there was plenty of both available in those days. That night, we ordered in pizza. Tom's parents had lots of money and a huge house, so they gave us free run of the basement. His father came down around 10:30 to see if we needed anything. He handed Tom some cash, wished us all goodnight and disappeared upstairs. We were all just hanging out, drinking pop, eating pizza, and talking."

Maggie was quiet for a while.

"I got up to go to the bathroom at one point. When I came back, Tom pulled me into his lap and said, 'There's our star.' He wrapped his arm around me and handed me a pop. I took a couple of sips."

She closed her eyes and began to speak quickly, like a freight train rushing through a station.

"I open my eyes, and I'm in a strange room. The walls are white. There is no window. I look down, it's like I'm on the ceiling, watching myself," she whispered. She took a sharp breath, and blurted, "And I'm naked."

She leaned forward, holding her head in her hands. When she spoke again, her voice had changed. It was dull, monotone; a robot reading the news.

"There are tubes in my arms and down my throat. The sheets are bloody. My face is bruised; the skin is broken across my cheeks."

She sobbed suddenly.

"My hair, my long black hair. It's gone. I'm bald. Completely bald. I don't even recognize myself. But I know it must be me because a woman comes into the room, calls me by name and changes the sheets. She is so kind. I want to ask her where I am and what happened, but I can't seem to make any sound."

Maggie leaned over her knees, rubbing her hands up and down her legs.

She raised her head and looked right through Sharon.

"I found out later I'd been dumped in an alley. Someone found me and called the police. I was in a coma for weeks. My head was shaved because of all the surgeries to relieve the pressure on my brain. No one was ever arrested because I had no memory of anything happening. I couldn't press charges. My girlfriends left the party before I did, so they claimed to know nothing. Everyone figured it was Tom, but when the police questioned him, he said I'd walked home, and his buddies backed him up. My parents posted a reward, but no one ever came forward with information. It took me months to learn to walk and talk again."

"What about DNA, Maggie? Wasn't there an investigation?"

Maggie shook her head.

"This was the sixties, Sharon. There was no DNA testing in those days. Besides, Tom's father was a hot-shot lawyer. Even if we'd been able to prove it, we didn't stand a chance. They had lots of money and they…I…we…"

Maggie took a deep breath and tried again.

"It was a small town. Everyone was…white. Except for me and my mother. Mom lost her status when she married my Dad. He's white."

She looked up and saw confusion in Sharon's eyes.

"It's complicated. Point is, I was the only Native kid in my school. I worked hard to fit in, to be liked. And I thought I was. One of them, I mean. Until it happened. There was no real investigation. Cops were white, my friends were white. Rumor was I'd asked for it."

She glared at Sharon. "But you and I both know that if it had happened to a white girl, there would have been hell to pay."

"Oh, Maggie. I'm so sorry. It shouldn't be like that."

"Got that right," Maggie said. "But that wasn't the worst of it."

Maggie wiped her face with her shirt sleeve.

"I was pregnant. Me, who'd never gone on a date, let alone been kissed. I begged my parents for an abortion. But it was illegal, and they didn't have the money to send me out of the country. They sent me to my aunties, Mom's sisters, up north for my 'confinement'", she added, fingers raised in air quotes. "I was taken to the Grace Home for Wayward Girls for the birth."

"Grace," she choked. "What a joke. The Sisters wouldn't even let me see the baby. They said it was better that way."

She began to cry again, sobs ripping from her throat.

"They … wouldn't … even … tell me," she spit out the words, "if it was a boy … or a girl."

She held her arms to her chest as she rocked back and forth. "Just to know that much. After all I'd been through. That's all I wanted. To know if it was a boy or a girl. And if it was healthy."

Sharon passed her the box of tissues. Maggie grabbed a few and blew her nose. She wiped her face and closed her eyes again.

"Breathe, Maggie. Just breathe. You are safe here."

Maggie glanced down and studied the patterns in the carpet, following the lines of stitching from left to right and back again. Like watching flames in a fireplace, or waves on the shore.

"Maggie?"

Maggie raised her head, not seeing Sharon.

"What did you do after the baby was born?" Sharon asked quietly.

"They sent me back to the reservation. I stayed there with my aunties for a couple of weeks. I don't know what I would have done without them. I missed out on the scholarship obviously. A whole year of my life gone. Just like that."

She snapped her fingers.

"My parents never really got over it. Small towns are tough. Everyone knew about the pregnancy. I think it was hardest on Mom. Her friends dumped her. The priest came to the house and told her she was no longer welcome in the church. He said my sin was a stain that could never be removed. That destroyed her."

Maggie choked down some water.

"We moved away. My so-called friends had already left for college. I never saw any of them again. I got a job in a restaurant and built a new life for myself. My mother died a few months later."

"What happened, Maggie?"

Maggie looked out the window, her voice as sour as green apples in vinegar.

"Pills. She was taking two a day for depression. That morning, after I left for work, she finished the bottle. I found her when I got home. Dad drank himself to death a few years later."

Maggie rubbed her eyes.

"I was their bright and shining star, and I killed them."

"Is that true, Maggie?"

Maggie glanced up. She shook her head slowly.

"Maybe not, but it sure felt that way for a long time."

"When did that change?"

Maggie leaned back against the cushion. She gulped more water.

"One day, after Dad died, I got mad. I decided that if I couldn't find the bastard who ruined our lives, then I'd damn well make sure it couldn't happen to anyone else. That's when I joined the fight for women's rights."

She looked up at Sharon.

"You've heard of the World Organization for Women?"

"Of course."

"I built that organization from the ground up. One woman at a time. We did good things for girls and women. We made the world a safer place. And now the President and his buddies are trying to erase fifty years of progress. I can't sit back and let them do that."

"What do you plan to do about it, Maggie?"

"You'll see."

Chapter Twelve

Jack read through the feature once more and sent it to his editor. The photos from Joanna highlighted key moments in the World Organization for Women, from the early protest days to current projects around the globe. He had tried to reach the other four founding members but came up empty. Two had died in the last ten years, one was living in Europe and the other, Alicia Mitchell, refused to meet with him.

"It's all water over the bridge," she said when he called. "Or is it under the bridge? I can never remember. But it's all in the past now."

He had pressed Joanna for a comment on the proposed abortion legislation and rumored plans by the government to eliminate women's access to birth control. She had responded cautiously.

"I can't comment on rumors," she said, "and as far as we know, the legislation is only in its proposal stage. We have been meeting with State Senators and the latest donation from Judge Power seems to be a good indicator that women's rights are valued and solid."

As Jack packed up his laptop, his cell phone buzzed.

"Hey Robbie," he said. "What did you find?"

He listened for a moment.

"No kidding."

He thanked his friend, hung up and called his brother. The phone went to voicemail. After the beep, Jack left a message.

"Brad, it's me. I checked into it and there's no official reason that guy was at your house. So, hang tight for a few days. I'll stop by your place on the way home and see if I find anything unusual."

He sent a text to Hannah.

Running late. Need anything?

A few moments later, his phone pinged.

Just you!

Jack drove past the house that Brad shared with Lena and another friend. Built in the sixties, it was a two-story faux brick with three dormer windows in the roof and a large picture window near the front door. He circled the block looking for a red Corvette.

Nothing.

He pulled up in front of the house and got out, checking up and down the street. He climbed the front steps two at a time. The front door was unlocked.

He stood in the entry, listening. The house was silent.

He walked through each room, treading softly. Nothing seemed to be out of order in the living room or kitchen. There were dirty dishes in the sink. He remembered his college days and chuckled.

Upstairs, he went into the bedrooms. Clothes on the floor in the boys' rooms, but Lena's was neat and tidy, except for the desk drawer which was hanging precariously open. He texted Brad.

At your house. Need anything?

There was an immediate response.

Everything! Safe for me to come over? At Conner's. There in five.

Jack thought briefly.

Sure. I'll wait.

He headed back downstairs and pulled a chair up near the window. Still no sign of a red sports car.

Jack met his brother at the door.

"Before you go racing up to your room," he said, "just do a quick walkaround and let me know if you see anything missing or out of place, okay?"

Brad nodded and wandered through the rooms.

"Everything looks normal," he said. "Want me to check Lena and Tony's bedrooms too?

"Sure," said Jack. "You probably have a better idea of what they usually look like. But be quick. I'll keep an eye on the street."

Brad was back downstairs, backpack under one arm and pillow under the other, in less than five minutes.

"Pillow?" Jack asked.

Brad grinned.

"It's comfy, what can I say?"

Jack gave him a gentle shove and asked if everything had seemed in order upstairs.

"As far as I can tell," he said. "There's something weird about Lena's desk drawer though. She's pretty neat and tidy and it looks like it's about to fall on the floor."

"I noticed that too," Jack said. "It's as if Westholt was looking for something. I wonder if he found it."

Brad locked the front door as they left, and Jack drove him to their parents' house.

"Best you stay here for a few more days, okay? Westholt wasn't there on police business. So, let's wait and see if he goes back. I'll pop by periodically and watch for any action."

Jack pulled into his own driveway. He opened the mailbox, pulled out a few bills and flyers. Nothing important.

At least not what he was looking for.

Jack set his keys on the kitchen table and tiptoed into the office, sidestepping the creaky board in the hall. He didn't want to wake Hannah and the baby.

He closed the door, settled into the armchair and began to read, scribbling a list of facts to check on a yellow pad of paper. An hour later, he sent the finished article off to his editor just as the baby started to squawk. He turned off the laptop and put the folder away.

Tiny arms and legs wiggled a greeting from the cradle as he hurried into the bedroom.

"Hello sunshine," he said. "I'm happy to see you too."

Evelyn stared at him with big dark eyes and plunged her fist toward her mouth.

"I know, you're hungry, and you want Mummy. But first we're going to change your diaper, okay?"

Hannah stretched and smiled sleepily at him.

"Thanks, hon. I didn't even hear you come in. I guess I was tired."

The baby started to wail as he set her down on the changing table.

"Now, now, you know the routine, precious," Jack murmured. "First I tickle your tummy, so you pee in the diaper and not on me like last time," he grinned at her, "and then quick as bug, I get you changed and ready for Mums."

He fluttered the fingers of one hand above her face to distract her. He tucked the wet diaper out of the way and set a fresh one in place.

"Here you go, Mummy."

Hannah reached out her arms and drew the baby close to her breast. She gently nudged her nipple toward the eager mouth.

"Atta girl. You're becoming a pro at this, Evy."

She glanced up at her husband who was sitting on the edge of the bed.

"No word today, I guess."

He shook his head.

"You can't rush these things, Jack. We don't know what her circumstances are. She may need some time to think about it."

She rested her free hand on top of his.

"I know how much you want this. But it's out of your control right now."

He sighed.

"I just want some answers. That's all."

"I know. You're like a terrier. You don't rest until you've wrestled a story to the ground. That's what makes you good at your job. But this isn't a job – this is your life. And you're going to have to be patient."

Jack nodded.

"I'll go start some supper. Let me know if you need anything."

Chapter Thirteen

The next morning after breakfast, Daniel told his driver to take him to his office at the Supreme Court. Along the way, he checked his messages. Still no word from Madeline. The President had bought his line about the donation, so he didn't need Madeline to fix that problem. But he did need to get her home by next week. The President had been clear about that.

Then he found a message from his mother.

"Shit, her birthday party. I totally forgot."

He checked his watch and called her back.

"Happy birthday, Mother. Of course, I didn't forget. I got busy, couldn't get away. Did you have fun?"

He listened for a while, scrolling through his emails on his phone.

"Mm-hmm? Sounds good. So sorry I missed it. Work comes first, as Father used to say. I'm sure you understand."

He hung up the phone and dialed Frank's number. Voice mail. He left a message.

"Frank, need an update on Madeline. Give me a call."

The driver let him off at the East Facade. He unlocked his office door, dumped his briefcase on the leather armchair and pulled open the side drawer of his desk. A shot of bourbon to calm his nerves. He swirled the amber liquid in the crystal glass before downing it in one gulp.

Opening the folder on his desk, he considered the cases for review. Nothing urgent, he thought.

The phone rang.

"Frank? Any news?"

He listened, frowning.

"She needs to be back home by Friday," he said. "No later. I don't care what you have to do to make it happen. Understand?"

He counted on his fingers.

"You have four days. Get it done."

He hung up the phone and smiled. His wife was no match for Frank. He checked her off his mental list and leaned back, resting his feet on the desk.

Lena grabbed a piece of leftover pizza from the fridge while Madeline poured herself a cup of coffee.

"Whoa, girl," Madeline said, "don't you want some breakfast?"

"What'll you make me?" she asked.

"Avocado toast? How's that sound?"

"Works for me," Lena said, plopping down in a chair.

She waited for Madeline to prepare breakfast. Once the plates were on the table, Lena burst out, "Okay, spill. You've kept me in suspense long enough. What's going on? Why are we at Auntie Max's apartment and not at the cottage? And why am I here at all?"

Madeline held up her right hand like a stop sign.

"One thing at a time," she said. "It's a bit of a long story."

She added milk to her coffee and stirred it with a spoon.

"Things are not as they appear to be," she began.

"No shit!"

"Language, Lena."

"Just get on with it," Lena mumbled, stuffing a slice of toast in her mouth.

Madeline shook her head.

"For starters, I am not who you think I am. In fact, only Auntie Max knows the full story. I will tell you part of it, the part you need to know."

Lena stopped chewing. She stared at her mother.

"I'm on a 'need-to-know' basis?"

Madeline smiled.

"Here goes. When Max and I were girls, we used to play a game. We'd see how long we could pretend to be each other before someone would notice. It was fun, like pulling a prank on our parents or our teachers. Thing is, we looked so much alike that no one seemed to notice, and then it wasn't fun anymore."

"But you're twins! Even I got fooled today at the train station. Just for a second though."

"What gave it away?"

Lena thought for a moment.

"You smell like Mom. Auntie Max smells different, more like lilacs. And you are… lavender."

Madeline nodded.

"Very few people would notice that so, well done! Anyway, we gave up the game when we were teenagers, but it came in handy when we went to college. We took turns attending classes and trading work shifts. That way the other one could sleep in or go out with friends."

Madeline sipped her coffee.

"I'll skip over some stuff and just say that Max and I had an understanding: we would always be there for each other, no questions asked."

"Fair enough," Lena said. "But what does that have to do with dyeing your hair gray, new cell phones and all this spy stuff?"

Madeline shrugged.

"For reasons I'm not going to explain, it's important for me to vanish for a while. Max will stay in Italy for the foreseeable future, and I've stepped into her life. It's like our old game again, only there is a lot more at stake than just trying to fool people. And this is where you come in. I need you to stay with me for the summer. We will head to Max's cottage tomorrow. And you'll have to refer to me as Auntie Max, not Mom, okay?"

She took a slice of toast and watched her daughter. Lena slouched in her chair; legs sprawled out.

"How long will we be at the cottage?"

"Until the end of August," Madeline replied. "Possibly longer. It really depends on how things unfold."

"What things, Mom?"

"I can't give you any details, but I can tell you that we're going to start a book club."

Lena rolled her eyes.

"Seriously? So lame."

Madeline winked.

"It's right up your alley. Books with strong female leads. Women who are unorthodox, unconventional for their time, and who don't take no for an answer. Books that the government wants to ban."

Lena sat up straight, her face glowing.

"Yes! I've got a whole list in mind already. From that women's lit course I took. Bring it on!"

Chapter Fourteen

Madeline eased her sister's car onto the gravel road.

"Not far now," she said.

She could feel Lena's excitement building as she bounced on the seat beside her.

Some things never change, Madeline thought. She had been bringing Lena to Max's cottage every summer since she was a child. Sometimes she would stick around for a few hours, but she usually let Lena and Max enjoy their time together. Madeline spent most of the summer at the country house, leaving Daniel to his own devices. He had never questioned where they went; he was glad to have the house to himself. And his hookers, Madeline thought.

"I see the lake, I see the lake!" Lena sang, pointing with her finger. "The first person to see the lake gets an ice cream, remember?"

"Okay, you win," Madeline said. "What flavor this time?"

"Can I have two scoops?"

"Hmmm, let me think..."

"M-o-m! Oops, I mean Auntie M-a-x!"

"Okay, two scoops, but this has to be the last time you call me Mom. Pinky promise?"

Madeline extended her right baby finger toward her daughter. Lena wrapped her left baby finger around it.

"Pinky promise, *Auntie* Max," she said, winking. "And I want the usual - chocolate and strawberry."

They sat in silence as Madeline eased into the laneway behind the cottages.

"One, two, three, four, five, six!" Lena called, counting the cottages. "We're here!"

She pushed the car door open and ran up to the back veranda. She reached under the doormat and found the key. Propping open the screen door, grabbed the brass handle on the faded blue door and turned the key in the lock. A quick shove with her hip and the worn wooden door groaned open.

"Hey cottage," she said. "I'm back!"

Madeline carried the groceries inside as Lena roamed from room to room, raising blinds and opening windows. Madeline set the bags on the kitchen table and stood still, inhaling deeply. The sharp scent of pine mixed with damp sand and musky lilacs welcomed her like a soft embrace.

"Thank you, Max," she whispered.

She went back out to the car to grab their backpacks and her laptop. When she stepped into the kitchen, Lena had already unpacked the food and was helping herself to some dill pickle chips.

"Want some?" she called, stuffing another handful into her mouth.

Madeline laughed. "You never stop eating, do you?"

She dropped the bags in their bedrooms.

"So, what's first on the agenda, M…Auntie Max?"

Before Madeline could answer, Lena added with a giggle, "After a swim and lunch, I mean!"

Wrapped in towels, they washed their sandy feet in the old metal pail by the door.

"That was a great swim," Lena said, tiptoeing across the floor, leaving puddles in her wake.

"Lena! Dry off before you go inside."

Lena looked back over her shoulder.

"Oops, forgot. I'll clean it up after I get changed."

She flashed a grin as she disappeared into the bathroom.

They hung their towels and swimsuits on the clothesline. Over egg salad sandwiches, Madeline went through the guest list one more time. Three men and three women, plus the two of them. A perfect mix for their first book club meeting.

"I need to pick up a few things in town for tonight. Coming? We can get your ice cream treat if you want."

Lena bounded into the kitchen.

"So ready," she said, a gleam in her eyes. "What are we serving the book club members?"

Madeline showed her the menu – homemade brownies, a vegetable tray with hummus, and some fresh fruit.

"I thought we'd pick up some blueberries and raspberries at the farmers' market," she said. "They should be in season now."

"And corn?" Lena said. "For supper?"

"Okay, kiddo, corn too. Grab some bags."

As they pulled out of the laneway, Madeline noticed a red sportscar in her rearview mirror.

Frank drove slowly down the beach lane. He glanced at his notebook for the address and continued, watching the number signs. He parked around the corner and surveyed the neighborhood. He could hear laughter and shouting punctuated by the crash of waves. The lake must be on the other side of the cottages.

He didn't see anyone around, so he got out of the car and wandered back toward the yellow and white cottage. He checked the yards on both sides before opening the gate to the back yard. He tapped on the screen door.

When no one answered, he wandered around the side. He leaned against the trunk of an old willow tree and looked toward the open windows. He could see dishes in the sink and some papers on the table. He strolled toward the front of the cottage and stood in the shadow of the honeysuckle-laden gazebo, watching children run in and out of the waves while their parents chatted or read, stretched out on beach chairs.

It was early afternoon. He figured the cottage owner, a Maxine Pelletier according to records, was either out on the beach or in town running errands. As he walked back to his car, he paused by the open window, his hand playing with something inside the pocket of his jean jacket.

There was a gap between the window and the old wood-framed screen. He juggled the screen out wide enough to get his hand inside and pressed a listening device under the sill. After wedging the screen back in place, he stuffed his hands in his pockets and walked quickly back to his car.

He headed to a local bar for supper. Beer and fries. As he waited, he checked his phone for messages. Nothing yet. Earlier that day, as he dug deeper into Madeline's background, he had found very little. A couple of sorority photos, a mention of her engagement to Daniel – all the celebrities and power couples from across the country had attended their wedding – but not much else. It seemed odd to him and so he pursued a different tack.

By calling in some favors and going through old college yearbooks, he discovered that there were two women with similar names. Based on the photos, he figured they were either twins or close in age. And there was a lot more information on Maxine Pelletier. In fact, she seemed to have had such an active social life that Frank wondered if the woman ever slept.

He had tracked Maxine to an apartment in a small town. No one was around when he visited the apartment. He asked a couple of neighbors who said they'd heard she was going to her cottage for the summer.

And here he was, sipping a warm beer in an empty bar in a sleepy beach town, waiting for the sun to go down.

Chapter Fifteen

After supper, Madeline waited on the back porch, welcoming friends and neighbors to the first book club meeting.

An older man and woman came through the gate.

"Max, so good to see you again! I didn't know you'd be back for the summer," the woman said.

Madeline gave her a quick hug.

"Plans change, Audrey," she said, smiling. She turned to greet Sam, Audrey's husband of forty years. "But you two never do."

She showed them into the kitchen.

"Make yourselves at home in the front room," she said. "There's a list of book ideas on the table if you want to take a look."

Once everyone arrived, Madeline latched the hook on the back door and Lena asked everyone to serve themselves in the kitchen.

"Lots of yummy munchies and juices," she said. "And if anyone wants coffee or tea, there's plenty to go around. We'll do proper introductions once you're fed and watered."

Madeline handed out a sheet of paper and a pencil to everyone.

"This is just a list of possible book ideas," she said. "Some of you may already have a book in mind, and that's great. But if you're not sure, this might help."

She sat down in her grandmother's wooden rocking chair and waited for Lena to find a seat.

"Thank you all for coming," Madeline said. "I thought we could start with introductions since some of you know each other but others don't. Maybe give your first name, and the title of the book you've chosen. And if you haven't picked a book yet, just say so."

She sat back and gestured to the woman on her left to begin.

"I'm Audrey," she said, standing up. "Me and Sam, that's my husband in the green t-shirt, we have the cottage two doors down. We haven't picked books yet, but the list here looks real interesting. I'm a bit slow at reading these days cuz my eyes are going, so I will need to get one of those audio books or big print. That being said,

I'm super excited to be part of this group. And can I just say that it's about time women got the attention we deserve. Not just in books either."

She fist-pumped the air before sitting down.

Lena winked at her mother. She went next.

"So, I'm Lena, and I'm here for the summer with my Auntie Max," she pointed to Madeline. "I just finished a course at college on women's lit, so that's where some of the book suggestions come from. Totally agree with you, Audrey; women authors and main characters are far too often overlooked. I think we're going to have a lot of fun. Oh, and the book I've picked is *The War on Women* by Sue Lloyd-Roberts. Not an easy read, but an important one."

Shelley raised her hand.

"I'm Shelley, and Lena and I've been besties for years. I wanted to say decades, but I guess we're not that old, are we?"

The group chuckled.

"Anyways, we've spent most summers together here at the beach. Me and my Dad, that's him with the beard and glasses, we have the cottage across the lane. The book I want us to read is *The Paper Bag Princess.* I know it's a children's book, but I think it's the first one I read that showed me girls can fight their own dragons."

Sam sat with his arms crossed and his legs stretched out in front of him. He lifted his chin and smiled at the group.

"So, like Audrey said, we're together. Have been for over forty years now. Not much surprises me anymore, but her decision to join this book club, and drag me along, I didn't see that comin'. Not that I mind. Don't get me wrong. I love to read. Why, my Mum said I had my nose in a book the day I was born. Might be a wee bit of an exaggeration, but…"

He paused for the ripple of laughter.

"Now I didn't have a book in mind when I got here, but having heard what everyone has said, I've gone and made up my mind. It's not on the list, but I think it should be. *Atlas Shrugged.* There's a book makes you think. And it does have a mighty strong woman lead. In fact, she makes me think of my Audrey in some ways – she speaks her mind, she isn't afraid to fight for the little guy, and she never gives up."

He cleared his throat and nodded in his wife's direction. Audrey beamed and blew him a kiss.

Brian grinned.

You two lovebirds," he said. "Get a room!"

Brian waited for the laughter to subside. He leaned forward in his chair.

"I've known Audrey and Sam, Lena and Max since I bought the cottage fifteen years ago. It's a really tight community here. Everyone looks out for each other. Shelley and I needed that after Sarah died. That's my wife. This place welcomed us with open arms. The people here are like family."

He rubbed his hand across his beard and cleared his throat.

"When Max mentioned this book club, I jumped at the chance. I'm a prof at St. John's. And believe it or not, I teach women's studies. Well, I co-teach the course with a colleague. She's the one who had the vision for a man and woman teaching the course together. She thought it would be good for students to get the dual perspective on women's issues. Since I see myself as a feminist, and we can get into the definition of that at some point if you want, it felt like a good fit. The discussions the class gets into are astounding. So rich and thought-provoking."

He stopped and looked at his daughter. Shelley was wagging her index finger at him.

"Okay, I see I'm getting the signal to wrap it up. Part of the challenge of being a teacher I guess – I like to hear myself talk."

He picked up the list from the table.

"I know you had women-focused books in mind, Max, but I think this book club needs to be about more than just women."

Brian held up a hand to silence the protests from around the circle.

"Hear me out, okay? I think the government's attack on women's rights is just the beginning, so I'd like to broaden our reading to include all forms of oppression. It's time we all faced what's wrong with our country, and books are a good first step in raising awareness. With that in mind, and with your consent, Max, I'm going to go with a recently banned book – *Stamped From The Beginning.*"

He set the paper down and turned to the woman at his side. "Next?"

"Okay," she said hesitantly. "I'm Janet. I'm the librarian in the next town over. And I hear you, Brian. I was going to choose my childhood favorite, *Little Women.* I love Jo, the main character. She's very much her own person, independent, opinionated and fiercely herself at a time when women were supposed to be docile and domesticated. But given what you've said, Brian, I'm going with a more recent book, *The Vanishing Half.* It will definitely create some good discussion."

She sat back in her chair; her face flushed.

"I guess I'm last," said the man beside her. "Well, except for you, Max. I'm Marshall. I'm Janet's neighbor, so we came together."

"Not that we're together," Janet added hastily.

Marshall glanced at her and grinned.

"Right you are. I'm a plumber by trade. Just retired last year. And I've been looking for something to do. I don't really have any hobbies. I do read a lot, but that's not a hobby, is it? It's a way of life as far as I'm concerned. I'm in the library all the time, and Janet and I were talking one day, and she mentioned she was joining this book club. And I said what a coincidence because I'd got an invite from Max as well, and so we decided to carpool. Long story short, I don't have a book picked out yet so I'll see what I can find on the list. Or, Janet, maybe you can see one here that you think I'd enjoy?"

"We'll talk later, Marshall," she said quietly.

Madeline smiled at the group. "So here we are. As you all know, I'm Maxine, Max to my friends. My book choice is *A Room of One's Own.* It is non-fiction and an older book, but I find the message particularly timely these days with the government's legislation. While the author focuses on the need for women's voices in the literary world, I think her ideas apply to all aspects of life. Virginia

Woolf was a thought leader, an early activist, and controversial. Exactly the kind of stimulation we need for our discussions here."

She sat back and thought for a moment.

"Now we need to pick a month for our books. I know Audrey and Marshall haven't chosen books yet, and that's fine. You can still select a month and give us the titles later this week. Since Lena is only here for the summer, can I suggest that we look at her book first? I'll pass around a sheet of paper, and you can sign up for the month that best suits you. Oh, and is everyone okay with sharing email addresses? Anyone not?

She glanced around the group.

"Alright then, I'll send out a group email tomorrow with the list of books, the months, and everyone's address so we can stay in touch. Sound good? Who wants to host the next meeting?"

Brian raised his hand, as Lena interrupted.

"Hey, before we go, I just had a thought. What'll we call the book club? I think we need a name."

After a quick discussion, they settled on The Cottage Lane Bookies.

Chapter Sixteen

As the group broke off into conversation, Madeline heard a knock at the back door. Lena came over to her quickly and whispered, "We're not expecting anyone else, are we?"

Madeline shook her head.

"You stay here and keep people busy. I'll take care of it."

She straightened her glasses and smiled at her guests as she passed through the living room into the kitchen. She turned on the porch light but left the screen door locked. On the back step, she could see a man of medium build with a neatly trimmed beard and closely shaved dark hair, speckled with white. In the yellow glare of the porch light, his eyes looked sunken and menacing.

"Yes?" she said.

"I'm Chief Inspector Westholt. I am looking for Lena Power. Her father has reported her missing and I have reason to believe she might be with you."

Bullshit, Madeline thought. Dan has not filed a missing person report. I know him too well for that.

"Wait here," she said.

She went back to the living room and motioned to Lena. She whispered to her and then accompanied her to the back door.

"Lena," she said, "this man says your father has reported you missing. Do you want to talk to him?"

Lena shrugged and stared at the man.

"Who is he?"

"I'm Chief Inspector Westholt," Frank repeated.

"So?" Lena said, raising an eyebrow. "Prove it. Show me your I.D."

Frank reached into his pocket and pulled out a card. He held it close to the screen so that both women could read it.

"Anyone could get a card printed," Lena said. "This tells me nothing. Is there a number I can call to prove you are who you say you are?"

Frank spoke in a low tone.

"Look, your father has reported you missing. I am here to find you and take you home. We can do this the easy way, or …"

"Or what?" said Madeline, raising her voice. The conversation in the living room stopped. She could hear footsteps heading toward the door.

"Are you threatening us?" she asked.

Frank stepped back from the door as the heavy-set shapes of Brian and Marshall filled the kitchen entry behind Madeline.

"What seems to be the problem here?" Marshall asked.

"This man claims to be a cop but won't give us a number to call to prove it," Lena said, keeping her eyes firmly on Frank. "He says my father has sent him to find me, but I doubt that very much because my father has never given a shit about me. Half the time he doesn't remember my name. So, I'm not inclined to believe this little toad."

Madeline stifled a giggle. Apparently, Frank had never been called a toad before. His face flushed and his eyes bulged. Out of the corner of her eye, she saw Brian pull his cell phone out of his pocket and press in three numbers.

Frank noticed as well.

"Look, just confirm that you are Lena and you're here of your own accord, safe and sound, and I'll be on my way."

"Fine, I am Lena, and I'm here because this is where I want to be. College is over, and I'm 20 years old, so I am free to make my own choices. You can tell my father that my life is none of his fuckin' business. Oh, and tell him that if he ever does anything like this again, I'll sue him for harassment."

"You heard the lady," Brian said. "Best be on your way."

He spoke into his phone.

"I'm calling to report an attempted abduction," he said. He gave the address and his phone number as Frank jumped backwards onto the path and was out the gate before Brian completed the call. "Oh, and he's driving a red Corvette."

Brian tucked his phone into his back pocket.

"That should keep him busy for a while," he said. "Nothing like a little excitement for our first book club night. Say, Max, where do you keep the beer? I don't know about you, but I could use a cold one!"

Frank's phone rang as the police officer was checking his license, insurance, and identification. He glanced down at the number and groaned.

"Look, are we done here?" he growled as the officer returned his documents. "I have urgent matters to attend to in the city."

The officer stared at him.

"I think you should step out of the car, sir. Now."

"You have got to be kidding me. Do you know who I am?"

"Just doing my job, Chief Inspector. Out of the car. Set your gun down on the seat where I can see it."

Frank rolled his eyes but did as he was told. The officer gave him a pat down before writing out a ticket for speeding.

"You are a suspect in a reported kidnapping attempt, so don't leave the state. We will be following up. And I suggest that you not return to this community unless you have a legitimate search warrant. It would be a shame to have to arrest you…sir."

Frank spun gravel at the officer's feet as he drove away.

"Rookies," he muttered. He had memorized the officer's name and planned to follow up.

He stopped at a gas station ten miles down the road so he could return Daniel's call.

"I know, I know, Dan, but I have good news and bad news. The good news is that I found Lena. Lena, your daughter? No, I haven't found Madeline. But Lena's fine. She is staying at a beach cottage on the coast. According to records, it belongs to her aunt Maxine. Maxine? Forget it. No, no sign of Madeline. Yes, I'll keep searching."

He hung up and drove off into the night.

After washing the dishes, Madeline closed and locked the back door but left the outside light on. Brian had suggested that she switch the light on and off three times in the night if the man returned.

"I'm a light sleeper and my bedroom faces the lane."

"I'm sure we'll be fine," Madeline said.

"Watching you and Lena in action, I'm sure you will be too," Brian said, chuckling. "I wouldn't come back if I were him."

His eyes grew serious.

"I know we talked to the police, but be careful, okay?"

"Will do," Madeline said.

She checked all the windows before she went to bed. It was too hot to close them, but she lowered them to make it harder for someone to climb in. She set up trip wires by the back and front doors and placed her grandmother's brass bells on the windowsills. Running her fingers under the living room window, she found the bug. She sat down at the desk, gloves on, to examine it more closely. Satisfied it was a local manufacture, she crushed and disposed of it.

Before going to bed, Madeline searched the rest of the house carefully.

Lena was sitting in bed reading as she walked past. Madeline leaned against the door frame.

"So," Lena said, "want to fill me in on what's going on?"

Madeline shook her head.

"Like I said before, there's only so much I can tell you. It's better for you that way."

"Dad didn't file a missing person report, did he?" she said, smirking.

"I doubt it very much. I think he's actually trying to find your mother," Madeline said with a wink. "And this guy was hoping that you'd be naïve enough to tell him where to find her."

She squeezed Lena's hand.

"You are a firecracker, you know? You handled the whole situation brilliantly. I'm proud of you."

Lena smiled.

"Thanks, Auntie Max. You weren't so bad yourself…for an old lady!"

Madeline gave her a playful swat on the cheek.

"I think we're good for tonight. Tomorrow we'll talk more. If you hear anything unusual in the night though, is your phone handy?"

Lena pulled her phone out from under her pillow.

"Right here. And I've got 911 on speed dial, don't you worry."

"That's my girl," Madeline said, kissing the top of her head. "Sweet dreams."

"Night, night, Auntie Max," Lena called as Madeline headed down the hall to her bedroom.

Madeline lowered the blind on her window. She pulled her laptop onto the bed and did a search. No missing person reports for her or for Lena. Frank had been lying.

I wonder if he recognized me, she thought. She closed the laptop and sat back against the headboard.

Chapter Seventeen

Rumors had been circulating all weekend that Congress had been called into session behind closed doors. Jack tried to get confirmation, but no one was talking. Even his usual leads were tight-lipped. One of his inside sources made the curious remark that 'all will be revealed on Friday'.

Friday morning, he got a call from his editor.

"The President has called a press briefing for today at 4 p.m., Jack. Be there."

At 3 p.m., he pulled his motorcycle into a parking spot in front of Swing's. A block from the White House, the coffee shop was a familiar haunt for journalists and politicians. He eavesdropped on a few conversations but heard nothing new.

Munching on a sugar donut, he strolled down the street. An area of the Rose Garden was sectioned off for the media in front of a podium. Jack nodded to his cameraman and pulled out his recorder. He found a seat near the front and chatted briefly with colleagues.

At 4 p.m. on the dot, the door to the Rose Garden opened. Several security officers came out first, surveying the area, followed by the President, Chief Justice Power, the Speaker of the House and the Senate Majority Leader. Two clergy members joined the group followed by additional security officers.

Daniel approached the microphone and jabbed it with a finger. A sharp clunk thudded through the air.

"I see it's working," he said with a grin.

He took some notes out of the inside pocket of his suit jacket and cleared his throat.

"Gentlemen," he began, and added after a quick look around, "and lady."

Jack glanced to his right. The only woman present was Amanda Chartright, reporter for *City Central*. Amanda caught his eye and waved. They had worked together on several projects.

"We are here today to announce a major legislative breakthrough passed last night by the unanimous decision of Congress. This legislation promises to build, promote, and sustain the strong family values that are inherent in our society and our Constitution. To provide a deeper insight into this impressive work by Congress, I present to you the President himself."

The group gathered behind the President applauded loudly as he walked to the podium.

"Thank you for coming. This is indeed a momentous occasion," he said. "Congress worked tirelessly over the last few days to debate, modify and approve the legislation that I am about to announce. It is their hard work and dedication to the people of this country that has made today's announcement possible."

He paused and looked down at his notes.

"I am honored to announce that Congress agreed unanimously, and I must stress that word, that our role as the elected representatives of the people of this great country is to uphold the values established by our forefathers. Namely: the importance of family; adherence to faith; and respect for life. As our faith leaders here today will confirm, the approved legislation has the support of the major faith groups in our glorious country.

"We have reworked the wording to ensure inclusivity; no one is excluded. This document, which shall go down in history as a turning point in the evolution of our country, represents many, many hours of hard work by Congress and Chief Justice Power. Together, they have crafted a magnificent legal document to serve our country as we move forward into the coming decades. We are calling this new law *"The Statute of Faith, Family and Freedom"*. It comes into effect immediately."

The President paused and looked at the media. Most were frantically taking notes. A few were busy snapping photos.

"I'm sure you are all eager to learn more about this impressive piece of legislative work. We will provide the highlights now, and details will follow in the coming days. A copy of the full document will be made available to the media following this press conference."

He gestured to Daniel.

"I now bring forward a man who needs no introduction. Chief Justice Power will brief you on the highlights of the document he has carefully reviewed."

Daniel stepped up to the mike.

"Thank you, Mr. President," he said, smiling and shaking the President's hand. "I am humbled by the endless hours of hard work that you and Congress have invested in this legislation. From a legal perspective, there is no finer document in existence. And from the perspective of a citizen, there is no greater assurance in our collective future as a great and glorious country."

He held up a ring-bound document with a blue cover.

"This, gentlemen…and lady, is the moment we have all been waiting for. It is our way of honoring the vision of our forefathers; their ambition and drive to make this country what it is today – a financially strong economy, based on faith, a good work ethic, and solid family values."

Just get to the point, Jack thought. He sensed the windup to a sucker punch.

Daniel set the booklet down on the podium and leafed through the opening pages.

"I will share with you the executive summary."

He cleared his throat and began to read.

Jack could not believe what he was hearing. He glanced at Amanda. She was stone-faced. If she had her way, Daniel Power would be six feet under, he thought.

He waited for the Chief Justice to finish so he could ask him about the donation to the World Organization for Women. But as soon as the presentation was over, Daniel introduced the Speaker of the House and the Senate Majority Leader who praised the legislation. They were followed by the faith representatives: two Christian clergymen.

Finally, the President approached the mike and announced that the conference was over. The media shouted out questions as the President strode back into the White House. None were answered.

Jack shook his head in disbelief. He turned to a colleague and said, "I think we just witnessed the end of democracy."

Amanda marched over to him, eyes blazing.

"Can you believe it? Not only are they trying to turn back time and shove women into a box, they wouldn't even take questions? What are they so afraid of?"

Before Jack could comment, she stormed to her car and drove off.

Jack texted Hannah.

Won't be home for supper. Working late. Big story.

His phone pinged right away.

No prob. Good luck.

He drove to the office and tapped on his editor's door. Ed was on the phone.

"Huge story, Ed," he whispered. "Save the front page for this one. I'll get it and photos to you as soon as I can."

Ed gave him a thumbs up and went back to his conversation.

Jack sat down at his desk, eyeing the laptop.

He pictured the layout on the front page and decided he would create a sidebar with bullet points. The main article would describe who was there and what was said, although he was determined to include what was not said. That's far more important, he thought.

He also wanted to get some reaction from Joanna, the CEO of the World Organization for Women.

"I wonder what Ms. Carpenter will think of this," he muttered, making a note to call Maggie.

Jack submitted the feature article just before the deadline. His editor had come by the office twice, rapping on the door. Jack waved him away. He had reached Joanna, but not Maggie. Joanna was stunned.

"You can quote me on this, Jack," she said, her voice quivering with rage. "The World Organization for Women is shocked and confused by this new legislation, particularly in light of the $1 million donation last week from Chief Justice Power. We can only assume that the donation was designed to buy our silence. If that was the intent, the government will be disappointed."

"What do you plan to do?" Jack asked.

He heard a click, ending the call.

Madeline and Lena stared at the computer screen as the live broadcast of the President's press conference wrapped up.

"I don't believe it," Lena said. "And yet I do. Just the kind of asshole thing Dad would do. No wonder you left."

"Your father isn't an asshole," Madeline said. "He's just easily manipulated. And he has some archaic views of women and their place in society."

"How can you defend him like that? This law condemns women to a lifetime of pregnancy and housework. That is not how I plan to spend my life – under the control of some man who thinks he's better than I am just because he's got a dick."

Madeline frowned.

"The frustrating part is that generations of women worked really hard to make sure you and your friends, Lena, would be free to chart your own course. Suddenly that's all gone."

Lena glanced at her. "We can't just give up. We need a plan. I'll call Shelley and…"

"Hold up, girl, not so fast. This has been very carefully orchestrated. We have to be strategic. We need to do some research, so we can use their facts against them. If you stick to facts, no one can dismiss you."

"How do you know so much, Mo…Auntie Max?"

"Long story. None of which matters at this moment. I think it's time for a swim, and tonight I have some work to do. Tomorrow morning, we will regroup and decide on next steps, okay?"

"Okay," Lena grumbled. "I don't see why we have to wait. But I could use a swim."

Madeline inserted the memory stick into the side of her laptop. She clicked on the file called "Draft 3" and read carefully through the document. It was an early version of the legislation Daniel had crafted for the President. Before she left, Madeline had spent months on Daniel's home laptop, downloading copies of various files she hoped would be useful in the days to come. For such an ambitious man, he was surprisingly sloppy with his online passwords. And the code for his safe. The photos she found in the safe had shocked but not surprised her.

"Karma sucks, baby," she muttered. "This is payback for all of Lena's dance recitals, school plays and parent-teacher conferences you were too busy to attend. And all those nights you were "working late".

Madeline shook her head, scrolled to the top of the document and started over, making notes in the margin.

Chapter Eighteen

Early the next morning, Jack rapped lightly on Maggie's front door. Her face fell when she saw who it was. She shrugged and motioned him inside.

He sat down and looked at her, frowning. She was pale with dark circles under her eyes. He noticed that her hand shook slightly as she reached for her cup, and she was still wearing pajamas under her robe.

"Are you okay?" he asked. "You look like you didn't sleep all night."

"Got that right," she replied, rubbing her forehead with her free hand. She took a sip of coffee, set the cup down and sat up straighter.

"Is this an official visit?" she asked. "Because what I'm feeling right now isn't suitable for print."

"Fair enough," he said. "The news about the legislation shocked the heck out of me. I can't imagine what you're thinking."

"You know, I'm not even sure," she said, attempting to smile. "I knew this could happen, especially with our current government. But I was hoping I was wrong. I never thought they'd go this far."

She shook her head.

"What's that expression? 'The more things change, the more they stay the same.' That's what this feels like. Fifty friggin' years of work. And here we are, back in the Dark Ages. I lay in bed last night, asking myself 'What's the point?'"

Jack sat in silence.

"There was a time, Jack, when something like this would've lit a fire deep inside me. I'd be hellbent for justice. Today, I just want to crawl into a hole and pretend none of this is happening. I've lost my drive. I think that worries me more than anything."

She cradled her cup in her hands.

"Look," Jack said, scratching his head, "I'm not sure if it's good or bad news, but I wanted to let you know the President has called another media conference this morning. I'm heading there now. Maybe we can talk after?"

Maggie shrugged.

"Sure. It can't get any worse, can it?"

Alicia pulled the newspaper from her mailbox after breakfast. She had a bit of time to herself. Jerry was still in bed, recovering from his first chemo treatment. She didn't have the twins today. She sat down at the kitchen table and poured herself a second cup of coffee. Within minutes, she was on the phone to Maggie.

"Mags, have you seen the paper? I know I said I wasn't going to get involved, but this is crazy. We have to do something."

"We, Ali? I thought you'd counted yourself out on this one."

She could hear the edge in Maggie's voice.

"Change of plans, Mag. I don't know how I'll find the time or the energy, but I can't sit back and do nothing. How can I help?"

"Want to join my book club?"

When Jack left Maggie's, he headed to the White House for the next press conference. He was surprised to see the First Lady accompanying the President to the podium.

The President introduced his wife, Magda, to the media.

"I believe the media, and all women, will find my wife's perspective on the *Statute of Faith, Family and Freedom* enlightening," he said before taking a seat at the back of the stage.

"This should be interesting," Jack murmured to a colleague.

Magda set her notes down on the podium and thanked her husband for the introduction.

Turning to the media, she took a deep breath. When she began to speak, Jack noticed she had a powerful voice. She was a natural on stage, pausing and looking at each member of the media individually as she spoke.

"I come before you this morning as the President's wife," she began. "We have been married for ten years and I never thought I would be standing here. You see, as part of our prenuptial agreement, he assured me that I would not have to speak in public. This morning that changed when he insisted that my perspective on this new law was vital to the future of our nation."

Jack was watching the President. He had seen more confident smiles on corpses.

The First Lady held up a piece of paper.

"This is the speech prepared for me by the President's speech writer. It reads as follows."

She cleared her throat.

"As the President's wife, I fully support the Statute of Faith, Family and Freedom because it will bring families closer together, restore a foundation of spiritual values in our communities, and ensure that our future as a country is solid and strong."

She looked up at the media, tore the speech in half and clutched the pieces in her right hand.

"I now stand before you as a woman. I cannot support a law that denies the rights of anyone in our country - regardless of gender identity, sexual preference, race, culture or faith, whether you are wealthy or poor, educated or illiterate, Native American or immigrant. And, by the way, we are all immigrants here. Including everyone on this stage."

Jack snapped a photo of the President as he gestured at the sound engineer, making slashing marks across his throat. The engineer was oblivious, captivated by what was happening on stage.

"In light of this new law, I declare August 26 to be Women's Choice Day, and I urge all people to take a stand to support women and our right to make our own choices. This is my final act as First Lady. And as the President's wife."

Suddenly the mike went dead.

She smiled, turned and dropped the shredded speech into her husband's lap along with her wedding ring. She strode off the stage, down the stairs and into a waiting limousine.

The media erupted in laughter as the President shot out of his seat and ran after her. He changed his mind halfway to the car and whispered to one of his security agents. Turning his back on the media, he disappeared inside the White House.

The President paced back and forth in front of the windows in the Oval Office. He turned toward the door at the sound of a knock.

"Yes?"

Ryan poked his face inside and said, "Security on line one, sir."

The President put his phone on speaker.

"Go ahead."

"We've located her. She was dropped off at the World Organization for Women headquarters downtown."

"For fuck's sake!"

"Sir? She wasn't alone. Your daughters were with her."

Silence filled the phone line.

"Sir? They had bags with them. Several bags each."

"What, are they moving in?"

"It appears so. Apparently, the building has self-contained apartment units, fully furnished. The place is built like a fortress. It covers two city blocks, surrounded by a 12' high brick wall with spikes along the top ridge, and there seems to be well-trained security on the gate and within the compound. We took a drone up to check out the options."

"Good work," the President growled. "Leave someone on watch 24/7. And keep me informed."

"Yes, sir."

The President ended the call and pressed another button. Ryan opened the door and approached the desk.

"We need to issue a media release. One that states, in no uncertain terms, that my wife is mentally unstable and cannot be held accountable for her actions today. You know the drill. Have it on my desk in 30 minutes. We need to get on top of this immediately."

Chapter Nineteen

Jack called Maggie as soon as the conference ended.

"You're not going to believe this," he said.

"Try me."

"The First Lady started reading a prepared speech in support of the new legislation. Then she tore it up and said that, as a woman, she couldn't support it. She announced August 26 as Women's Choice Day and asked people to come out and show support."

"No way! What did the big man say to that?"

"He cut the sound to her mike. But she just stormed off the stage, dropping the speech and her wedding ring in his lap."

"Yes!" Jack could hear a smile in her voice. "Where did she go?"

"No one knows."

"Maybe it's not too late," she said slowly. "I spent the last few hours researching. I think I know what's behind their grand scheme; the reason they are so focused on women, especially white women. Maybe you should drop by."

Jack checked his watch.

"I'll be there in fifteen."

When Jack arrived, Maggie handed him three pages.

"Take a look at the top one. Current population stats, broken down by gender and race."

Jack skimmed the page. He looked up at Maggie, with a raised eyebrow.

"You're going to have to explain," he said. "I see what this says but I don't understand what it has to do with anything."

Maggie grabbed the paper and pointed with her finger.

"See this? According to the national census, women outnumber men in this country and have for at least the last fifty years. The same is true for most countries in the world. There's strength in numbers, Jack. Imagine what could happen if women actually used the power we hold."

She pulled out the next page.

"Within twenty years, white people will no longer be the majority racial group. Who's been in power for over 200 years? White men. Who's in power now? White men. This chart shows that the current racial minority population will grow by almost 75% in the next three decades. You can bet the government is running scared of this stat. What will happen to their cushy jobs when they are no longer the majority?"

She held up the third page.

"Look at this. The majority of women having abortions are white and unmarried. If the men in power want to hold on to their control, they need to put a stop to abortion and contraception and persuade young white women to get married to white men and have lots of white babies. Are you getting it now?"

Jack looked blankly at her.

"Sounds like a conspiracy theory."

"Oh, Jack! Don't be so naïve! What would happen if women put our numbers advantage to good use? And if non-whites knew they're on the verge of becoming the majority population in our country? Think about it. Everything, and I mean everything, could change. And change for the better, I think.

"We could finally have a just society where all people had equal rights, equal opportunity, equal choice. Where the government would represent everyone in the country and not just wealthy white men. It could be a real government of the people, by the people, for the people, instead of one that only pays lip service to those democratic ideals."

Jack sat back on the couch, smiling.

"I thought you said you'd lost your drive," he said.

Maggie chuckled.

"Okay, you caught me out. What I have here is solid gold. But I am not in a position to do anything with it."

She gave him a sideways glance.

Jack stared at her.

"What are you suggesting?" he asked.

"It's obvious, isn't it? Being the cutting-edge investigative reporter that you are, if you happened to come across stats like this in the course of your research, you'd probably write about it, wouldn't you?"

Maggie smiled.

"I've read your stuff over the years. You're good, Jack. If anyone can find a way to get this information out to the people, you can."

Jack crossed his arms over his chest. He looked out the window and watched the daylilies dancing in the wind. He could feel excitement rumbling in his chest like an approaching thunderstorm. He stretched out his arms and placed his hands on his knees.

"This could be a dynamite series," he said, almost to himself. "I'm pretty sure my editor and publisher would go for it and cover my back. The government wouldn't like it though."

He turned to Maggie.

"Give me those pages. I'll research it further and if it looks like there's something to this, I'll put an article together. I always protect my sources, so you don't need to worry. But if you think of anything else, let me know. It really could provide a plausible explanation for this legislation. If I expose them though, there could be repercussions. I'll need to talk this over with my wife and make sure we have a backup plan. I've been threatened before, but that was when I was single. Now with Hannah and the baby, I need to think differently."

He grinned.

"It will be so worth it if you're right."

Maggie gave him a high five.

"Trust me, Jack, this is just the beginning."

Chapter Twenty

When Jack got back to his office, he found a new media release sitting on his desk. It was from the Office of the President, questioning the First Lady's mental wellbeing. Jack whistled.

"Let the games begin."

He crafted an article for the front page on the First Lady's remarks. Underneath, as an addendum, he added a small section with the memo from the President suggesting that his wife was experiencing a mental breakdown and asking the public to respect the family's privacy during this "challenging time." Before he submitted the article and photos, he checked his phone messages.

Joanna had called. He could hear a ripple of laughter in her message. He called her back and changed the title on his article to *First Lady Has Last Word.* At the bottom of the memo from the President, he added an editorial note mentioning that sources indicated the First Lady and the President's daughters had sought refuge at the World Organization for Women.

He set up an interview appointment with the three of them for the next morning.

Jack was humming as he walked into the house. He wrapped his arms around Hannah and gave her a hug.

"Hello, beautiful," he said, kissing her softly on the lips.

"Hello yourself," she replied, resting her head on his shoulder.

"How's your day been?" he asked.

"Too long. Really glad you're home. Evy has wanted to eat every couple of hours, so I haven't had time to rest let alone make dinner. Do you think you could pull something together?"

"Consider it done," he said, massaging her neck. "Just let me wash up and I'll get on it. Go put your feet up for a bit."

Hannah wandered into the living room. She stretched out on the couch and stuffed a pillow under her head.

"If I fall asleep, Jack, wake me. I'm starving."

Within a few moments, she was snoring. Jack smiled and opened the fridge, looking for inspiration.

He whipped up a cheese omelet, cut up some apple slices and toasted some bread. After setting it on the table, he walked quietly over and touched Hannah on the shoulder.

"Supper's ready, Sleeping Beauty," he whispered.

She groaned and rolled over. Pushing herself to a sitting position, she held her head in her hands.

"Have you checked on the baby?" she asked.

"Just did. She's still sleeping so come and eat while it's hot."

They finished their supper in silence. Hannah pushed her plate back, scanning Jack's face.

"Okay, you're positively vibrating," she said. "Spill."

Jack laughed.

"You won't believe what happened today. The President called a media conference, and it was his wife who spoke."

"His wife? She's never said boo before. She just shows up at events in tight, skimpy dresses and hangs on his arm. I always thought she was a bit of a floozy."

"Not at all," Jack said. "Turns out she's an excellent speaker and today she went totally off-script. You should have seen the President's face. I thought he was going to have a stroke. She announced that she could not, as a woman, support the new legislation, and she called on all citizens to stand up to support women's rights on August 26. She declared it to be Women's Choice Day. By that point, the President had her mike turned off, but it didn't stop her. She tore up the speech he had given her and dropped it and her wedding ring in his lap. She marched off the stage and got into a limo."

Hannah clapped her hands.

"Where did she go?"

"This is the best part," he said. "She's staying at the World Organization for Women. And…she took his daughters with her."

Hannah laughed.

"Alright! That's what I call leadership. Honestly, Jack, if I didn't have you to talk to, I wouldn't have any idea what's going on out there. I'm so wrapped up with the baby these days."

Tears filled her eyes. He reached over and took her hands in his.

"It'll be okay, Hannah. Remember the nurse said there would be days like this. And you know you can always call my Mum to give you a hand. Or Beverley next door. She said she'd be happy to pop over. All you have to do is say the word."

Hannah looked down at the floor.

"I should be able to do this, Jack. It's supposed to feel natural. But some days, I just want out. Am I a bad mother?"

"You are the best mum Evy could have," he said gently. "Remember you're not a superhero though. I don't see an 'S' on your chest."

Jack lifted her to her feet and nudged her back to the couch.

"As soon as Evy wakes up, I'll change her and bring her to you. Just rest for now, okay?"

As he cleared the table and started the dishes, the baby began to cry. The rest of the discussion would have to wait.

Early the next morning, Jack parked his motorcycle a block away from the headquarters of the World Organization for Women. He wanted to check the layout before he went inside for his interview with the President's wife and daughters.

He crossed the street to a café to grab a bagel and coffee. He and Hannah had been up late talking about the implications of the articles he wanted to write. They agreed on a safety plan, and she had packed bags for the three of them, just in case.

He stood outside the coffee shop, noticing the details of the building that loomed in front of him. An institution of some sort originally, he thought. The high brick walls topped with spikes suggested a prison. Behind the wrought iron gate, wide enough to drive a tank through, he could see a paved space, almost like parade grounds. The building itself was impressive – seven stories high, gray brick, ornate bars on the windows, and small towers at each of the four corners. Watching closely, he saw slight movement at two of the towers. Security, no doubt.

He sat down at a table in front of the café to eat his bagel. Anyone arriving at the building had to be buzzed in by security at the gate. He decided to walk around the outer perimeter of the property to see if there was another entrance.

He completed the circuit and returned to the main gate. There was no other way in or out apart from a locked parking garage. He had noticed security cameras along the walls, in addition to uniformed personnel on the sidewalk at each corner. He wondered why the organization needed such tight protection.

At 8:55 a.m., he approached the front gate, showed his media badge and explained to the guard in the gatehouse that he had a 9 a.m. appointment with Joanna Price. The guard took his badge and closed the partition. He could hear a low murmur as she spoke on the phone.

She returned his badge to him and pressed a button to open a small door in the gate.

"Please wait here," she said. "Someone will be with you shortly." She returned to her post in the gatehouse.

Jack looked around. There was little activity in the square behind the gate. He saw a few security vehicles parked to one side, and half a dozen personnel near the main door to the building. One of them was walking toward him.

"Mr. Winthrup?" the woman said. "Please follow me."

She used a fingerprint scanner to open the main door. He followed her down a long corridor and up one flight of stairs to an office. There was no name plate. She opened the door and motioned for him to go inside.

He stepped into a spacious room furnished with a couch, several armchairs, and a low table with a pitcher of water and five glasses. Before sitting down, he walked over to the window. It overlooked a large central courtyard with raised gardens, benches, large shade trees and a splash pad where children played under the watchful eyes of their mothers.

"Jack," a woman said. He turned and saw Joanna walking toward him. Three women followed.

He reached out and shook Joanna's hand.

"Good of you to set this up," he said.

"Anything for an old friend. Besides, I think we have the makings of a good story here."

She introduced the women.

"Jack, I would like you to meet Magda, the President's soon-to-be-ex-wife, and his daughters, Tina and Becky."

Jack shook their hands.

"And this is Jack Winthrup, probably the best journalist in the country," Joanna added. "Let's all have a seat, shall we?"

Joanna poured water for everyone and turned to Jack.

"Where would you like to start?"

Chapter Twenty-One

After gathering some background information, Jack turned to the President's wife.

"That was quite a speech yesterday," he said. "And a dramatic exit."

She smiled and said nothing.

"It was obvious that it didn't go the way the President had planned. What caused you to go off-script?"

Magda hesitated.

"We," and she indicated the President's daughters, "are going to give you an exclusive story. The full story. I trust you will use it appropriately."

She paused and watched his face. He gave a slight nod.

"There were a number of incidents that culminated in yesterday's media conference," she said. "Most involved me directly. One focused on these young women. I will tell my story, and they will tell you as much of their story as they wish."

She glanced at her stepdaughters for confirmation. They nodded.

Magda cleared her throat and sat up straighter, holding her head high.

Over the next half-hour, Magda explained that she had been raised in another country with the awareness that, one day, she would be required to marry a man of her family's choosing. She was groomed for the role, well educated, taught how to run a household, and introduced to society at the age of twenty-one.

"It was a debutante ball," she said. "We were paraded around like prize horses at a breeder's auction, dressed in our finery, showing ourselves to advantage. The invited guests were mostly men, eligible bachelors from the wealthiest families in the world. They were accompanied by mothers or aunts looking for the best catch for their family. It was all about political connections."

She pressed her lips together.

"I thought it was ridiculous, but I had no choice. This was the culture in which I was raised, so I put on a good show. My family did not realize that the President had sent a representative to find him a third wife. Apparently, I fit the bill – a healthy white broodmare."

She agreed to the marriage but stipulated that there be a prenuptial agreement.

"My father and I worked on it together. He had spent his career in international law," she said with a slight smile. "The President had already been married twice and had a reputation as a womanizer; chances for divorce were high. We had the family lawyer deliver the agreement. Apparently, the President barely looked at it. Just signed. And that was that."

For the past ten years, she had raised his daughters, run the household and provided sexual services as required, as she put it.

"I was well aware of his attitude towards women," she said. "As Tina and Becky became older, I knew I would need to take a stand. I wasn't too worried for myself, but once he was elected, it was clear his plans could have disastrous consequences for them."

She added that, in the last three years, the President had become insistent on having more children. He said the country expected it.

Magda shook her head.

"I used contraception for a long time because I did not want to have children with a man who saw women as a convenience. One day he found my pills and became incredibly angry. He tossed them in the garbage and threatened to hurt me if I got another prescription. I tried avoidance, saying I had a headache or wasn't well, but that didn't work for long."

She was silent for a few minutes.

"I did get pregnant. Three times. And each time I miscarried. It's the worst thing to go through. The pain, the blood, the despair…" Her voice grew hard. "And now with this new law, women who miscarry will have to be examined by a doctor to prove it was natural and not an attempted abortion. Only a man could come up with such an abhorrent concept."

Magda's eyes narrowed.

"He forced me to give the speech yesterday. He said it was my duty as his wife, and that any prenuptial agreement could be preempted in emergency situations. For him, it was an emergency, an act of desperation because he needs people to buy into the legislation. So, I saw my opportunity to make a difference, and I ran with it."

She laughed gently.

"He didn't see it coming. I guess I wasn't the catch he bargained for after all."

Magda paused, waiting for Jack to finish taking notes.

"My last miscarriage was six months ago. Recently he's been hassling me to get pregnant again. He keeps saying he needs sons to carry on his legacy. His dynasty is more like it. I suspect that he is preparing to toss me aside like his last two wives when they no longer served his purposes. I thought I was protected – in the prenup, he cannot divorce me. The only way he can remarry is if I die."

"What are you suggesting?"

Magda gave him a long look.

"I doubt very much that the clause about miscarriages in the new law is a coincidence. All he'd have to do is get me pregnant again. I'd likely miscarry. He'd get one of his doctor friends to examine me, declare the miscarriage deliberate, and I'd be tried for murder. I would, of course, appeal, and eventually the case would make it to the Supreme Court where his dear friend, Chief Justice Power, would overturn my appeal. It's the death penalty for convicted murderers in this country. I'd be dead, and he'd be free to remarry."

Jack sat back in his chair, his mind leaping.

"That's a frightening analysis," he said. "I don't want to believe it's possible, but I can see where you're coming from."

"You don't know him like I do. He'll do anything to get what he wants."

Jack made some more notes and turned to Tina and Becky.

"Is there anything you want to add?"

The two girls looked at each other. Tina shrugged and said, "I'll go first."

She explained that their father had commanded them to meet with him three days ago, prior to the announcement of the legislation.

"He sat us down in his office and told us that, as the daughters of the President, we had an important role to play in the future of the country. He made it sound like we were special, that people looked up to us, and we needed to set a good example."

Becky chimed in.

"He said it was time we got married. That was news to us. Turns out he's already chosen our husbands – some billionaire techie for Tina, and Ryan, his assistant, for me. He said we'd be married in a joint ceremony. It would be the "social event of the year", she said raising her fingers in air quotes. "If we were good girls and signed the document on his desk, we could have the wedding of our dreams – the dresses, the flowers, the music … anything we wanted. So very generous of him," she added, rolling her eyes.

"I read through the document," Tina added. "It was written in legalese but I'm not stupid. We had to agree to go out on two very public double dates, marry these men in a televised ceremony, and have at least four children each. Under the new law, we would not be allowed to use any form of contraception. And we definitely could not continue our education. Our job was to become model wives and mothers. Period."

Becky shook her fist in the air.

"We told him to stuff it. And refused to sign."

"He yelled at us and said we were grounded. He made Frank lock us in our rooms. He said we couldn't come out until we signed. What a loser."

"What did you do?" Jack asked.

The girls looked at Magda.

"A long time ago, I had extra keys made for all the rooms," Magda said. "I heard the yelling and opened my door a crack just as he was threatening to keep them locked up until they signed. I waited until he had fallen asleep, and I unlocked the girls' doors. I told them to pack a bag and wait for me downstairs in the morning. I'd already arranged for a limo, so I got them into the car before he woke up.

Then I relocked their doors and went to the media conference. The rest you already know."

"What happens next?" Jack asked. He looked at Joanna as well as Magda and her stepdaughters.

They all smiled and refused to comment.

Before leaving, Jack asked the First Lady if she was aware that the President had issued a media release suggesting that she was experiencing a mental breakdown.

"He will stop at nothing," she scoffed. "Men in power are all the same. He is trying to undermine my words before I can do more damage. It won't work. Do I seem mentally unstable to you?"

Joanna told Jack that she was scheduling a video conference in two days.

"I want to give you a heads-up so you can save room in the paper," she said. "We will be announcing next steps and details for Women's Choice Day."

He asked about the tight security in and around the building. She explained that the World Organization for Women dealt with controversial issues around the world; issues that harmed women and enabled men to maintain a rigid control of their wives, daughters, and female family members.

"Because we are successful in making changes, we also attract a certain amount of attention. Death threats are not uncommon. Towards our staff in the field and here at headquarters. We have had people attempt to plant bombs on the premises and along the outer wall. We are committed to ensuring the safety of our staff and everyone who enters our gates."

She added with a wink, "The donation from Chief Justice Power came in handy. I won't specify what it was used for, but we have been able to upgrade protective measures on all levels. Given this new law, I think we may need it."

Chapter Twenty-Two

Lena sat wide-eyed, looking from the computer screen to her mother and back again. She shook her head and sipped her pop. She glanced at the screen once more, her mouth gaping.

Madeline laughed.

"Close your mouth. You look like a fish out of water."

Lena sat still, barely breathing.

"What, you didn't think I had it in me?" Madeline said.

She shut down the computer, locked it in a desk drawer and stood up.

"C'mon, let's take a walk."

Lena followed her down the path through the sand dunes to the beach. They turned and began to wander away from the cottages, toward the point.

"Uh, I, I don't know where to start," Lena said. "It's like discovering I've been living in a world of make-believe. I don't even know what's real anymore."

She scratched her head.

"So, all this time, you've been living two lives?"

"I guess that's one way to put it," Madeline said.

"How? Why? I don't even know what to ask," Lena said. "When did this start? And who knows?"

"Breathe, girl, just breathe. To answer one question, only you and my sister know. And someone we work closely with. Since I don't know if the cottage is bugged, it's best for us to have this little chat out here, away from everyone."

Lena stopped.

"Bugged? You're serious about all this spy stuff?"

Madeline put her hands on Lena's shoulders and looked her straight in the eyes.

"Yes. Very serious. That was no cop the other night. And he could be just the beginning of a much more dangerous game. The only reason I'm sharing this with you now is you're involved whether you want to be or not. I'm sorry. I thought it out very carefully, and the only way to keep you safe is to keep you with me."

Lena held her gaze.

"Don't be sorry. Honestly. It beats spending the summer in the city."

Madeline smiled and started to walk again, picking up bits of sea glass and colored stones. Lena walked in silence for a while. She bent down to examine a shell and as she stood up, she asked, "How did this all start? I mean, were you ever normal? You know, just an ordinary teenager?"

Madeline looked up at the blue sky. When she turned to Lena, her dark eyes were sparkling.

"Define normal. I already told you how Max and I would trade places, right? At college, we got involved with some interesting people and one thing led to another. I guess they were impressed with how well we could become each other and decided to let us in on a much bigger game. It turned out to be private training school. Only a select few were allowed in every year and when you completed the training, you were assigned a task as a trial run. We always worked together, Max and I, during the training and in the years after. We're quite the team."

Lena slowed down. She picked up a stone from the beach and tossed it back and forth between her hands.

"What exactly were you trained to do?"

"I'm going to gloss over some things here because the details aren't important and I'm not at liberty to share them. I will say that, basically, we were trained in high-level espionage."

"No shit!"

"Lena, language, please."

"Come on. You can't tell me you're a spy and expect me to be calm about it. With all the disguise stuff you were pulling in the city, I thought you'd gone a little weird, but it's for real?"

"Yep. For real. Curious to know why it surprises you so much."

"Well for starters, you're my moth…aunt. And I thought I knew you. Where does my useless father fit into this?"

Madeline hesitated.

"Let's just say that he's part of a long-term project and when I learned what I needed, it was time to go."

"You were spying on him?"

"More like investigating, Lena. He's always been power-hungry and determined to climb to the top. Which he has now done. He's close to the President. In fact, they are stepbrothers, but that's not public knowledge. They have been careful to keep their relationship squeaky clean."

"Why?"

"Not important. All that matters is that your father has harmed a lot of people over the years, people who matter very much to me. Living with him gave me the chance to gather information; information I can use to bring him down."

Lena shook her head.

"All this time, you were spying on him, and he had no idea. That's so cool. Can you teach me? I want to be like you."

Madeline smiled.

"You definitely have a role to play. We've only just begun this battle and there may be a war ahead. One thing though, you need to keep all of this to yourself. If you want to talk, suggest a walk. I've changed the locks on the cottage, and set up a new security system, but it's important to be careful and cautious."

Lena nodded.

"No prob. You can count on me, Auntie Max."

Chapter Twenty-Three

Jack hesitated before knocking on the door. He straightened his shoulders and rapped firmly.

The door opened.

"Oh, hello," the woman said. "I wasn't expecting you.

"I know," Jack said. "Can I come in? Just for a few minutes. There's something we need to discuss."

"Why don't we sit out on the veranda?" she suggested. "It's cooler there. I'll get some water."

"Actually, I think it would be better if we were inside," he said. "It's personal."

She glanced up at him, shrugged her shoulders and led the way into the living room.

"Suit yourself. I'll get us some water."

When she returned, he cleared his throat.

"I'm not sure how to say this."

"Oh, whatever it is, just get it over with," she said gruffly with a wave of her hand. "I've got things to do."

"Okay, then. Does the name Mary Magdalen mean anything to you?"

She frowned.

"You mean the one in the Bible?"

"No, a baby born on March 31, 1968."

Maggie caught her breath. No one knew that date, not even Alicia. Her face flushed. She gripped the arms of the chair.

"What's this about?" she asked, her voice low and firm.

"My mother was born on that date. Her given names are Mary Magdalen, and the family name on the birth certificate is Charbonneau. She was born at a place called the Grace Home and given up for adoption the same day. I have reason to believe you are her birth mother."

Maggie closed her eyes, breathing quickly. Her mind raced. The date and location were right, and the baby had her maiden name. But...

She opened her eyes and stared at Jack.

"But you're ... " she took a deep breath and blurted, "you're Black."

He laughed.

"So is my father."

She shook her head, trying to clear the confusion.

"So, I have a..." her voice broke as her tongue danced around the unfamiliar word. "A daughter?"

"Yes. So, it seems," he said softly.

"What does she look like?"

Jack reached inside his wallet and handed her a small photo. Maggie's hand trembled as she reached out. She wiped her eyes with the back of her left hand. A middle-aged woman with dark wavy hair smiled up at her. Maggie traced her features with a finger.

"She looks like my mother."

Looking up at Jack, she asked, "Does she know you're here?"

Jack bit his upper lip.

"Yes and no," he said. "She knows I've been searching. And she's okay with that. But I didn't want to say anything to her until I talked to you. I wasn't sure how you'd feel about all this."

Maggie looked down at the photo. Her daughter. She'd be 57 now. Maggie had kept track of each birthday, marking it on the calendar and making a small cake with candles every year.

"I can't imagine what she must think. I didn't have any choice, you see."

Then she caught her breath and looked up at Jack.

"You are her son," she said.

Eyes wide, she reached out to touch his arm.

"You're my grandson?"

She began to laugh softly, shaking her head.

"All these years, I thought I was alone. And in the space of five minutes, I gain a daughter *and* a grandson."

Jack waited for a moment, and added, "Actually, you have two grandsons. I have a younger brother."

He watched as Maggie tried to absorb the news. She closed her eyes, rocking slightly, tapping one hand on her knee.

Jack took her hand in his.

"You also have a great-granddaughter."

Maggie sat up straight, her eyes wild and flickering. She bolted from the room. Jack heard a door slam. He waited but heard nothing more. He tiptoed in the direction she had gone and peered into the kitchen. Through the window, he could see her sitting on the back steps, arms wrapped around her shoulders, back rounded, head between her knees. She was rocking but making no sounds.

He walked softly back into the living room and sat down.

Fifteen minutes later, she returned, blinking hard.

"Do you, do you have a photo of your daughter? My…great-granddaughter?" she asked, a quaver in her voice.

He took out another photo and gave it to her.

"This is your wife?" she asked, pointing to the woman holding the baby.

He nodded.

"That's Hannah. We've been married for four years. And that's Evelyn, our daughter. She's two months old now."

Maggie gazed at the photo, memorizing every feature of the baby's face.

"I, I don't know what to say. You probably have a lot of questions, but I'm going to need some time."

She sat in silence for a while.

"How did you find me?" she asked, handing the photo back to him.

"Well, I am an investigative reporter," he said, grinning. "It's my job to find things out. Plus, I've been working on the family tree for a while. When Mum said she was adopted and didn't have any info on her birth parents, I got curious. I filed a request with the adoption agency board and got a letter back a few days ago, saying the birth mother was open to meeting. I followed up and they gave me your maiden name. It didn't take me long to find out your married name was Carpenter. I couldn't believe it because we'd already met. For other reasons."

Maggie nodded.

"I gave my permission years ago, just in case," she said. "I didn't know if I'd ever hear anything, but I wanted to leave that door open. I never knew if the baby was a boy or a girl. And I never had a chance to hold … her."

She pressed her fingers against the tip of her nose. A single tear rolled down her cheek.

"No matter what the circumstances, your heart doesn't forget, you know."

Jack reached out and touched her arm.

"Are you okay if I talk to Mum and let her know we've met?"

"Maybe give me some time first. It's a lot to take in."

"I know. I keep pinching myself. For now, let's keep this our secret? Hannah knows I got the letter from the agency, but not who you are or even that we've talked. I want to keep it that way until you and Mum have a chance to meet."

"My lips are sealed."

Jack stood up.

"I've got to get back to the office."

He stopped with his hand on the doorknob.

"I hate to ask when your head is probably spinning, but I may need your help with something."

Chapter Twenty-Four

Jack pulled into his parents' driveway. He hoped his brother was there. He needed to talk to them all at the same time.

He knocked twice and opened the door. They really need to learn to lock it, he thought. His mother called from the kitchen.

"Jack? Is that you?"

"In the flesh," he replied, giving her a hug. "Where's Dad? And is Brad here?"

She pointed down the hall.

"They're in the office. Brad's trying to help Dad set up a social media account, although goodness knows why. I've been hearing a lot of laughter and swearing."

Jack went into the office where the two men were hunched over the laptop. He tapped them both on the shoulder.

"Hey guys, I hate to interrupt but we need to have a family meeting."

Brad groaned and followed his brother to the kitchen. Their father joined them a few moments later. They all sat down at the table while his Mum poured four cups of coffee.

After she sat down, Jack said, "Something important has come up at work and I need to talk to you because it could affect all of you."

"Sound ominous, son," his father said, winking at his wife.

"I'm serious, Dad. I wish we didn't have to have this conversation, but here goes. You've seen the news about the new law, right?"

He looked around the table and they nodded.

"I'm about to publish a series of investigative pieces that the government will not like. Not at all. In the past, when I've done work like this, I have received death threats. Now, Mum, don't look so shocked. You know it happens in my line of work."

He waited for them to take in the words.

"It's different this time. There is a lot more at stake for me personally, with Hannah and Evy. If I know the current government, they will go after the people who matter most to me. That means all of you."

His mother gasped. His father frowned. Brad yawned.

"So, what I need you to do is pack a bag and go away for a while. I've booked a furnished cottage under a different name and the three of you will stay there until things blow over."

"What about Hannah and Evy?" his mother asked.

"I have different plans for them," he said. "I want to keep you in separate places. I think you'll be safer that way. They will be in a place that no one will think to look. And I can't tell you because the less you know, the better it is."

"Such a drama queen," Brad said, raising an eyebrow.

"Brad, I can't stress enough how dangerous this could be," Jack said. "You've never had to deal with things like this. I have. So, for my peace of mind, please do this. If something happens to you, I will never forgive myself."

He paused and took a deep breath before continuing.

"Think of it as war. A war against women for now, but against democracy in the long run. As in any war, there will be casualties. This law will affect Hannah and Evy directly. It will affect you to a lesser extent, Mum, because you're past childbearing, but there are more details to come which will restrict the way you live your life. And, Brad, if you care at all for the women in your life, and I don't just mean Mum, Hannah and Evy, this is a battle you need to fight in your own way. My way is through writing, and the pieces I need to write this week will cause repercussions, I guarantee it."

He sat back in his chair.

"Time to pack your bags."

His parents sat like statues. Brad rolled his eyes.

"First that cop, now this," he muttered as he stood up and sauntered into his bedroom. They could hear drawers opening and closing.

"Cop?" his mother asked. "What's this about a cop?"

"Nothing to worry about, Mum," Jack said, laying his hand on hers. "He broke into Brad and Lena's house and Brad found him there. Brad hightailed out and came to my place, and that's why he's been staying with you. I'm afraid it's just the beginning though. So, will you please go pack your bags?"

They all stood up. His mother's face was pale, and she was tugging on her curls. His father's eyes flashed, and his jaw was set.

"Come along, Mary," he said, wrapping an arm around his wife's shoulders. He led her down the hall to their bedroom.

Chapter Twenty-Five

Over the next few days, Jack researched and wrote articles using Maggie's statistics as the foundation. He created a three-part series, and the message was clear: wake up, citizens, and recognize the real intention behind the new legislation.

The response was immediate and overwhelming. The newspaper had to reprogram their phone system to handle all the calls; letters to the editor were submitted in numbers never seen before; social media went wild. Links to the articles were posted and reposted, receiving millions of hits, and plenty of comments for and against.

The first death threat arrived on Jack's personal cell phone within hours. The second by email from a secured account. The third showed up on his desk.

He called his publisher and editor into his office. Pointing at the note, he suggested that they call the police.

"I haven't touched it," he said. "But I did read it. The message is consistent: stop writing lies or your family will suffer."

"You're…" began his editor. Jack held up his hand. He wrote something on a notepad and showed it to the two men. *The office might be bugged. Don't say anything more here.* The men nodded. He waved them out of the room and walked toward the large storage room at the end of the hall. Opening the door and turning on the light, he ushered them inside.

"You're staying at the office tonight," his editor said. "Just like in the old days."

Jack nodded.

"I brought a bag with me this morning from home."

"We'll beef up security on the building," his publisher added. "And check all the cameras. I wonder how someone got that note in here. We'll do a sweep of the building as well. Code names only between us if using the phone."

"What about your family?" Ed asked. "Do you need them to go to a safe house?"

"Already taken care of," Jack said.

He opened the door and headed back to his office to get his laptop. He pulled a new cell phone out of his briefcase and sent texts to his parents and Hannah. As a precaution, he had purchased new phones for them as well.

All is well, Hannah replied.

Enjoying the view, was his father's response.

Each day brought more details of the legislation. Madeline was shocked at the depth of the impact. Daniel's final document was much more detailed than the draft she had copied from his laptop.

"You've outdone yourself this time, Danny boy," she muttered as she scanned the newspaper. "I didn't know you had it in you."

"What, you're praising him now?" Lena asked.

"Sarcasm, my dear, note the sarcasm. Although I do have to admit he seems to have written an airtight document. I wonder how much bourbon was involved."

She snorted, making notes as she read.

"What's the list for?" Lena asked.

"Facts, Lena. If you want to win the war, you've got to fight with facts. You start by noticing how they justify their position. Then you do your own research. That's how you come up with a document that sounds just as convincing as theirs but is based on facts. Not fantasy. Most people can't be bothered investigating the truth of a statement, so we do that for them, and then present it in a way that everyone can understand. Unlike the legal gobbledygook your father has used."

Lena pulled the paper in front of her.

"How can they make contraception illegal?" she asked. "Do they really want a baby boom?"

"Yep, but preferably white babies. And they're being very generous – look at the baby bonus women will get per child, especially white women. Like you and Shelley."

Madeline hoped Lena could hear the sarcasm this time.

"But if there are going to be more babies," Lena said, "why are they cutting funding to daycare centers and reducing the number of spaces? Who's going to look after the children if both parents are working?"

She sat back in her chair.

I can almost hear the gears clicking into place, Madeline thought.

"No way!" Lena exclaimed. "They're going to force women to stay home. They're stopping us from working, from having a career. They are choosing for me what my future will be."

She slammed her fist on the table. The coffee cups danced and dribbled.

Jack sent Hannah a message.

Ask Maggie to text me on your phone. Thx

A few minutes later, his phone pinged.

Dr. Watson at your service, Holmes.

Jack grinned. Maggie hadn't lost her sense of humor.

Do you have anything else for me? What's your take on govt stance?

Suddenly his phone rang.

"Yes?"

"Couldn't be bothered texting. Is it okay if we talk instead?" Maggie asked.

Jack ended the call and sent a text.

Text only for now. Checking building for bugs.

Insects?

He rolled his eyes. Maybe Maggie was too old to understand.

Before he could reply, another text arrived.

Lol. Gotcha!

Not too old, he thought, chuckling, typing a longer message.

Thanks for taking in Hannah and Evy. Helps to know they are with you. You haven't told Hannah about the family connection, have you?

My lips are still sealed, Maggie replied.

I have someone watching the house btw, Jack texted.

Thought so. Thx

Maggie said she had nothing more for him yet, but she was following the developments closely.

Good articles. Big boys running scared. Stick to your plan. They will start making mistakes.

Maggie erased the text conversation and set the phone down. She could feel Hannah's eyes on her.

"Yes?" she asked without looking up.

"What did he say? Is he okay?"

"It's all good, Hannah. He was just checking in to see if I had anything more for him."

"Like what?"

Maggie sighed.

"Here's the deal. When I was younger, much younger, I was what you would call an activist. For women's rights. In fact, that's probably been the theme of my life. So, when this new legislation came down, I did what I do best – I researched. It's like riding a bike – you never really forget. I pass stuff along to Jack. If it's useful, he uses it."

She picked up her phone, shifting it from hand to hand.

"Gotta admit, it feels pretty good to be in the thick of things again. You probably think I'm crazy."

Hannah shook her head.

"Not at all. It's a bit of a surprise though. I mean, when Jack dropped us off here, all he said was that this is a safe house, and no one would think to look for us here. So, do you two go way back?"

Maggie stared at the phone in her hand.

"I guess you could say that."

She pursed her lips. "There's something I have to do. Make yourself comfortable. And let me know if there's anything you or the baby need."

She touched Hannah lightly on the shoulder as she left the room.

Maggie closed her bedroom door and texted her therapist. While she waited for a response, she tapped her foot on the carpet.

"Thank God," she breathed when she saw the answer.

She headed back to the kitchen.

"Hannah, hate to do this to you when you just arrived, but I have an appointment. I won't be back for lunch, so see what you can find in the fridge. I'll pick up some groceries on my way back. Oh, and don't answer the door."

Chapter Twenty-Six

"Thank you for making time for me at short notice," Maggie said, as she walked into Sharon's office.

"Not a problem, Maggie. What's up?"

Maggie rocked gently back and forth on the edge of the couch.

"I don't know where to start," she said. "It's everything I wanted, and terrifying at the same time."

She grabbed a tissue and blew her nose.

"Last time I spoke to you about the baby."

"Right, I remember," Sharon said.

"Well, it's a bit complicated, but it turns out, the baby was a girl. I have a daughter," Maggie said, shaking her head. "And two grandsons, and a great-granddaughter. Just like that. Over fifty years of not knowing anything and, poof, instant family."

Sharon was quiet for a few moments.

"That's a lot to process, Maggie. How do you feel?"

Maggie raised her head and looked at the ceiling. She exhaled with an explosive puff.

"I don't know. It's amazing, wonderful, extraordinary. But it's also scary. I haven't met my daughter yet, so I don't know what she thinks, or if I should tell her the whole story. I don't think I should, but what if she asks, and then there's Jack and his baby, and don't they have a right to know about their past, but I don't actually know who the father was, so I really can't say anything definite, and maybe it would be better if I just pretend it was ..."

Sharon interrupted.

"Slow down, Maggie. Take a breath. Your mind is galloping like a horse heading back to the barn. Let's pause for a moment."

She poured a glass of chilled cucumber water and handed it to Maggie.

"Take a few sips," she said. "And then we'll talk some more."

They sat in silence for a few moments.

"Okay then," Sharon said, "let's start at the beginning. Tell me how you found out about your daughter. And who is Jack?"

Maggie took another deep breath.

"Jack is the reporter from *The Nation Today* who came to interview me about the World Organization for Women. The organization is celebrating fifty years in September and, like I told you last time, I was one of the founding members."

"So, this reporter told you about your daughter? How did he even know you had a child?"

Maggie laughed.

"That's the amazing part. He showed up at my door a few weeks later and said there was something we needed to discuss. I figured it was a follow-up to the story. Did you see the feature article by the way? It was really well done. Anyway, where was I?"

Sharon waited as Maggie drank some more water.

"Right, so Jack comes back to see me. We sit down, and he asks me about the name Mary Magdalen. I thought he was going all religious on me and I was ready to show him the door. Don't you hate it when those evangelical types knock on your door and try and sell you their religion?"

She glanced at Sharon but didn't give her a chance to respond.

"Turns out, that's the name that was given to my child. Those nuns had a twisted sense of humor. Jack knew the birth date, the hospital, and my maiden name from the adoption agency, because I had given my permission a long time ago. He did more searching and came up with my married name. And realized we'd already met. Isn't it a small world? Just imagine. I might have passed my daughter in the street a thousand times and never known. Where was I going with this?"

Sharon smiled.

"Jack found you."

"Right. These days my thoughts are so muddled. Too much going on. So, Jack has been searching for a while. He and his wife had some questions about family health history when they were expecting Evelyn. Did I tell you…no, I won't get distracted. Jack asked his Mum about her parents and found out she was adopted. And she had no information about her birth parents. That's when he decided to investigate."

"When will you meet your daughter?"

"I don't know. My daughter –– oh it gives me such a thrill to say the word! I don't know yet if she calls herself Mary or Magdalen or Mary Magdalen. I must ask Jack. I don't want to put my foot in my mouth."

Maggie swirled the water in her glass.

"Oh, did I tell you that Jack's wife and daughter are staying with me?"

Sharon shook her head.

"Why is that? Do they know the connection?"

"Jack's been writing all these articles, and they've caused quite a stir. He's had death threats, and he needed a safe house for Hannah and Evelyn – that's his wife and daughter. No one knows the connection, not even Hannah, so nobody would think to look for them at my place. Can you believe it?"

"How is that for you, Maggie?"

"That's why I needed to see you today. It's hard. Jack made me promise to keep things a secret until he tells his Mum. And he wants to wait until things get back to normal. Whenever that is."

She wrapped a few strands of hair between her fingers.

"The baby. Evelyn. She's so precious. I haven't held her; not sure I want to."

"Why not?"

"I'm afraid I'll drop her, and she'll break. Or I'll break. I've always been good at secrets, but this one is slippery."

"One step at a time, Maggie."

Sharon looked at her notes.

"At some point, you will meet your daughter. Shall we talk a bit about what you will say when that happens?"

"Oh, yes," Maggie said, clasping her hands in front of her chest. "I'm so worried. I don't want to mess things up. What do you think I should say?"

"It's not what I think that matters, Maggie. What feels right to you?"

"Well, I want to be honest but not give too much information. So, I was wondering about saying that I got pregnant unexpectedly, my parents wouldn't let me keep the baby, and I had to give her up for adoption. Everyone told me she would be raised in a loving family, and I had to believe them. I was only 17 and, in those days, being pregnant and not married was a sin."

She thought some more.

"Or maybe I want to tell her how much I loved being pregnant with her. Okay, not at first. But when I was staying with my aunties, they helped me see things differently. In our tradition … I think I told you my mother was Mohawk, and it was her sisters I stayed with, up north, on the reservation?"

Maggie sat quietly for a few minutes, rubbing her hands together.

"They taught me my baby was a gift to the world, no matter the circumstances, and helped me connect to my child while she was still inside me. I started to talk to her. I sang her songs and told her about myself. I spent time with her in my dreams, although I didn't know she was a girl then. It helped me accept what had happened. And it helped me heal – just focusing on the love I felt for the baby."

Sharon nodded.

"And if she asks who her father is, what will you say?"

Maggie frowned.

"That's the hard part. I don't know who he is, but if I don't explain what happened, it sounds like I slept around. Which isn't true. Just the opposite."

She bit her lip.

"Maybe I could say that, for reasons I can't share, I cannot reveal her father's identity. I don't know if that's okay. It's possible with DNA testing that they could find out if they want, right?"

She stopped suddenly, her hand on her mouth, eyes wide.

"Oh my God."

"Talk to me, Maggie," Sharon said.

Maggie shook her head slowly.

"If they can find out through DNA testing, then I'll know who did this to me."

She stared at her therapist.

"But only if his DNA is on file, right? Right?"

Maggie began to choke.

Sharon crouched down in front of her.

"Look at me, Maggie," she commanded. "Count your in-breath with 1, 2, 3, 4, 5, 6…hold 2, 3… and exhale 2, 3, 4, 5, 6. Good. Again."

Maggie willed herself to count as she struggled to take air into her lungs. She could feel her body trembling, heart racing, her mind catapulting into the distance.

"Keep focused on the breath," Sharon said.

Maggie nodded slightly. As her pulse slowed, the dull throb of a migraine emerged at the base of her skull. She reached for the glass of water and took a sip. Then she dug in her bag for her pain pills.

"Just a sec," she said to Sharon and downed a pill with some more water.

She sat back on the couch; eyes closed.

"How are you doing, Maggie?" Sharon asked after a few minutes.

Maggie shook her head. She rubbed her hands together and pressed them on her knees.

"I don't need to know who it was, do I? They might find out, but I can ask them not to tell me. I don't want to know. Not after all these years. It wouldn't change anything. Not for me."

She swayed awkwardly back and forth like a pendulum that has forgotten its rhythm.

"But maybe I would want to know? For closure? And what if they found out, and started to spend time with him, how would I feel about that? And what if Evelyn got married and he was there? And what if…?"

"Maggie," Sharon interjected. "That's a lot of 'what ifs'. And you know what we say about that."

"If I'm going to imagine what might happen," Maggie recited in a monotone, "I might as well imagine the positive. Because there's no way of knowing the future."

"That's right. Focus on right here, right now. You know you have a daughter. And you will meet her at some point. That's enough for now."

"Got it," Maggie said.

"And how will you handle having Hannah and Evelyn around?"

Maggie sat back on the couch; arms folded across her chest.

"I guess I'll just take it one day at a time. I don't have to hold the baby. Hannah hasn't asked, so maybe it won't come up. I'll try to pretend that she's just the daughter of an old school friend. That's the story Jack suggested to keep them safe. Hannah's okay with that."

She tilted her head.

"The way I see it, I didn't even know they existed a week ago. What's another few weeks or months?"

Maggie grew silent, chewing on her lower lip. Sharon waited.

"It's still possible I could find out who did this," Maggie said slowly. "It scares me to think about it, but maybe you could help me sort that out? Next session?"

"Okay," Sharon said. "It is fresh in your mind right now though. Shall we give it a try?"

Maggie took a deep breath and nodded.

"So, Maggie, let's imagine I'm handing you a piece of paper with a name on it. Turn the paper over and tell me what you want to do."

Maggie's hand shook as she took the imaginary paper from Sharon's hand. She peeked at the other side and sat back on the couch, eyes darting around the room, breathing hard.

"Maggie?"

"Give me a minute," she said.

She calmed her breathing and added, "It's strange. Knowing wouldn't change anything, really. I'd have a name, someone to blame, but that's not what I want."

"What do you want, Maggie?" Sharon asked.

Maggie stared past Sharon at an abstract painting on the wall, not seeing shapes or colors, her thoughts twisting and turning like sheets hung to dry in the summer sun. Ideas flirted, beckoned and vanished. She searched for something, anything, that would satisfy decades of grief and rage. When she spoke, her voice was low and hard.

"I want justice, but not in the usual way. Just sending him to jail, even if I could after all these years, wouldn't be enough," Maggie said. "No, he took away my family and my future. The things that mattered most to me. That's what I would do to him. Find out what's important to him and take it all away. Permanently.

"And do it in a way that he would spend the rest of his days looking over his shoulder, wondering who he can trust, and knowing life will never be the same again."

Chapter Twenty-Seven

Jack closed his fourth-floor office door at *The Nation Today* and clicked on the media conference link from the World Organization for Women. He glanced at his watch. He still had another ten minutes. He grabbed his coffee and walked over to the window.

The street below was bustling with shoppers at the market in the city square. As he took a sip, a sudden movement on a roof across the street put him on full alert. He stepped back from the window into the shadows just as the glass shattered. The force of the blast pushed him backwards. He landed in a heap on the floor, coffee splattering his blue shirt and jeans.

The door flew open.

"What the hell…?" Ed shouted, looking at the broken glass.

"Get down," yelled Jack.

Ed ducked behind the desk and crawled over to him.

"Are you okay?"

"I'm fine," Jack groaned. "A bit shaken, nothing's broken. Someone shot at me from across the street."

Ed was already on his phone calling the police. He covered the phone with one hand and asked if Jack needed an ambulance.

"No. I'm fine. And that video conference starts any minute. Can you reach my laptop?"

As he spoke to the police, Ed reached on top of the desk, grabbed the laptop, and brought it down to the floor. Jack leaned against a chair and propped the laptop on his legs. The conference was starting. His legs were shaking.

"Notepad," he whispered. Ed felt blindly across the top of the desk and pulled down a pen and pad of paper.

"Police on their way," he mouthed.

Jack turned up the volume. Joanna was introducing the women who would be speaking. Magda, of course. And two women he didn't recognize. One was the head of media relations for the World

Organization for Women. The other was a university professor who specialized in the history of women's movements.

She'll be out of a job as soon as this conference is over, he thought.

The presentation focused on Women's Choice Day, set for August 26. Each of the women shared their perspective. Joanna explained that, in light of new legislation, the organization wanted to support the call of Magda McCarthur, the President's wife, for women to stage a one-day general strike.

"On August 26," Magda announced, "we are asking all women to spend the day celebrating the contribution we make to society. As women we have many roles, most of which are unpaid or underpaid, unnoticed, and unappreciated. Our contributions include household activities such as cooking, cleaning, laundry, child-rearing, and driving children to sports activities, as well as job-related contributions by the millions of women who are part of the workforce."

She looked straight into the camera and said slowly and clearly, "We are calling for women to opt out of the system. A general strike. We will withdraw our services at home, at work and in the community on August 26. Services to be withheld may include sex. Your body, your choice."

Joanna smiled.

"And that concludes our media conference," Joanna said. "Thank you for tuning in. If you have any questions, you know how to reach me."

The screen went blank.

The police arrived and cordoned off Jack's office. They allowed him to take his laptop and key files with him but told him to stay close so they could question him.

Ed pulled him into his office and closed the door.

"Look, we've been talking, Bob and I."

He waved his hand toward the publisher who was sitting in a chair in the corner of the room.

"We don't want you to get hurt. Or killed for that matter. We've made a decision."

"Hold on a minute!" Jack said. "You're not pulling this story. It's getting bigger by the minute. Wait until you hear what the women have planned."

Bob held up a hand and motioned for Jack to take a seat.

"It's okay, bud, we understand. We're not pulling the story so relax. But we do need to find a way to protect you. That was too close for comfort and way beyond what our insurance will cover."

He shook his head.

"Here's the deal. You can find your own safe house for the foreseeable future, or we will set you up in the Cave. No windows, you can sleep there, there's even a connected washroom and kitchen. Internet is a bit tricky in there, but I've talked to IT and they're going to swing it somehow. What do you say?"

Jack thought about it.

"Well, maybe for a day or two," he said hesitantly, "but the longer I'm here, the more dangerous it is for everyone. If they have tried to shoot me and missed, I'm afraid the building will be their next target. I need to be somewhere else."

"Fair enough," Ed said. "Any ideas?"

"Leave it with me. For now, I'll use the Cave, and I'll let you know when I have something else set up. Thanks, guys, for sticking with the story."

"The attempt on your life is going to make great front-page news, Jack," Ed said with a grin.

After speaking with the police, Jack wrote a text to his parents and Hannah.

I'm okay. Don't read the papers.

Then he realized it would just make things worse. He deleted the text and tried again.

All is well. No matter what you see in the papers. I'm safe.

He hit Send.

Chapter Twenty-Eight

News of the attempted murder ignited the country like wildfire after a lightning strike. The rumor mill spun stories about the President ordering the shooting because Jack had been sleeping with his wife. The fact that Jack was investigating the reasons behind the new legislation raised red flags for even the most oblivious of citizens.

Maggie heard snippets of conversation at the grocery store.

"Maybe that reporter's right. This could be much bigger than we realize."

"I hear he's gone into hiding. I bet we won't read anything from him in a while.

"Serves him right, pointing fingers at the President. We elected him fair and square."

Maggie wanted to shake the naysayers and tell them what she thought of them. But she kept her head down and focused on her grocery list.

Daniel and Frank joined a hastily convened meeting with the President, his senior advisors, the Speaker of the House and the Senate Majority Leader. The President thanked them for coming at short notice and launched into a disjointed monologue.

Daniel stifled a burp. He had not been sleeping well since Madeline left and had been surviving on takeout food. He tried to focus on what the President was saying but could make no sense of it.

The President had moved from women to the benefits of obedience training for dogs, hands flailing in all directions as he stormed around the room.

"Religion, that's the ticket!" he said. "I should have invited the clergy too. Nothing like a little hellfire to put the fear of God into people and make them toe the line. Make a note for our next meeting," he said, pointing at Ryan.

"Men, I need you to brainstorm," he said. "These women, they don't get it. They don't see what we're trying to do here, how it's going to benefit them. How do we get that message across? And quickly before they turn off the tap, so to speak."

He winked and pretended to clutch his crotch. The men shifted uncomfortably in their chairs.

"This day of protest they've announced is next week, so we don't have much time. Not that we need it. We're good at handling crises, and they're just a bunch of chicks. We're smarter than they are. And we outnumber them, no matter what that useless newspaper says. Speaking of which, we have to do something about that paper too. Are you with me?"

Daniel nodded. He wondered what he was getting into.

"Sir?" asked one of the advisors. "Could you buy off the newspaper? Or get that journalist fired?"

"Just might work," the President said. "Look into it, Ryan. Frank, how do we stop their protest?"

"Well, sir, one idea is to insist that all protests or marches have to get written authorization from the Chief of Police. Otherwise, their action is illegal. I've seen it tried in other places."

"Brilliant! What else?"

Frank shrugged and looked at Daniel.

"You could sign an Executive Order that women can't gather in groups of two or more without a man being present," Daniel suggested. "If a man is around, they won't be able to plan anything that we don't know about."

"Good idea! What else, gentlemen?

He glanced at the grandfather clock in the corner of the room.

"Time flies when you're having fun. Work on your ideas and get back to me by 8:30 a.m. tomorrow. Frank, can you stay for a few minutes?"

after the others left, Frank approached the President's desk. "Sir?"

The President told Ryan he could leave and waited for him to close the door.

"What happened yesterday?" he asked in a low voice. "I read about it in the papers. How could you miss?"

Frank straightened his shoulders.

"I put our best man on it, sir. He only missed by a hair. Apparently, the mark stepped away from the window a split second before the hit."

"Where is he now?"

"We believe he's still in the building. Trying to confirm."

"Let me know as soon as you know anything. And his family?"

"No sign, sir. His wife and baby are not at home and haven't been all weekend. His parents have left as well. We've tried to track them, but nothing has come up."

"It's not like you to let me down, Frank."

"I will keep trying."

"Trying isn't good enough, dammit!" the President yelled, slamming his fist on the desk, his face crimson. "I want success, do you hear me?"

He leaned forward, his face inches from Frank's.

"Do I need to remind you of Daniel's private photo collection?"

He smiled as Frank flinched.

"No, sir."

"Well then?"

"If the reporter doesn't surface, we could target the building. He may be holed up inside."

The President nodded. "That's more like it."

"We did not have this conversation," he added, waving Frank toward the door.

Jack was in the "Batcave" as he had taken to calling the basement space at the newspaper building. It was a large rectangular room with glaring lights and no windows. Some of the older reporters claimed it had been built as a bunker during the Cold War, designed to withstand bombs because, of course, the newspaper must always meet its deadlines. Staff used the space when there was a big story and Bob wanted everyone to work in the same place.

He was surprised to see an émail pop up on his laptop. It was from Joanna at the World Organization for Women.

Hey Jack,

Read about you in the paper. I may have a solution. Message me.

He texted her.

Curious. Text me at this number.

Within ten minutes, he was packing up his equipment and clothes. He left a vague voicemail for Ed and Bob, using his code name as agreed.

Jack packed everything into his saddlebags and guided his motorcycle out of the underground parking. He drove quickly along back streets, checking his mirrors. There was a black and white Mini Cooper in the distance, keeping a steady pace. He turned sharply down a narrow alley and out on to the main road where he picked up speed. No sign of the Mini.

He circled the block to the back entrance of a gray building and pressed a code into the keypad. The door opened. As he coasted down the slope into the parking garage, he glanced to his right. The Mini appeared, the passenger window opening quickly.

He revved the engine and raced into the garage, rounding the corner as the first three bullets struck the metal door frame. The large door slid back into place, two more bullets pinging off it. Jack jumped off the bike, jabbed at the kickstand with his foot and ran to the stairwell door, pressing the buzzer as fast as he could. When the door opened, he raced up four flights of stairs before pausing to listen. No sounds.

Breathing heavily, he pushed open the door and stepped inside. A young woman greeted him by name.

"Welcome to the World Organization for Women, Jack. Bit of a close call, was it?"

She smiled and held out her hand.

"I'm Brigitte. Joanna has asked me to bring you upstairs. Please follow me."

Chapter Twenty-Nine

Maggie stood in the center of the produce aisle, holding a head of broccoli in her hand. Moments before, the radio station had been playing easy listening music from the eighties. Now a manifesto was being read as if it were nothing more than the weather report.

She looked around the store. Everyone was standing still, confusion spreading across their faces as their plans for the day crashed to the floor.

Open Letter To The Wealthy White Men in Power

Your days are numbered.

We are coming for you.

We ... are the women of the world.

We are your grandmothers, mothers, daughters, and granddaughters. Your sisters, wives, lovers and friends. The women who birthed you, held you, fed you, and loved you.

Without us, you would not exist.

For centuries, you have stolen our bodies, our power and our voices. When we still would not be silent, you murdered us and buried our remains to hide your shame, calling us witches, bitches and whores.

And yet we thrive.

Our roots are deep, our spirits even deeper.

We have been patient for far too long.

We are coming and we are not alone.

We are joined by all those who believe in justice, equality, integrity, and choice. United, we stand for a just society that embraces human beings of every gender, age, race, culture, background, faith, and ability. A healthy society that lives in harmony with Earth, our only home.

Consider this fair warning.

We have seen the future.

And it belongs to us.

Magdalen

"Yes!" Maggie shouted, clapping her hands, as the voice grew silent, and music flowed through the store once more. She tried to catch the eyes of other shoppers. Most lowered their heads and resumed their mute shuffle past the bins of cabbages and carrots, staring blindly at the lists in their hands. A young woman with a toddler in her cart held her gaze, raising a fist. Maggie nodded and smiled.

As she walked home with her bags, Maggie noticed people gathering in small groups. In outdoor cafes, men and women concentrated on the front page of newspapers, oblivious to their phones and lukewarm coffee. She stopped at a nearby newsstand.

"What's up?" she asked the vendor.

"Sold out," he said. "Big letter on the front page."

Shop owners stood in their doorways engrossed in conversation with customers. The streets hummed, not with traffic, but with the steady drone of voices.

"Did you hear…?"

"Did you see…?"

"Magdalen. That's the name."

"Sounds like she's got an army behind her."

"Auntie Max! Check this out."

Lena handed her phone to Madeline.

"All my social media pages are the same," Lena said.

Madeline showed her the front page of the newspaper. Lena glanced at it.

"It's the same letter as on my phone. What's going on?"

Madeline gestured toward the beach and added loudly, "Oh, look at the time! We planned a walk this morning right after breakfast, remember?"

She winked at Lena.

"Oh right, I forgot."

Lena slipped on her flip flops and followed her mother out the door to the beach.

The waves frothed and crashed on the shore. Seagulls cruised and called overhead. The two women walked along, scanning the beach for shells, until they were past the last cottage.

Lena raised her head, a calculating look in her eyes.

"It's you, isn't it?"

Madeline shrugged.

"I have no idea who Magdalen is."

Lena shook her head.

"Not buying it. Even her name sounds like yours."

"Maybe so, but it's not me. You'll have to take my word for it. Look, I think it's incredibly good timing, and someone out there has a powerful voice, but I can't take credit. I think we may be able to use the situation to our advantage though."

"How so?"

"That letter is a call to action. Perhaps even a catalyst for an uprising. And it will trigger a reaction; you can count on that. But on its own, without behind-the-scenes support, it will be nothing more than a blip on the radar and soon forgotten."

"So, what do we do?"

Madeline leaned forward and whispered in Lena's ear. A smile spread slowly across her face as she listened. When Madeline was finished speaking, Lena jumped up and down, clapping her hands.

"Let's get started!"

Lena raced back to the cottage. Half an hour later, she skidded into the kitchen and flapped a piece of paper in Madeline's face. Madeline studied it carefully and gave her a hug.

"Good work, kiddo," she said.

She pointed to some names in the middle of the list: *@magdalenknows, @therealmagdalen.* "Start here, and let it build gradually, okay?"

Lena nodded and grabbed an apple from the bowl on the table.

"How long until lunch?"

Madeline groaned. "I can whip up grilled cheese sandwiches in about ten minutes. Is that soon enough?"

As the President's aides briefed him on their failed attempt to buy *The Nation Today*, the widescreen television above the fireplace switched from the drone of the morning news to a close-up of a typewritten letter. A computer-generated female voice read the contents out loud.

The men moved closer to the screen. Ryan scrolled through news channels on his phone.

At the end of the broadcast, the President grabbed the remote and muted the television.

"Sir? We have a problem," Ryan said.

"No shit!"

The President paced around his desk; hands clasped behind his back.

"Who the hell is Magdalen? That letter's a threat against me, I mean against the government. It's treason, that's what it is, and I won't stand for it."

The aides stared at the floor. Ryan cleared his throat.

"Sir? This letter, it's on all the news networks. And not just across the country. Around the world."

The President hurled the remote across the room. Batteries scattered as the plastic case broke open.

"Who has that kind of power? It's got to be China."

He glared at his aides.

"Don't just stand there! We have a crisis on our hands. We need a plan. Now!"

"Sir? Is this a matter for the police? I mean, treason is a criminal offense."

The President studied the young man. A graduate of Harvard law; fine family background; scrupulously dressed in a dark pin-stripe suit and matching blue shirt and tie. A keener, he thought, when he hired him.

"And how do you propose to find out who this 'Magdalen' is?" the President roared. "We don't even have a last name."

The young man swallowed noisily and suggested that the police might be best equipped to handle that as well.

"Fine," he thundered, "get Frank and Daniel in here on the double. And you three? Out on the streets. Find out what people are saying and report back."

As they turned to leave, he shouted, "Not dressed like that! Put on, I don't know, jeans or something. You have to blend in. Bloody hell! Do I have to think of everything?"

Frank caught up with Daniel as he arrived at the White House.

"No sign of your wife yet," Frank said.

Daniel shrugged. "Who cares? I think we've got bigger fish to fry now."

Four security guards flanked the two men as they walked down the hall to the President's office. The President was standing by the window, looking out at the Rose Garden.

Without turning, he asked for their updates.

"That reporter is staying at the World Organization for Women," Frank said. "We tailed him, and nearly stopped him, but he got away. The place is built like a tank – nothing goes in or out without surveillance."

The President turned and glared.

"Change in plans. Frank, find this Magdalen bitch and stop her. That's all that matters. And Daniel? Stay for a moment. We need to talk."

The President waited for Frank to leave. He turned to Daniel.

"I need more legislation. How quickly can you pull it together?"

"Whatever you need. What's it about?"

The President explained what he had in mind.

"That won't be hard. Some of that already exists. I just have to update it for the present circumstances."

"Good man. That's what I want to hear."

Chapter Thirty

Jack drummed his fingers on the top of the desk. Joanna had arranged for him to have a small office with a pull-out couch and a private bathroom on the top floor of the World Organization for Women complex. A single window overlooked the hallway.

"No one can find you here, Jack. The hall overlooks the courtyard, not the street, and we only use this floor for special guests. It's self-contained. In fact, it doesn't exist according to the floor plan of the building or the elevator buttons. You are invisible."

Invisible but accessible, he thought. High-speed internet meant he could stay up to date on events in the outside world, focus on research, and file his stories.

He got up and walked around the room. The letter on the front page of the paper had set off fireworks. Bob and Ed had sent him a panicked message. How had someone broken into the secure system at the paper? And at all the papers, radio, and television stations around the world? The text had even been translated into different languages.

I have to find this Magdalen, he thought.

He stopped in the center of the room and frowned.

He sent a text.

Time for a call?

When Jack didn't hear back from Maggie, he called Hannah. They chatted briefly about the baby. Jack asked if Maggie was around.

"Is that the only reason you call me these days, Jack? I thought Evy and I were your priorities."

He could hear the smile in her voice.

"You know you are. But I need to talk to Maggie about some of these developments."

"She's been in her office all morning with the door shut. She left me a note on the kitchen table to make myself some lunch. I'm sure she'll get back to you as soon as she's done. Did I tell you she's invited me to join her book club? Next week is the first meeting."

"Hey, that's great. It'll do you good to be around other people. What's the book?"

"I think we're all supposed to pick a book when we meet on Tuesday. Looks like the theme is books with strong female leads. Maggie gave me a list of ideas, but I already know which one I want to discuss – the one I've been reading lately. You know the one with fifteen suggestions for raising a feminist daughter?"

Jack chuckled.

"Could make for interesting discussions given what the government's been up to this week. How's Maggie going to introduce you to the group? It's important that there be no connection to me or the paper."

"We'll use your suggestion – I'm the daughter of a friend and I've just moved to the area. I'm staying with her until I find a place."

Maggie picked up her phone and set it down again. Alicia had said she wanted to get involved, but did she mean it? Only one way to find out. She grabbed her phone again.

"Ali? Maggie. Have you seen the letter in the paper? The one from Magdalen."

Maggie listened and interrupted, "Of course it's not me. Why would you think that? Listen, I know you said you wanted to do something, but how much time do you have? Realistically speaking."

After a brief pause, she added, "Because I think this is our big break. I don't think they saw this coming, so if we act fast, we have the advantage. Can you come over this aft? I've got some ideas. Bring your laptop."

Maggie and Alicia huddled over their laptops at the wicker table. It was a perfect summer day – blue sky, sunshine glowing through the branches of the oak tree. A gentle breeze danced through yellow and burgundy flowers in Maggie's back garden, but the two friends were oblivious to their surroundings.

Maggie sat back and took a sip of coffee. She placed her hand on Alicia's for a moment.

"Thank you."

"For what?" Alicia asked.

"For deciding to get involved. It's like old times."

"Kinda, sorta." Alicia shrugged. "I mean, we're more in the shadows this time."

"Is that okay?"

"I miss the excitement of the front line," Alicia said, "but this is actually more fun. I feel like a kid plotting mischief with my best friend."

She gave Maggie a quick hug.

"Hey, do you remember that time in grade 7? Mr. Williams' science lab."

Maggie snorted. "How could I forget?"

"We thought we were so brave, hiding in the bathroom after school until everyone left, and sneaking into the lab," Alicia said.

"It took us five trips to release all those mice and frogs out the side window," Maggie said. "Some of the frogs kept jumping from the windowsill back into the room."

"It was so worth it. Dissection was cancelled for the rest of the term."

"Guess we were rebels even then," Maggie said. "Too bad you moved away after grade 8. Imagine the chaos we could have caused in high school."

They laughed and bent over their screens again.

"Mags?"

"What?" Maggie kept typing.

"This woman and kid staying with you, are they … can we … does she know?"

"She's part of our book club, but that's the extent of it. She's got a lot on her plate, so I haven't shared any of this with her. She doesn't need to know."

"Where is she now?"

"She's sleeping with the baby. I checked. As long as we keep our voices down, she can't hear a thing from the front bedroom."

"Who is she?"

Maggie sat up and rested her hands in her lap.

"She's like … family. I promised a friend I'd give her a place to live for a while. That's all."

She turned back to her screen and continued to type.

"How about this?"

Alicia turned her laptop toward Maggie.

"The Magdalen Club," Maggie read out loud. "Perfect. Send me the link and I'll share it with my contacts."

Alicia stood up and stretched her arms above her head.

"You've got a gorgeous spot here, Mags. Very private with all the trees. A corner of paradise in the middle of the city."

Maggie didn't reply. Alicia began reading over her shoulder.

"There," said Maggie. "I think we're ready to go."

Alicia clapped her hands and squealed.

"GNN. Love it. Sounds like a real news network. What do the initials stand for?"

Maggie smiled and pulled a notebook out of her pocket. She flipped through a few pages and pointed to something.

"One day you joked about being a gray-haired granny. You said age made us invisible. I think invisibility is a great superpower, don't you?"

She winked at Alicia.

"Introducing …" Maggie pummeled the edge of the table in a drumroll crescendo, "the Granny News Network."

Chapter Thirty-One

The next morning, Jack received a text from Maggie. He called her back.

"I hear you're organizing a book club."

"Oh, I guess Hannah told you. But that's not why you wanted to talk to me, is it?"

"No. I'm wanting your thoughts on Magdalen," Jack said.

"Why?"

"You're well connected in the women's movement, so I figured you might have an idea of who she is."

"No, I don't," Maggie said. "Anything else?"

"Well, let me ask you this. What's your full name?"

Silence. Followed by peals of laughter.

"Thank you for the compliment, Jack," Maggie said as she tried to regain her breath. "You made my day. But as you already know, my full name is Margaret Ellen Carpenter, Maggie to my friends. Good luck finding Magdalen."

Maggie looked up from her laptop as Hannah came into the kitchen, still in her pajamas.

"Baby down for a nap?"

Hannah nodded and yawned.

"Maybe you should rest too," Maggie said.

"Probably, but I've been doing that for weeks. I want to get back into a routine, so I thought I'd start by folding laundry. It never seems to end with a baby."

Maggie pulled out a chair and gestured.

"Put your feet up for a bit first. Laundry, like dishes, can always wait."

She filled a glass with water and set it in front of Hannah.

"Tell me what you used to do before you had Evelyn. Were you working? Going to school?"

Hannah took a sip of water and sat back in the chair.

"Not much to tell really. I graduated from college with a degree in journalism, like Jack. In fact, that's where we met. Before we got married, I worked for a few years as a reporter with a local paper while Jack was building his career with *The Nation Today*. We moved into the city three years ago and I worked part-time for a while at another newspaper. And along came Evy."

Maggie pushed a plate of blueberry muffins toward Hannah.

"Fresh from the oven. Help yourself."

Hannah picked one up.

"Still warm, mmmm."

She broke the muffin in half and nibbled on a piece.

"Do you bake a lot?" Hannah asked.

"Only if I have guests. It would take me a while to get through a dozen muffins on my own."

Maggie tugged on a loose thread on her shirt sleeve.

"So, what do you enjoy doing when you have free time?" Maggie asked.

"Gardening. I could spend hours, days even, in my backyard," Hannah said, her face glowing in the sunlight drifting through the window. "I spent the first couple of years in our new house, digging and chiseling through the clay. I was determined to create a garden oasis even though there was no topsoil."

"You added peat moss, right?"

"You got it!"

Maggie chuckled. "Been there. Done that. Too bad Jack wants you to stay inside for now. You'd love my yard. I bet you'd know most of the plants."

Hannah glanced out the back window.

"I can see a lot of familiar faces," she said.

Hannah sighed and picked up another muffin.

"I hope this will soon be over so Evy and I can get back home. I do appreciate your willingness to take us in, Maggie, but there's no place like home, is there?"

The media conference on Women's Choice Day took place from the headquarters of the World Organization for Women. Joanna invited Jack downstairs to sit in on the video conference. Jack sat off-camera facing Joanna, Magda, and her stepdaughters. Joanna signaled the countdown to going live with her fingers.

"Three, two, one … Welcome to today's media conference from the World Organization for Women. I am Joanna Price, director of the organization, and I am here today with Magda McArthur, the First Lady of the United States, and the President's two daughters, Tina and Becky."

She nodded at the women beside her.

"The purpose of today's media conference is to talk about the upcoming Women's Choice Day. First the context. As of last week, abortion is a criminal offense, and miscarriages will be investigated for illegal activity. Any woman found guilty of these offenses will be charged with murder; any doctor performing an abortion or participating in a planned miscarriage is subject to a fine of $50,000 and a prison term of up to 99 years."

She paused, took a sip of water, and continued.

"Contraception is banned. White women who have more than two children will receive financial bonuses based on the number of additional offspring they produce. All non-white women are restricted to a maximum of one child. Women who choose to work outside the home will have their salaries capped, and maternity leave shortened to 30 days. The number of childcare spaces has been cut in half and all public funding for childcare has been eliminated."

Joanna looked directly into the camera.

"The government's purpose is clear – take away our independence and force us into servitude. But they've forgotten one important thing - women outnumber men in this country. It's time to put our numbers to good use and stand up for our rights, as women and as human beings."

Magda outlined the plan for the day of celebration.

"Women's Choice Day is a one-day general strike by women to highlight the many ways in which we contribute to society. Please reflect on all you do within your family and workplace to provide direct support to men. Withdraw those services. All of them. And, yes, that can also include sex in any form."

She glanced at her notes.

"Bring your children. Bring a friend. Events have been organized across the country. Please check your local chapter of the World Organization for Women for details in your area. Here in the Capitol, we invite you to Lafayette Square. Pack a picnic lunch; bring a blanket and games for the children if you wish. People of all genders are invited to join us to support the rights of those who identify as women. The rest of the day's agenda will be shared at 9 a.m. on August 26. We look forward to seeing you there."

When the news conference was over, Jack headed for the stairs. Joanna called his name. He turned and waited for her to catch up.

"Come with me," she said. "There's something you have to see."

She led him back into the room and over to a large window.

"Look out there."

Jack's eyes followed her finger to an orange banner flying across the front of the community center.

"Where did that come from?" he asked.

"I have no idea. Things like this are springing up everywhere. I saw an electronic billboard on the way into work this morning. It kept flashing *United We Stand*. And in the middle of Constitution Ave., there's a huge poster that reads *Your Days Are Numbered*. Just like in that manifesto."

They both watched as the wind caught the banner. Three words sprawled across its length in black letters at least seven feet high.

Magdalen is watching

Jack shivered.

Chapter Thirty-Two

The President called an emergency session of the Senate. Upon his arrival in the Chamber, he shook a few hands and took the seat of the Senate President.

"Gentlemen, I have called this extraordinary session because of the threat to national security. The so-called Magdalen Letter is a call for violence. It urges citizens to take to the streets and overthrow the government. That's treason, plain and simple. We must deal with this immediately for the safety and protection of all Americans. Therefore, I am asking you to pass the following legislation. Copies are on the table in front of you.

"First, the Civil Obedience Act. As we discussed by teleconference, women shall not gather in groups of more than two without a man present. In addition, all large group gatherings must apply for, and obtain, advance authorization from the Chief of Police. All funding is immediately revoked from any organization that does not support the government's stated mission of protecting our people, keeping our jobs and communities safe, and upholding strong family values. By that, I mean expressly, the World Organization for Women."

The men nodded their approval as they scanned the document.

"Second, I present the new and improved Emergency Measures Act. In the interest of time, I asked Chief Justice Power to review the existing act and update it for current circumstances. The document in front of you permits me, I mean the government, to use whatever means necessary to ensure the safety and security of our country."

"Why haven't we seen this document ahead of time?"

"What right do you have to make these decisions without consulting us?"

The President's eyes rested on each man in the room, one by one. He raised his voice over their angry muttering.

"I don't think I need to remind any of you of your commitment to this government, and of my personal commitment to you and your interests."

The men fell silent.

"We don't need to discuss this further, do we?" the President paused and watched their faces. "I didn't think so. We also don't need a recorded vote. All in favor of passing both pieces of legislation? Unanimous? That's what I thought. Well done, men. And in time to have lunch with your families."

The President smiled and shook the Senators' hands as they left the meeting.

"Ryan? Draft a press release and bring it to me for review. And call a media conference for 4 p.m. this afternoon."

The press conference began outside the White House with Daniel introducing the President. The President strode to the microphone, smiling at the crowd. As he glanced around, he saw women pushing strollers in the park, and children playing with a ball.

"Look around you," he said, pointing to the activity in the park. "Families, enjoying a lovely summer day. Lots of women and babies. That's what our government is here to protect. The key to a strong society is happy children, solid parental bonds, and adherence to the values that make our country great."

He glanced at his notes and added, "And it's this stability that Magdalen has threatened. We will find her; you can count on that. No one has the right to hijack the media and bypass rules of order for the sake of a personal vendetta. This is treason of the highest sort, and she will be stopped."

Behind him, the men on stage clapped politely. He gestured behind his back, and they ramped up the noise, whistling, cheering, and stamping their feet.

The President nodded and began to list the details of the new legislation.

Jack watched the President's media conference via remote access. He had a mike connected to a wire in the cameraman's ear. As he listened to the President go on about the threat to the country and the need for an emergency response, Jack scanned the background.

"Hey, Mike. Take a quick look around. Anything unusual?"

He watched closely as the cameraman took a slow scan of the crowd.

"Stop."

A group of children in the park tossed a bright red ball back and forth. It took him a minute to make sense of the words on their shirts. *United we stand.*

Jack grabbed a copy of Magdalen's letter from the desk.

"Holy crap, Mike, the words on the kids' shirts? They're from the letter."

Jack took the stairs down to Joanna's office. Her assistant waved him in.

"Jack? What's up?"

"Just finished watching the President's latest media conference. Did you see it?"

"No, anything new?"

"He's announced more legislation. Women can't meet in groups of more than two without a man present. Large gatherings must have signed permission from the Chief of Police, and funding has been cut from organizations that don't support the government's policies. Like yours. Wondering how you're going to handle this for Women's Choice Day?"

"Is this an official interview?"

"Not at this point," Jack said. "Just giving you a heads-up."

"Okay, thanks. I'll keep it in mind. Could you close the door on your way out?"

Jack looked back as he passed the assistant's desk. Joanna was already on the phone.

Chapter Thirty-Three

Audrey, Sam, and Janet were in the kitchen at Brian's cottage talking about the Magdalen letter and Women's Choice Day when Lena and Madeline arrived for the second meeting of the Cottage Lane Bookies. Marshall was in the living room helping Shelley set up refreshments. Brian set a plate of cookies on the counter and leaned back against the sink to listen to the conversation.

"Everybody's talking about it. Why, I was in the bank today, and all the people in line were going on about women's rights, and what the government is doing, and …"

"Has anyone figured out who Magdalen is?"

"No one knows. Mike at the gas station said he thinks it's a government set-up so they can justify clamping down on the big women's celebration. Sounds like something they'd do."

"Hey, Brian, what do you think? You're the one teaching women's studies, right?"

Brian frowned.

"Not anymore. The college cancelled the program today. Pressure from the government. And not just our college. Right across the country."

"No way!" Audrey said, slamming her hand on the counter. "They've gone too far, messing with education."

Lena glanced at Madeline. "I wonder what that means for my course."

"And that's not all," Janet added. "Most of the books we're reading here are now banned. They've been pulled from public libraries. We'll have to be careful."

Shelley came into the kitchen and tapped Audrey and Sam on the shoulder.

"I hate to interrupt, but it's time to get started. Grab something to drink and come on in."

They found seats around the coffee table and pulled out their copies of *The War on Women*.

Marshall raised his hand. Madeline shook her head.

"It's okay, Marshall, we're not in school here, so you don't have to put your hand up."

"Just wanted to say something before we get started, if that's okay."

Madeline nodded.

"I know you suggested that we just choose one chapter and focus on it, but I ended up reading the whole thing. Anybody else?"

A few people raised their hands.

"I gotta say, this was the toughest book I've ever read. I had to put it down so many times. All those shocking stories about how women are treated around the world. And not just by men; sometimes by other women."

He shook his head.

"I know it's not just "over there", he said, using his fingers to make air quotes. "It happens here too, although maybe it's more hidden. But reading these stories made me glad I was born a man. I don't know if that's considered politically correct these days, but I just had to say it. Being a woman in any of the countries in this book just plain sucks. And I sure hope that none of you women here feel like we think you're only good for one thing."

"Thanks for starting the conversation, Marshall," Lena said. "It is a difficult book and that's why I chose it. We had to read it for one of my courses and I remember feeling terrified, and sick to my stomach. Mostly though, I felt rage. And maybe that's a good place to start tonight. Rather than give us the details of what you read, can you share one word that sums up how you felt about the book?"

"Shocked."

"Depressed."

"Ashamed."

"Motivated."

"Motivated to do what, Shelley?"

"To change things. In fact, given the legislation that was passed last week, I'm not sure that women here are any better off than the women in the book."

"Bit of an exaggeration that, don't you think?" Sam asked.

"Actually, no, I don't think it is, Sam," Shelley said. "By repressing women's choices, the government has begun to suppress civil rights. Today it's women; tomorrow, it could be Black people, immigrants, Indigenous people. Just like that Magdalen letter said, the government is run by wealthy white men, and they will stop at nothing to keep their stranglehold on power."

"I think this book club is very timely," Janet said. "Maybe our discussions will help us understand the current political situation in a different way."

"For those of you who read all or most of the book, I'm curious what you saw as a common thread in the stories," Lena said. "Auntie Max, do you want to start?"

Madeline nodded.

"The obvious theme was the oppression of women, but I think it's important not to get stuck there. What struck me was the collusion of women within a given culture. This isn't a man versus woman issue; it's a mindset, and that's something we need to keep in mind as we watch our own country in the coming weeks."

"I agree," said Brian. "It's almost a cult-like acceptance, an unquestioning belief that 'this is the way things are'. How do people get to that point?"

"Oh, that's simple," Audrey said. "Those in power undermine your confidence, your sense of truth and justice, and your ability to speak up or fight back. It happens gradually. It's about pitting one group against another."

"*Divide et impera*," said Janet. "Divide and conquer. It's a military strategy that goes back to the Greeks, I think. Used successfully by Julius Caesar and Napoleon. And I believe Machiavelli even wrote about it in *The Art of War*."

"Am I the only one feeling a little lost here? Are we talking about the book or ancient history?" Sam asked.

He looked around the group.

"Anyone else confused?"

"It's okay, Sam," Madeline said. "Sometimes fact and fiction overlap. And I think that's the case here."

"Getting back to the book," Lena said, "what was your take on it, Sam?"

"I hated it."

Lena sat back and frowned.

"Can I ask why?"

Sam leaned forward.

"I skimmed through a bunch of chapters. I could never finish any of them because I got so mad. Audrey told me to stop reading and get out for a walk to clear my mind, so I did. But it didn't help. And I'm sitting here tonight listening to you go on and on about men and women, and how men are trying to control women and it's driving me nuts. I mean, I'm not like that, am I, Audrey?"

She shook her head and started to speak but he continued.

"I was raised to be a gentleman. Now, maybe that's old school, but I was taught to respect girls and women. That's why I open doors for Audrey and pull out her chair when we go out for dinner. I think women are amazing creatures, and none of us would be here without them, right? Just think of what our mothers went through to bring us into this world and then raise us. Sure beats the hell out of what a man can do."

He cleared his throat, lifted his chin, and crossed his arms over his chest.

"I appreciate what you have shared, Sam," Lena said, "but what if women want to open their own doors? Or what if we want to be paid the same salary as men when we do the same work, or decide whether or not to have children? If men are making those decisions for us, how is that respecting us?"

Sam leaped to his feet. He shook his finger at Lena and said, "If this group is only about making men feel bad when we try and do something nice, I want none of it. Your book, young lady, paints us into a corner. Makes me ashamed to be a man. It suggests that all I think about is sex when I see a woman, and that I would be capable of doing the terrible things that happen in the book. I like women. I respect 'em. And if any man ever tried to hurt my Audrey or our girls, he'd wish he was dead."

He stormed out of the room. As the screen door slammed, Audrey stood up.

"Don't mind him," she said with a wave of her hand. "He gets himself all worked up over things sometimes. He means well. By morning, he'll be right as rain. You'll see."

She picked up her purse and her copy of the book.

"I'd better get going. He's going to feel bad leaving like that, and he'll need to talk it out."

Lena flung her head into her hands.

"It's all my fault. I baited him, didn't I? I didn't mean to."

"It's okay, Lena. It's an intense book," Brian said. "I'm wondering if we should consider setting up some ground rules for our group. I do that kind of thing all the time in my classes. It helps everyone feel safe and comfortable having difficult discussions."

"Good idea. Maybe we could meet in a few days to do that?" Janet suggested.

Madeline offered to send out an email suggesting the date.

Marshall stood up.

"Before we go, there's something I want to say. And I don't think it can wait until next time."

He glanced around the room for approval.

"I don't have a way with words like some of you, so what I'm going to say may be a bit jumbled, but here goes. I've been listening to the whole conversation, and it seems to me we're all missing the point. Janet said something about divide and conquer. And I think maybe that's what the government is trying to do. I think the book does the same – it's about men versus women, and sometimes women versus women. Either way, it's all about differences."

He rubbed his hand across his wrinkled forehead.

"Even within this group, we're feeling it. Sam made a good point. I've been sitting here feeling awkward about being a man after reading that book, and I really hope that the other books aren't like this one. If they are, I'm outta here.

"I think it comes down to this. We're human first and foremost. Whether we're men or women, Black, white or something in between, gay or straight, a professor or a plumber, none of that matters. Seems to me we need to focus on what we have in common. And if we stick together, we'll outsmart the buggers."

He sat down hard, pulled out a handkerchief and blew his nose.

Madeline reached over to a pile of books by the coffee table and pulled one out. She held it in her hands for a moment and then passed it to Marshall.

"Based on what you just said, Marshall, you might want to consider this book as your choice."

Marshall read the title out loud, "*Girl, Woman, Other*". He frowned and turned the book over to read the back.

"What's it about, Max?" he asked.

"It's a novel about the lives of Black women in the UK. You said it's important to find what we all have in common regardless of gender, race or religion. Here in this beach town, we all look the same. It's hard for us to imagine the world through someone else's eyes. The stories in this book look at life from multiple perspectives. I can guarantee you will find it challenging, Marshall. But it will get us talking about differences and help us find similarities, which is exactly what you just suggested."

Marshall glanced at Janet.

"Do you know this book? What do you think?"

Janet smiled. "I think you're up to the challenge, Marshall. We all are."

"Okay, Max, I'll do it. Mark me down for this one."

Brian insisted on walking Madeline and Lena across the lane to their cottage after everyone left. Lena raced inside. Madeline dropped her book on the kitchen table and moved slowly down the hall. She knocked on Lena's closed door.

"Come in," was the muffled reply.

Lena was lying face down on the bed, a pillow over her head. Madeline lifted the pillow up and touched her daughter's shoulder.

"Hey," she said.

Lena rolled over. Her face was wet with tears.

"Oh, sweet girl, it's not that bad."

"I blew it. And Sam was so mad, he left. It's all my fault."

She covered her face with her arms.

Madeline got up and closed the window and the door.

"Listen," she whispered. "That's exactly what needed to happen. So, thank you for getting things stirred up on the first night."

Lena opened her eyes and stared at her mother.

"Who are you kidding?"

"The whole point of the book club is to generate discussion, preferably by pushing people out of their comfort zone. And that's what happened brilliantly tonight, thanks to you."

Lena shook her head.

"But Sam's so upset he won't come back."

"They'll all be back. This book club is the most interesting thing that's happened around here in a long time."

Madeline grinned.

"I know you don't believe me right now, but people have to get mad before they're willing to consider new ideas. They resist, you persist, and walls come down. Think of our book club as a miniature version of society. As we explore the ideas within the books, we'll find the walls that separate us. And that will give us valuable insights for the larger battle. If you know what I mean."

She winked, and Lena began to smile.

"So, it's not just a book club," she said in a low voice.

"Nothing is ever what it seems. It's all part of a much bigger plan."

She sat on the edge of the bed and leaned closer to Lena.

"Picture a giant chess board that stretches around the world. Each book club is one of many pieces on the board. Each move counts. Every move is connected. Just like in chess. And the best part? Our opponents don't even know they're in the game."

Chapter Thirty-Four

Frank hung up his phone and scowled. Finding this Magdalen woman was like looking for a pebble on the beach – all the stones look the same, and then a wave comes along and covers them with sand.

He had spoken to his contacts at intelligence agencies around the world. The feedback was consistent – someone had managed the perfect hack. No one was able to trace the source. It was as if the hacker had opened a door, slipped the message inside, and locked the door, leaving no fingerprints or footprints behind.

Even the message had vanished from the online world. Just like one of those Banksy paintings, he thought. One minute it's there and some fool has spent millions of dollars to buy it, and suddenly the painting shreds itself.

Daniel's wife, Madeline, was another one who had disappeared into thin air. At least he had found her sister, Max, and Lena, as well as the President's wife and daughters, not that their location was good news.

He slumped over his desk. A knock at the door.

"Come in."

Four of his top agents stood in front of his desk.

"You want to see us, sir?"

"Right."

He yawned and pointed at one of the men.

"That house you've been watching at the beach. Anything new?"

"No, sir. The woman and girl spend time walking on the beach, reading, or shopping. They're part of a book club. The club meets at different cottages, but it's all the same people."

"Who's in it?"

"An elderly couple who are neighbors. A father and daughter – he's a college prof, she's a student. The local librarian, and a plumber."

Frank frowned.

"I haven't picked up anything new from the bug, so she must have found it," he said. "That means she's hiding something. I want you to keep watching them, and plant some more devices. Get inside when they're not there and see what you can find out."

He gestured to the next agent in line.

"Nothing to update, sir. The reporter is still inside that women's organization as far as we know, and we can't get a bead on him from anywhere. He's publishing articles from there. And the President's wife and kids have been busy with news conferences about that Women's Day thing."

Frank ordered him to keep watching, especially the reporter.

"He might show up at the event," Frank added. "It's right up his alley."

He assigned the other two the task of researching women named Magdalen.

"Or any variation you can think of: Magdalena, Magdalene, Magda. You get the picture. Bring me a list with contact info. I want to know their backgrounds too. That letter was written by someone with a good education and a big hate on for men. Get Joe to pull together a psychological profile while you're at it."

"What scope for the name search? Local, national, international? And how soon do you want a report?"

"I've already got contacts doing an international search, so focus on local and national. Let me know what you've got by the end of the week."

Madeline pushed her chair back from the desk with a sigh. She reread the latest posts on the book club network. It was a private chat site set up for book club hosts to share the insights from their meetings. Madeline monitored the central site and passed key information on to Maggie and Joanna to be used in their strategy development.

The book clubs had only held a few meetings so far, yet the feedback was invaluable.

Just like we hoped, she thought, tapping her fingers on the arm of the chair. People are identifying what divides us. And coming up with some cool solutions.

She leaned forward and began to type a message to the general group.

"We can't do this alone. Need to find ways to include men as allies. The government is focused on a divide-and-conquer strategy. How do we counter this? Also need cross-sectoral approach – bridge gaps created by race, economics, gender identity, religion, and education. This is a human rights issue, not just a women's issue."

A message popped up in the chat room within seconds.

"So glad to see this comment about bridging gaps. Our book club is all older white women. The book choices are typical. And the discussions often gloss over important issues, Example: Gone With The Wind. A favorite in our group because they see Scarlett as a woman showing spunk and learning to stand up for herself. But they don't see the treatment of Black people, and if they can't see it, we can't talk about it. Suggestion for book clubs just forming – get a diverse mix of people as well as a mix of authors/books. We can't bridge gaps if we don't see them."

When she got up to make a cup of tea, she noticed the light was on in Lena's bedroom. Madeline looked at her watch. It was 2:30 a.m. She cracked the door open. Lena was sprawled on the bed, her laptop beside her. She scrolled through her phone and began to type rapidly.

"Just a sec," she muttered, glancing up at Madeline.

Madeline sat down on the edge of the bed and leaned forward, trying to read over her daughter's shoulder. Lena pulled away and hid the laptop with her body.

"I said, just a sec!"

She smirked and added, "All shall be revealed…"

Lena typed for a few more minutes and closed her laptop.

"Can we talk about this in the morning?" she asked. "I've got a lot more to do and the clock is ticking."

"Shouldn't you be sleeping?" Madeline asked.

"Shouldn't you?"

Lena bounced into the kitchen at sunrise. Madeline was sleeping with her arms cushioning her head on the table. Lena tapped her on the shoulder.

"Wake up, sleepyhead. Time for a walk."

Madeline groaned.

"What time is it?"

"Six-thirty."

"Coffee first," she muttered.

Lena was silent as they headed to the beach, but Madeline could feel her excitement building like a pressure cooker on high heat. Lena sprinted ahead, and waited for Madeline by the old willow, springing up and down on a low-hanging branch.

"Okay, what's up?"

Lena grinned.

"Promise you'll just listen? Don't say anything until I'm done, 'kay?"

She explained that, at college, she and Tina, the President's oldest daughter, had developed a phone app as part of a class project.

"It was pretty basic at the time, but Tina and I decided to take it one step further. We wanted to get away from the constant monitoring of Dad and the Secret Service. With the app, we could make plans without being shadowed by bodyguards."

She picked up a tiny shell and cradled it in the palm of her hand.

"I don't think the Women's Choice protest is going to be a one-off, do you?

Madeline shook her head.

"Since we're no longer allowed to gather except in pairs, I think we're gonna need a way to connect and plan online," Lena continued. "So, I've been working on expanding the app to allow for broader use. I just need a couple more days and it will be ready to go."

"You never cease to amaze me, girl. But how do you make sure it doesn't get into the wrong hands?"

Lena tossed her head, eyes sparkling.

"Tina figured that one out. I don't fully understand, but she says it's cutting edge. And since she's living at the World Organization for Women, she's going to share it with the director. They have chapters across the country and around the world so anyone who wants to organize a protest event will be able to do it in secret."

"Do you have a name for the app?"

Lena danced a jig on the sand.

"OMG."

Madeline raised her eyebrows.

"Spill."

"That's the name. OMG. It stands for 'On Magdalen's Guard'. We may not know who she is, but we're with her all the way."

As they headed back to the cottage, Madeline noticed a man walking through the front garden of their cottage. She pulled out her phone and called Brian. Then she called the police.

"Keep walking, Lena. Let Brian and the police handle this."

Brian was out the door before he got off the phone. He jumped down the front stairs and raced across the laneway. When he got to the gate, he stopped, raised his phone and starting filming. A tall man, dressed in jeans and a t-shirt, was peering into the window of the kitchen door, his hand shielding his eyes from the early morning sun. The man placed one hand on the doorknob and tried to turn it. The door was locked. He pulled something small out of his jeans pocket and inserted it between the door and the frame. Brian waited until he opened the door.

"Can I help you?" Brian called, still filming.

The man jerked his head around, dropping his hand to his side.

"Ah, no, just stopping by to pick up some things for a friend," he said, smiling. Then he saw the phone.

"Hey! What are you doing?"

As he strode toward Brian, they both heard the sirens.

Brian backed to the far side of the road. The man jumped in his car and sped away.

When the police arrived, Brian showed them the video footage including the closeup of the car, the license plate and the man's face. Then he sent a quick text.

Safe to come home.

Chapter Thirty-Five

"Update me."

The President sat in his leather chair, staring out the window, his back to the room. His aides, as well as the Chief of Police, Daniel and Frank lined up facing his desk like prisoners awaiting execution.

No one wanted to go first.

The President swiveled the chair around. He pointed.

"Well, sir," Ryan began, "we've been out on the streets. People are talking – about the letter, legislation, the Women's Day event. They seem afraid, and excited at the same time. No one knows who Magdalen is but there are some guesses."

"Go on."

"Someone wondered if it was your wife, sir. Her first name could be a short form for Magdalen."

The President slammed his fist on the desk and pointed to the Chief of Police.

"Arrest the bitch! We need to send a message."

"We have no proof, sir."

"Then get it! Frank, what the hell have you been up to?"

Frank explained that he had senior officers watching headquarters of the World Organization for Women, as well as monitoring the activities of Daniel's daughter, and two staff dedicated to investigating women across the country with names similar to Magdalen.

"I've asked them to check their backgrounds. And I've ordered a psychological profile so we can narrow it down. As soon as we have a list, I'll bring it to you."

The President grunted.

"But you don't know who it is?"

"Needle in a haystack. We only have the words in the letter. The letter has vanished from cyberspace. No traces of anything that could lead us to the writer."

"And what about their big protest day?"

"Everything is under control, sir," said the Chief of Police. "I have not given my signed authorization, so they cannot proceed legally. If they do, we can arrest them."

"In addition," Daniel added, "they can only meet in groups of two unless there are men present. It's women organizing this, and it will be women attending if it goes ahead, so we can arrest them for civil disobedience."

"Our special forces will be joining the police to monitor the situation," Frank said. "At the first sign of trouble, we will get them off the streets. But it won't come to that. We've considered all the possibilities."

The President turned his chair to face the window.

"I hope you're right," he said. "I don't want any trouble. Don't give them any reason to escalate things. Just keep an eye on the situation. With a bit of luck, it's a one-day event and then we can all get back to normal."

There was a lengthy pause. The men in the line looked at each other, wondering if they were free to go.

"By the way," the President added in a low voice, "has anyone looked into those bright yellow signs in the park? Or that plane that's flying overhead right now, pulling a long banner? My eyesight may not be the best, but it looks to me like they all say, '*Magdalen is watching*'. I've also heard there are billboards across the country that say, '*United we stand*'."

His voice grew shrill.

"And t-shirts with slogans from that goddamn letter!"

He stood, faced the men, and slammed both hands on the desk.

"Make it stop!"

Maggie had been bustling about all day, preparing for the first meeting of her book club. She had tidied up the living room, added a few extra chairs from the kitchen, baked muffins and cookies. She handed participants a sheet of paper and a cup of coffee as they walked in the front door.

"Lots of chairs," she said. "Make yourself at home."

The group chatted among themselves. Hannah came downstairs with Evelyn, stopping briefly in the entrance to the living room. She looked around. No one she knew. No connection to Jack.

Maggie started the discussion, holding up a thin hardcover book.

"Since I'm hosting this book club, I thought I should set the tone," she said, grinning widely. "I love the title of this book as much as I do the author. *The Truth Will Set You Free, But First It Will Piss You Off* by the incomparable Gloria Steinem. Really speaks to my rebel nature."

She handed the book to Hannah and asked her to pass it around.

"So many dynamite quotes in this book. Very inspiring, especially these days," Maggie added. "I was thinking that maybe we could all pick one quote or passage that speaks to us and discuss why."

She glanced around the circle.

"I'm also curious to hear the books that you have chosen. There's a list of possible titles on the paper I gave you, but a word of warning. As of this morning, most of those books have been banned. So if you'd rather choose a different book, that's fine. You do what's best for you. Hannah, do you want to go next?"

Hannah snuggled Evelyn close to her chest.

"Hi everyone, I'm Hannah, and this sweet little bundle is Evy. She's just nine weeks old, and I might need to feed her soon, but I'm really happy to be a part of this group."

She glanced at Maggie.

"In order to understand my book choice, I need to give you a bit of context. I hope that's okay?"

Maggie nodded.

"My parents raised me to work hard … and watch my back. Looking around this circle, I think most of you know what I mean."

She glanced down at the baby, sleeping comfortably in her arms.

"I want a better world for her. One in which she can live openly, joyfully and safely as a Black woman. I want her to be welcome wherever she goes and have a huge cheering section around her every step of the way. That's why I have chosen this book."

She held up a small book with a vibrant cover.

"*Dear Ijeawele, or A Feminist Manifesto in Fifteen Suggestions.* The author wrote it for a friend's baby girl, and one day, I will give a copy to Evy. And to my son if I am blessed with one. Because I think it's a powerful message for everyone."

As if on cue, Evelyn wriggled and began to make sucking noises with her mouth.

"I guess that's my signal to head upstairs," Hannah said. "I'll try and get back down before the end of the meeting."

Alicia looked around the group.

"Guess I'm next," she said. "I'm Alicia. Maggie and I have known each other since we were little. My parents moved here from Tokyo when my brother and sister were toddlers. I was born a year later. Given my background, it might surprise you to learn that my book choice is *Anne of Green Gables*. At least it hasn't been banned. Yet."

She picked up a worn copy from the table.

"Anne is extremely popular in Japan. It was my mother's favorite book. In fact, my middle name is Anne. With an 'e' of course," Alicia added, smiling. "One of our first trips as a family was to Canada to see Green Gables on Prince Edward Island. My mother was so excited. She insisted that we all read the book before we went. When my daughter turned ten, I gave her a copy of the book, and now my twin granddaughters are reading it for the first time."

She picked up a muffin and broke it in half.

"I have always loved Anne for being unpredictable and spunky. I think she's a great role model for young girls. Especially girls who are considered different, like me. Anne didn't dress like the other girls, and she didn't think or act like them. She was fiercely herself, and that's why I want to discuss this book with the group."

She nodded at the woman beside her.

"Hi everyone," she said. "I'm Amrita, and I'm here with my husband, Paul."

She gestured at the tall blond man sitting beside her.

"When Maggie sent out the invitation, I immediately knew the book I wanted to talk about: *I Am Malala.* For me, it's a story about the courage it takes to be a girl or a woman in this world. Men don't understand the intense scrutiny and pressure that we are under all the time. I thought that here, in America, we would be accepted and valued as human beings. But this new legislation has shown me that women's choice is just an illusion. Men have always held power over us and intend to keep doing so. I make a point of rereading Malala's book regularly these days to keep myself motivated and ready to fight. I suggest that we all do."

Paul applauded quietly as she finished speaking. He cleared his throat and leaned forward.

"Look, I might be a man but I don't understand what the government is doing, and I definitely don't support this legislation. In fact, I don't get what's in the minds of men who want women to shut up and put out, so to speak. You might think my book choice a bit odd under the circumstances. I read *Angry White Men* because I wanted to try and figure out where these men are coming from, what motivates them. I think we need to do that if we want to find a way to neutralize their power."

He looked at Maggie.

"I know you said the books were to have a strong female lead. So, I can choose another book. But I think it would be shortsighted not to explore their perspective."

Maggie glanced around the group.

"What does everyone think?"

After a brief discussion, Maggie turned back to Paul.

"Looks like we'll be reading your book."

Maggie gestured at the woman sitting to Paul.

"Jeannie? What book have you chosen?"

The dark-haired woman shifted in her chair and held up a book with a brightly colored cover.

"I'm really glad you started this whole discussion with Gloria Steinem's book, Maggie," she said. "It made me feel more comfortable about suggesting this one. Sara, here," she nudged her wife, "she thinks it's too in-your-face for a book club. But you know me, I'm not one to shy away from controversy."

She handed the book to Sara.

"Pass it around, hon. I just love the title: *The Seven Necessary Sins for Women and Girls*. Doesn't that make you want to read it?" she chuckled.

"Seriously though, it's a deliberately thought-provoking book, and since the theme of our books is strong women, I think it fits right in. It's kind of a manifesto, a guidebook for women to break out of the box of stereotypes most of us were stuffed into at birth and make some noise. Stir things up. Give the patriarchy something to fear."

Sara grinned. "She keeps telling me she doesn't hate men but…"

"No, it's true, I don't. And it's not about men," Jeannie said. "It's about the patriarchy. There is a difference. It's this rigid structure designed to keep everyone in their assigned place. It's not good for any of us, and it has to change. Am I right, or am I right?"

Maggie smiled.

"I think you've done a good sales pitch on your book, Jeannie. Sara? What have you chosen?"

"Actually, Jeannie insisted that I read one of Lee Maracle's books. She gave me a list to choose from, so I'm going with *Bobbi Lee, Indian Rebel*. To be honest with you, I haven't read it yet, so I can't say much about it, but Jeannie said it would make for good discussion here. She's usually right, as you know."

Jeannie blew Sara a kiss.

Alicia raised her hand. "Maggie? I have an idea."

"Sure, go for it."

"I was looking at your book list and listening to all the ones we've chosen. There are so many good ones, and we can't possibly cover them all. Maybe we could put together a reading list, and keep adding to it?"

"Great idea!" Sara said.

"One more thing," Maggie said. "In order to make our gathering legal under the new legislation, we need two more men to round out our numbers. So, put on your thinking caps and let me know who you'd like to invite."

Hannah slipped into the room.

"The baby's asleep. Did I miss anything?"

Chapter Thirty-Six

The next morning, Hannah peeked into the kitchen where Maggie was reading the paper.

"Maggie, can you keep an eye on Evy for me? I just put her down, but she doesn't want to sleep, and I need a shower."

"Are you afraid she'll crawl out of the crib? She's not that old yet."

Hannah giggled. "I know, but I'd feel better if I knew you were there. And I really want to do my hair."

Maggie went into the front guest bedroom and sat on the bed. She and Evelyn stared at each other. Maggie shrugged.

"Hey, kid," she whispered. "How's it goin'?"

Evelyn wiggled and gurgled.

Maggie got up and stood at the side of the crib, watching every move. Evelyn turned her head from side to side and yawned.

"Sleepy, are we?"

She reached in and rested her hand lightly on Evelyn's tummy. The baby gazed up at her, arms and legs growing still. She yawned again and closed her eyes. Maggie stood quietly and watched Evelyn's chest rise and fall in rapid succession. She was still standing there, her hand warm on the baby's body when Hannah came in.

"She's gone to sleep? Oh, you have a magic touch!"

Maggie quickly withdrew her hand, like a child caught with her hand in the cookie jar.

"She was tired. Yawned a couple of times and was out."

She stomped to the door and disappeared down the stairs.

Twenty minutes later, Hannah came into the kitchen for breakfast. She sat down at the table across from Maggie, sliced a banana into a bowl of cereal and added some milk.

"Thank you," she said.

"For what?"

"For watching, Evy. I don't feel comfortable leaving her alone when she's awake. I guess that's silly."

Maggie picked up her mug. "Nonsense. You need to do whatever works for you. No judgment here."

Hannah chewed for a while.

"Maggie? Have you ever been married? Do you have kids?"

Maggie sat back in her chair and set her mug firmly on the table.

"Yes. And no. I was married for five years. We couldn't have kids. We wanted to but…"

"Oh, I'm so sorry. That must have been hard."

Maggie sniffed. "Harder than you know."

She hesitated, running a finger around the top edge of the mug. Round and round. Hannah watched and waited.

Maggie set her jaw and pressed the palms of her hands together, lifting them to her mouth as if in prayer and then dropping them in her lap. She shifted in her chair, staring at the floor. After blinking a few times, she straightened her back and raised her head.

"Okay, here goes," she said, holding Hannah's gaze. "What I'm about to tell you doesn't leave this room. Ever."

Hannah nodded.

"I met John when I was in my early twenties. He was ten years older. A car mechanic, and a good one. He could fix anything. In fact, that's how we met. I took my Beetle in for repairs and we got to talking. One thing led to another and six months later we got married."

She gazed out the window.

"A year later, I went to the doctor to find out why I couldn't get pregnant." Her voice faltered. "Long story."

She rubbed her nose with the back of her hand and got up. She poured a cup of coffee and held the pot out to Hannah. Hannah shook her head. Maggie stood at the counter for a few minutes and returned to her chair.

Maggie glanced at Hannah.

"I'd been pregnant before, you see. A very long time ago. It wasn't … planned. I was very young."

Hannah put a hand on Maggie's arm.

"Can you keep a secret?" she asked.

Maggie nodded.

"I got pregnant when I was sixteen." Hannah said, biting her upper lip. "I…I had an abortion. It was the only way. I wanted to finish high school. I had plans. And being a teen mom was not part of it."

She leaned in closer to Maggie and whispered, "Jack doesn't know. It was long before I met him. I know it was the right decision at the time, but some days it's hard to live with."

Maggie sat back in her chair and crossed her arms. She stared at the floor.

"I would have given anything for an abortion," she said quietly. "It wasn't allowed in my day. I had to go away until the baby was born. When the doctor did the c-section, he tied my tubes. Without telling me."

She frowned. The next sentence came out in a hurry.

"It happened a lot to girls like me."

"What do you mean?" Hannah asked.

Maggie glared at a spot on the ceiling.

"I've never liked labels. I think they make us focus on what's different. It's easier to bully someone or isolate them if you can point at the difference. These days, everyone wants to know how you "identify". Thing is, I identify as a human being. Plain and simple. I wish we all did. But I guess our society just isn't there yet."

A dark cloud scudded across her face and vanished. She fiddled with a spoon on the table.

"You see, my mom was born on the reservation and forced into an Indian Boarding School when she was six. My grandmother had no choice but to let her go, and my mother never talked about it. I only know she ran away from the school at fifteen and met my Dad two years later. He was a carpenter. I was raised in the city, a good Catholic girl, but I got to spend a bit of time each summer with my mother's family on the reservation."

She stared at the floor. Her next words came out bitter, like biting into a fresh lemon.

"I grew up hearing all the slurs, mostly directed at my mother. Because of my Dad, I can pass for white. Some would say that makes me lucky. I don't know about that. All that's ever mattered in this world is that I'm not white. That's why the doctor thought he could go ahead and tie my tubes, without asking what I wanted. Girls like me had no voice. No power. No choice. And now, with what the government's doing, it's like we've gone back in time. Only now it's about controlling all women; not just me."

She slammed her mug on the table.

"Not on my watch."

Chapter Thirty-Seven

Women's Choice Day brought blue skies and sunshine. As Maggie looked out her bedroom window, she felt a familiar thrill bubbling through her body. She dressed quickly, pulling on jeans and a t-shirt. She left a note on the kitchen table for Hannah and headed to the park.

Joanna tested the mike and surveyed the gathering crowd. It was only 8:30 a.m., but Lafayette Square was already full of women, men, and children. Many families had blankets spread out on the grass. Children played tag and kicked soccer balls as parents chatted in small groups. She watched Carole and other staff set up the refreshment table and spread newly printed t-shirts along another table.

"You've got a beautiful day for it."

Joanna turned at the sound of a familiar voice.

"Maggie! It's so good to see you."

"Been a while."

"I'll say. I was thinking of you this morning, wanting you to be at my side to experience this. If not for you and all your work years ago, we wouldn't be here right now."

"Nonsense, Joanna. The tide has turned, and you have risen to the occasion. I only wish it wasn't necessary."

"Maybe this time, it will be different."

Joanna gestured to the mike.

"Will you join me on stage?"

Maggie shook her head.

"I'm just part of the crowd today."

Lena and Madeline had been arguing for half an hour.

"We have to be there," Lena insisted.

"Not happening."

Madeline turned away and started washing the breakfast dishes.

"But Shelley is going. So is Brian."

Madeline said nothing.

"Oh c'mon, Auntie Max, after all I've done for you."

Madeline turned and drew her finger across her throat.

Lena rolled her eyes. She slumped down at the kitchen table and stared out the window. Madeline washed the last cup, grabbed the towel, and threw it onto the table.

"Dry the dishes. We have some errands to run."

Lena picked up the towel and scuffed to the counter.

Madeline came out of the bathroom as Lena was slamming plates into the cupboard. She tapped Lena on the shoulder and bent her index finger in a come-with-me gesture. Lena plodded behind her to the car.

"We have to get some groceries," Madeline explained as they left the house.

"Big deal."

As they drove into the parking lot at the town mall, Madeline glanced at her daughter.

"I know this seems unfair to you."

"Totally."

"But there are a few things you need to understand."

"Such as?"

"There will be police there. You heard what the President wanted to do to his daughters, right? Forced marriage. I wouldn't put it past your father to do the same to you."

"He couldn't!"

"Oh yes, he could. And the President will want him to set an example. If you show up at this event today, and they can find a reason to arrest you, you're as good as married and pregnant. Think about it."

Lena slid down in the seat. She crossed and uncrossed her arms. Shaking her head, she sat up straight.

"He can't do that to me. I'm twenty. I'm an adult."

"You're a woman."

"I've got rights."

"Not anymore. Your father put an end to that for you, me, and all women."

"So, I can't go."

"Do you want to take that risk?"

"Yes! If I stay here, it's like I'm hiding. He wins."

"No, he only wins if he gets his way."

"This is so unfair!"

"Yes, it is. And that's why we are going to fight it. There's a lot we can do behind the scenes. There are plenty of people like Shelley and Brian who can be out there, front and center, standing up for our rights."

Lena crossed her arms again, her eyes blazing.

"Alright then, if I can't go to the park, you'd better have a plan for getting the bastards."

At 9 a.m., Joanna approached the microphone. She glanced at her security staff stationed along the park perimeter. Thumbs up all around. She sighed with relief. They had already notified her of the undercover police across the street surrounding the outer edge of the park.

She welcomed participants and outlined the agenda for the day. As she spoke, a uniformed police officer came up to the podium. She continued speaking as he walked toward her.

"Your permit, please," the officer said.

"One moment," Joanna said to the audience. She pulled a piece of paper out of her backpack and handed it to the officer.

He scanned it and frowned. She pointed to the signature on the bottom of the letter. He shook his head and handed the paper back to her.

"Please take this copy," she said. He grabbed the paper and thumped off the stage.

Joanna stared across the street at the undercover officers and raised her voice.

"Just to be clear, this is a peaceful gathering in accordance with the First Amendment. We are in a public park." She paused for effect. "And, we have a letter of authorization signed by the Chief of Police."

She smiled and returned to her welcome speech.

"Now, as I was saying, you are free to enjoy all that Lafayette Square has to offer. It is a public space, after all. Built and maintained with taxpayers' dollars. The World Organization for Women is happy to provide you with refreshments today. There is a refill station for your water bottles, and we have plenty of fresh fruit on the table to my far right. Directly beside the stage, we have t-shirts, just like the one I am wearing. For sale by donation. We have a special family deal, so just ask staff at the table if you are interested. And for those who want a little exercise today, we suggest a walking tour in the vicinity of the White House. Perhaps wearing your new t-shirts."

A wave of laughter swept through the park. People began to line up at the shirt table.

"However, since we want to make sure all our activities are legal, please walk in groups of two. If you want to walk in larger groups, there must be one man for every two women. You do the math."

Lena curled up on her bed, laptop open beside her. On the way back from shopping, Madeline told her about an invitation she had received by email. A new social media group called The Magdalen Club.

"It's set up as a secret account. I accepted the invitation so now I can invite you as well. I like the look of it, and I think you and your friends could contribute a lot."

She scrolled through the posts. Madeline refused to say who was behind it. Lena's excitement peaked as she read a meme about women's empowerment and a quote by Malala Yousafzai:

"We realize the importance of our voices only when we are silenced."

Lena went to her own collection of favorites and pulled out a quote.

"Women's empowerment is intertwined with respect for human rights." ~ Mahnaz Afkhami

With a click, Lena added the post.

Frank swore loudly.

"How the fuck did they manage that?" he asked the police officer.

The man shook his head.

"She had the original and gave me this copy. It looks legit to me."

Frank picked up his phone and called the Chief of Police.

"We have a problem."

When Frank and the police chief entered the President's office, he was on the phone. He waved them to chairs.

"I hear you. It's just for today. Close up shop if you have to. Take a holiday. Whatever you need to do."

He slammed down the phone.

"You'd better have some good news. That was the head of the largest union in the country. Businesses can't open, factories have shut down, banks have closed, schools are closed, mail isn't being delivered …all because those stupid women didn't show up for work."

He glared at the two men.

"One day, right? Just today and then we get back to normal."

He jabbed his finger at the police chief.

"You said they couldn't gather without your authorization. So, what the hell is going on out there?"

The police chief winced.

"They have a letter. With my signature."

The President frowned.

"Did you give it to them?"

"No, sir. I have no idea how they got it. One of my officers brought it to me. It is my signature and my letterhead. Beats me."

"They forged it. That's against the law."

"Actually, it's not a forgery, sir. It is my signature. And it was signed with my personal pen. I know that because I use a fountain pen. With a peacock blue ink cartridge."

The President stood up and paced, deep in thought.

"Okay, forget the letter. What about the other rule, no more than two women together at a time?"

"Our officers have done a rough headcount," Frank said. "There are enough men in the crowd to balance out the numbers."

"There are men there? Find out who they are. Traitors. Every one of them. Take photos. Get names."

Frank raised both hands in the air.

"We can't do that, sir. No one has done anything illegal yet. They're in a public space. They have the right to peaceful protest. They've chosen not to go to work, and they'll have to deal with their employers about that. If we start arresting people, someone will take us to court. You can count on it. And it won't look good on you, sir."

The President stopped pacing and faced Frank.

"So, there's nothing we can do?"

"Like you said on the phone, it's just for today. If we're patient, it'll soon be over. Let them have their day in the sun and then everything will return to normal."

Jack watched the scene in the park from the camera Joanna had installed at the back of the stage. He wondered what the President would think of the authorization letter.

Only one way to find out, he thought, picking up his phone. He called the President's office and was told he was in a meeting.

"Set up a time for an interview, Ryan. I need to get his perspective on the Women's Choice Day event. Before 3 p.m. so I can include it in the front-page article. Otherwise, I'll just have to say that he had no comment or refused to respond. And you know how that looks to readers."

Ryan said he would do his best and hung up.

Jack smiled. Either way, he would have a good story.

Joanna returned to the stage.

"Hello again. Take a look around you. There's a sea of white t-shirts that say, '*The Future Is Ours*'."

The crowd clapped and cheered.

"And we have sold out! Across the country!"

Whistling and applause.

"Thank you for your inspired support. We will have more soon. I will let you know when they arrive."

Daniel slammed his phone on the bedside table.

"Bloody hell!"

He had called his mistress to invite her over for a morning quickie. He was describing what he wanted her to do when suddenly she burst into laughter.

"Oh, honey, haven't you heard? There's a sex strike on."

The President opened Ryan's office door with such force, the hinges rattled.

"Ryan! Get in here."

Ryan reached for his pad and paper and ran into the room.

"Take a look out that window and tell me what you see."

On sidewalks near the White House, there were small groups of men and women, some pushing strollers, others walking arm in arm, talking. Groups of two or three, wearing white t-shirts, all heading in the same direction but not noticeably together. Secret Service officers were stationed inside the wrought iron fence surrounding the White House, watching closely. The crowd seemed oblivious.

"And what do you hear?" the President demanded.

Ryan opened a door facing the Rose Garden. At first, all he could hear was distant traffic. As the branches swayed, the wind carried another sound. A song. He could barely make out the tune, but it sounded like hundreds, no, thousands of voices singing together. The words became clear with repetition – "We…shall…overcome…"

He turned to face the President.

"I see a lot of people out for a walk on a sunny day, sir. It is a bit odd that they are all wearing white t-shirts and walking around the White House. And they probably could have chosen a better song."

He braced himself.

The President burst out laughing and clapped Ryan on the back.

"I didn't think you had it in you, boy. Well done! I think you just made my day. 'They could have chosen a better song'. That's a good one."

He grew serious.

"Damn right, they could have. The press will be all over this. How do we turn this in our favor?"

Chapter Thirty-Eight

Jack read the media release from the Office of the President. He scrambled to make room on the front page beside the photos Joanna had sent of the crowds in the park.

He chuckled as he typed the headline - *President Applauds Women's Choice*. That should get a reaction, he thought. He rearranged the photos to highlight a group of men and women wearing the t-shirts. The group included the local mayor and her husband, several female lawyers, and a judge. Joanna said they had insisted on including their names with the photo.

"It's time we made a statement," one of the lawyers said when Jack called her. "And if the President tries to get us fired, there'll be hell to pay."

The media release had a few quotes from the President praising the women and the organization for holding a peaceful event.

"It was good to see families out, enjoying the day. I spoke to business leaders and corporations, all of whom respect their employees taking one day to express their views. We live in a democracy, after all."

The release went on to suggest that he looked forward to everyone getting back to normal routines and reiterated that government and business had gone out of their way to be supportive and understanding.

"Change is not easy. People need to voice their concerns. We are happy to have provided the opportunity. Now it's time to move forward, working together to create a country we can all be proud of, strong in family values and our collective vision."

Early the next morning, Maggie sat in her rattan chair on the front veranda reading the paper. It was already too hot to sit in the sun. The cicadas began to hum as she turned the page. It was clear the President expected to move forward with his plans despite the widespread turnout across the country for Women's Choice Day.

"This is so not over," she muttered, tossing the paper onto the coffee table. She drummed her fingers on the arm of her chair. Her mind flashed back decades as her gut roiled. She didn't hear the footsteps on the stairs. A voice split her reverie.

"Mornin'."

"Whoa, you startled me! Where did you come from?"

Alicia laughed and gestured to her car parked in the driveway.

"Where were you?" she asked. "Another world?"

She glanced at the table.

"Oh."

Maggie pushed back her chair and stood.

"Have a seat. I'll make us some coffee."

Alicia studied Maggie over the rim of her cup.

"I know that look, girl," Alicia said.

Maggie grinned. "Do you now?"

"I'd say you're plotting our next move," Alicia said.

"You'd be right."

Alicia waited, but Maggie was silent.

"Do I have to tease it out of you?" Alicia asked.

"I'm still mulling. There's something I haven't quite worked out."

"I only have half an hour but maybe I can help," Alicia said.

"Okay, so here's what I've got."

Maggie leaned forward and dropped her voice.

"I've been thinking back to the tactics we used in the 70's and 80's. What worked and what didn't. I figure we need to catch them off-guard. They control the power, the money, the courts, and the police. What do we have that they don't have? And how are they expecting us to act? If we can answer those two questions, we'll know our next move."

Alicia sat back, a smile slowly stretching across her face.

"You look mighty pleased with yourself," Maggie said.

"I just thought of something," Alicia said, "although I don't know what to do with it. Last night, we watched one of Jerry's favorite movies, R.E.D. You know the one about the spies who are retired and come back for another kick at the can?"

Maggie shrugged. "And?"

"Do you remember what R.E.D. means?"

"The color?" Maggie asked.

"No, silly. The initials. Retired, Extremely Dangerous. That's you! The government has no clue who they're dealing with. I think it's hilarious."

"Hmmm," Maggie said, tapping her fingers on the table. "You might be onto something there. Leave it with me."

Chapter Thirty-Nine

Joanna organized her papers and started the weekly video call with the chapter leads for the World Organization for Women. She knew them all on a first-name basis.

"The numbers are in from across the country, and I'm delighted to announce we had over two million people turn out for Women's Choice Day. The t-shirts were a huge success, so please extend our thanks to your staff and volunteers."

She sipped water and asked the question on everyone's mind.

"Where do we go from here?"

Over the next hour, each chapter provided thoughts generated from staff meetings and event surveys.

"I'm hearing there's a strong desire to keep the pressure on, is that correct?"

Joanna suggested that each chapter proceed in the direction they felt best.

"We don't all need to be doing the same thing. Unpredictability can be an asset. Although I would recommend that we do a few things in common: t-shirt sales, an email and phone campaign, and a rotating walk-out approach. Organized chaos. You decide when it's happening for your region. Spread it out over the next month. If people get fired or reprimanded, keep track. We have a plan for that nationally. Share ideas and results through the network. Organize through the OMG app. And add to that social media page – The Magdalen Club."

Jack knocked on her office door as the meeting ended.

"Come in," Joanna said, closing her laptop.

Jack sat down in an armchair near the desk.

"What can I do for you?" she asked.

"Curious to get your take on the big event," he said, pulling a pen out of his pocket and holding it over his notepad.

"I'll be sending out a media release shortly."

He tapped the pen on the pad.

"Okay then, what did you think of the President's comments?"

"I think the media release will cover that as well."

Jack stared at her.

"So, we're back to a cat-and-mouse game?"

Joanna smiled.

"When I have something for you, Jack, I'll let you know."

"Fair enough."

He headed back upstairs to his office.

Madeline was setting up for the book club meeting as Brian carried a whiteboard and easel into her kitchen.

"I hope you don't mind, Max," he said to Madeline. "I stopped by the college and picked this up. I used it a lot in my seminars for discussing ground rules, so I thought it might help us out tonight."

"Sounds good." Madeline nodded, turned back to the cupboard, and pulled out a few more coffee mugs. "By the way, I'm sorry to hear your class was cancelled."

"To be expected, I guess," Brian said.

"What will you do now?" Madeline asked.

Brian shrugged. "Wait and see, I suppose. The college has told all of us we will be reassigned, but I'm not holding my breath. I have a few feelers out in the private sector. I don't expect anything in the near future though. Everyone seems to be keeping a low profile. Guess they're all afraid of being the next target."

He headed into the living room to set up the easel. He came back into the kitchen just as Shelley came through the door, carrying a plate of cookies.

"Max? There's something I'd like to discuss with you before the others arrive."

Madeline turned and leaned back against the counter; her arms crossed, watching Brian closely.

"I think it would be best if you and Lena moved in with us for a while. We have lots of space, and you'll be safer. I don't like all these guys snooping around your place. I worry about you two."

Madeline grabbed a tray and set the mugs on it. With her back to Brian, she tried to relax her jaw. She forced a friendly smile and turned to face him.

"Brian, we have been good friends for years and I have always appreciated your willingness to help out when needed."

"My pleasure," Brian said.

Madeline's smile faded. "But neither Lena nor I need a man to protect us from things that go bump in the night."

"I didn't…"

She raised her right hand, index finger high.

"It would be best for you to listen, Brian."

Her icy tone drove Lena and Shelley out of the kitchen. Brian stepped back.

"I don't expect you to understand where I am coming from on this. You're a man and I'm a woman. There's a world of difference and has been for centuries. And it's not just a matter of genitals."

Brian raised his hand.

"I know, I know, you call yourself a feminist, whatever that means to you. I acknowledge that you mean well, Brian, and I don't want to lose sight of that. But…"

She took a breath.

"…to come into *my* house and tell me what *I* should do so that *you* can feel more comfortable…"

Her voice cracked with rage. She closed her eyes and waited for her body to stop shaking.

When she looked at Brian again, he was pale.

"No one, and I mean *no one*, especially a man, has the right to tell me what's best for me. Do…you…understand?"

They stared at each other, unblinking.

Brian dropped his eyes and shifted his feet.

"I hear you, loud and clear. I just want you and Lena to be safe."

"And you figure we aren't capable of taking care of ourselves."

He flung his arms in the air. "When you put it that way, it doesn't sound so good. Look, I was just trying to help."

Madeline shook her head.

"You're missing the point, Brian. No matter how 'feminist' you claim to be, you will never be a woman. I'm white and straight, so I will never understand what it's like to be Indigenous, Black, gay or trans. I can ask how to be supportive, I can use my privilege to raise awareness, but I can't fight their battles for them. And you can't fight mine for me."

She watched him for a moment.

"We can, however, be allies. You can start by asking what would be helpful. Don't assume you know what that is."

She stepped forward and tapped his arm.

"Look, we both need to focus on doing what we do best. You, for example, are good at organizing and making sense of ideas. So, can I count on you to lead our discussion tonight?"

Lena was sitting at the breakfast table the next morning when she saw a text from Shelley.

Can I come over?

Sure.

Madeline had joined her for a cup of coffee earlier but disappeared into her room, saying she had work to do.

"If I'm not back out by lunch, go ahead and make yourself something."

Shelley knocked on the door and let herself in.

"Hey," Lena said.

"Wanna see something?" Shelley asked, setting a folder on the table. "Go ahead. Open it."

Lena peeked inside and caught her breath.

"What is this, Shel? Did you draw it?"

She held up an intricate design of a butterfly. The wing on one side of the body was in muted colors; the other was a shimmering mix of hues.

"I've never seen anything so beautiful."

Shelley blushed.

"I did it last night," she said. "After the book club meeting. There's been so much going on with Sam storming off, Marshall's comments, the protest day, and then the argument between Max and my Dad. It's all been spinning around in my head."

She handed a typewritten sheet to Lena.

"I did some research. I remembered Marshall and Max saying how we need to see the differences yet find what we have in common."

Shelley played with the end of her ponytail as she talked.

"Last semester, one of my profs was talking about gynandromorphy."

"Gyna-what?" Lena asked.

"Gynandromorphy. It's rare but it happens in butterflies and some other species. Once in a while, a butterfly emerges that is half male and half female; split down the middle as if two butterflies were fused together. Just like the one in my design. It's one butterfly with the colors, shapes, and qualities of two genders. I got to thinking that maybe this is what we need – a symbol that represents gender unity and diversity."

Lena glanced up. "Go on."

"Well, here's the thing," Shelley said. "There's nothing threatening about a butterfly. But, factoid drop, scientists say that even the tiny flutter of a butterfly's wings in one part of the world can affect the weather somewhere else. For such a fragile creature, they're pretty powerful. Anyway, I figure it could be used as a logo. And we could make stickers, and posters, and signs and…"

She stopped. Lena was grinning.

"I think it's brilliant. I mean, who would suspect a butterfly of leading a protest movement?" Lena said.

They burst into laughter.

Lena opened her laptop and clicked on The Magdalen Club page and gestured to Shelley.

"I've got something for you too. Have you seen this?"

Chapter Forty

Jack was itching to get back out on the street. He felt like an eagle chained to the ground.

"Sorry bud," his editor said over the phone. "We've checked, and there's somebody watching your building. They might be doing surveillance for a different reason, but we have to assume they're waiting for you to resurface. And we can't take that chance."

Jack grumbled. At least Ed had offered to send a photographer wherever he wanted. And he was able to do interviews by phone. But it wasn't the same as tracking down the story himself. Plus, he missed Hannah and Evelyn.

He checked his email. Joanna had sent out a media release as promised. As he read it, he rubbed his hands together.

"Here we go," he whispered to himself.

The President's phone buzzed as he arrived at his golf club.

"Just a sec, guys, gotta take this."

Daniel, and two security officers nodded and got out of the limousine.

"This had better be good, Ryan. I'm about to shut off my phone."

Ryan read him the press release from the World Organization for Women.

"For shit's sake! Don't those bitches know when to shut up? We gave them their day and I was even nice about it. If they think their little protest is going to carry on, they can forget it. Send me a copy. I'll talk to the guys about it and I'll meet with you when I get back. Get Frank there as well."

He stormed out of the car and glared at Daniel.

"We need to talk."

The President was in a foul mood when he returned to the White House. The golf game had been disastrous from his first swing. His mind kept swirling with images of angry CEOs once they found out the women planned rotating strikes and walkouts over the next month. The very men who had supported his last campaign in exchange for a promise of lower taxes, and higher profits.

Each time he tried to focus on the ball, all he could see was that black bitch from the women's organization grinning triumphantly from the front page of the newspaper. What was her name? Joan? Jean? Janet?

I'll get Frank to dig into her background, he decided. I'm sure he can find some dirt on her.

Lena set her phone down and grinned at Shelley.

"Green light!" she announced. "The director of the World Organization for Women says if we send her the original butterfly design in print-ready format, she'll get t-shirts and stuff printed. I offered to set up a website for sales and all proceeds will go to their organization. She'll link it to their website and promote it globally. Ready to roll?"

"You bet!"

Within two days of launching, the "Rebel Butterflies" website imploded under an avalanche of sales. Lena and Shelley posted a brief "under construction" message thanking people for their orders and their patience and stayed up all night upgrading the site. Madeline and Brian kept them stocked with food and drinks.

"C'mon, you two," Madeline said at 2 a.m. "You need a break. Get up, walk around."

'Just five minutes more," Lena said.

Madeline rolled her to the edge of the bed.

"You've been saying that for an hour. Up you get!"

Lena groaned, sat up and stretched.

"Hey, Shelley," she whispered, "how about a quick swim?"

Shelley ripped off her t-shirt and shorts and raced to the back door.

"First one in gets the next bag of chips," Shelley called.

"That's cheating! You had your bikini on under your clothes."

By 6 a.m., they relaunched the site with a brief message on The Magdalen Club page: *Butterflies soar once more*.

Orders flooded in from around the world. Book club members ordered t-shirts. Over the next few weeks, butterfly stickers appeared in windows of supportive shops and restaurants. People hoisted butterfly flags on poles in front of their houses. In Lafayette Square, children and parents flew large butterfly kites. Hannah told Jack that Maggie had a ceramic butterfly hanging from a hook in her front garden.

"I saw her putting it up yesterday morning. She was humming. When I asked her where she got it, she just smiled."

At daycares and summer camps, children painted butterflies or made origami chains to decorate walls, light posts, and benches in front of shops.

"What's with all the butterflies?" the President demanded.

Ryan shook his head. "No idea."

"I've got a bad feeling about this. Find out what's going on."

Madeline continued to research and draft background documents. She sent everything to Joanna. The World Organization for Women used the materials as the foundation for a court challenge to the abortion legislation. It was rejected by the lower courts. The appeal was to be heard by the Supreme Court, presided by Chief Justice Power.

"You will find grounds to dismiss it, Danny boy," the President said.

"Of course."

Women began to gather daily along the side streets and in the parks around the White House. Wearing white t-shirts with one of the Magdalen slogans, they walked slowly in pairs from Lafayette Square and stood in silence facing the White House. After about fifteen minutes, each pair turned in unison and continued along the sidewalk, encircling the President's residence in a somber funeral march. They were there by sunrise each day; by sundown, the streets were empty.

For the first few days, the President turned his back to the windows and focused on paperwork. On the third day, he switched offices with Ryan. He still felt the pressure of hundreds of eyes. He moved his files upstairs into his private sitting room, closed the heavy satin curtains and worked with all the lights blazing. When he went to sleep at night, silent shapes marched through his dreams; their muffled shuffle echoing in his head.

A month into the protest, he met with his four aides, Frank and Daniel.

"What are all those women doing?" he asked Frank. "What do they want?"

"I don't know," Frank said. "They don't have any signs. They don't even talk. They are completely silent."

"But, they're women," the President said. "Talking is what they do. They get together with their chick friends and they talk. About us."

He glanced at the men in the room.

"Am I right?"

The men nodded in unison.

"So why aren't they talking? Can we arrest them?"

"For not talking?"

"For anything! Make them stop staring at my home. Make them go away."

"They haven't broken any laws, sir. It's not a protest; it's just a bunch of women getting together. They aren't blocking traffic, and they're always in groups of two which is what we legislated. There's nothing we can do at this point."

As the crowds increased in streets near the White House and capitol buildings across the country, the President ordered Frank to solve the problem.

"Whatever you need to do. Break it up."

Over the next few days, government supporters appeared among the protestors on Pennsylvania Avenue, chanting slogans, carrying placards. The President watched the live stream on his laptop as Frank flew a drone above the crowd, zooming in on the signs.

Family First!

Men and Children Matter Too!

The Future Belongs To Our Children!

Frank raised the drone back up so they could see movement of the whole crowd. The President grinned as his supporters began to infiltrate the silent protestors.

"You see, sir," Frank said, "our people are like mosquitoes – irritating and annoying, buzzing around the protestors' heads until they have to react. And when they do, we can arrest them for breaking the peace."

As the two men watched, the government supporters began to shake their signs and bump into people. Suddenly, everything changed. It was like watching the tide go out. The silent groups moved outward, leaving government agitators stranded in the middle of large circles like grounded fishing boats.

Outside the circles, people were calm and silent. The louder the agitators became, the wider the circles grew. A couple of men and women walked through the crowd and into each circle.

"What's going on, Frank?" asked the President.

"I don't know. This wasn't part of the plan."

Brian approached two men with placards inside one circle.

"Hey guys, how's it going?"

"Hey yourself."

The men waved their signs, and shuffled back and forth, glancing at each other. He read one of the slogans out loud.

"Life is Life. What does it mean?"

"Is this part of the deal? Or are you with them?"

The man in the denim jacket pointed at the protestors outside the circle.

Brian shook his head.

"Nah, just curious."

The tall, bearded man stared at him.

"So, this is part of the scene?"

Brian laughed.

"Whatever works."

The men smiled.

"Okay then. But they didn't tell us about this on the bus."

Beard Guy shook his sign at Brian and pumped his fist in the air.

"Life is Life!" Denim Guy shouted.

Brian took a step back and raised his hands in mock protest.

"Very impressive," Brian said. "I was just on my way for a coffee. Can I buy you one?"

"Coffee would be great," Beard Guy added. "Especially if you're buying."

Brian led them to a coffee shop down the street, away from the crowds.

They placed their order and sat down at a table on the patio, setting their signs on an empty chair.

"So where are you two from?" he asked.

"Small town. Next state over. You?"

"I live here. Off work for a few months," Brian said. He paused and sipped his coffee. "It's Thursday. How come you're not at work?"

"Factory shut down. Owners couldn't keep it going with women not showing up for work. Got a chance to make a bit of cash here so we jumped on it," Denim Guy said.

"How so?"

"Ad in the local paper. They said it was for a movie shoot. Needed people to be part of the crowd. All we had to do is show up for the bus this morning."

"A movie? Any big names?" Brian asked.

"They didn't say. Just gave us all these signs and told us to get into the middle of the crowd, shout a little, maybe push people around. There's a bonus if we can stir up some trouble."

"You get paid for this? Where do I sign up?"

Denim Guy pulled a crumpled piece of paper out of his pocket.

"Here's the number if you want to call. It sounds like they'll be doing this for a while. When the bus leaves here at 11, we're heading to another location."

"How much do you get?" Brian said, leaning forward.

"$500 per day. We got $150 upfront when we got on the bus. We get another $150 when we get back to the bus if we still have our signs. And the balance at the end of the day. Easy money."

Brian whistled and took a photo of the ad with his phone.

"Really glad I bumped into you guys. Maybe I'll see you on the bus tomorrow," he said. He stood up and held out his hand.

"No problem, man," Denim Guy said, shaking his hand. "Thanks for the coffee," Beard Guy added.

Brian shared the number with Madeline who passed it along to Maggie. The next day, GNN featured an article entitled *Government Caught Buying Support*.

The President issued a furious rebuttal on social media, accusing protestors of deliberately trying to damage the government's solid reputation.

@officeofthepresident We don't need to buy support. We already have the support of the people.

The response was swift.

@Magdalenknows Which people?

Chapter Forty-One

Jack focused on tracking the progress of the women's protest and the government's reaction. In press releases, letters to the editor, and media interviews, Joanna referred to participants as champions of equality and freedom of choice. The President called them rabble rousers and terrorists, seeking to undermine civil liberties and overthrow the government.

"You elected your government to protect you and preserve your way of life. We stand strong for your rights as citizens of our great country. We will not be intimidated by a bunch of whining women led by a Black lesbian anarchist."

Jack began to feature profiles of women's organizations every day. One weekend, he ran a feature article on the Women's Coalition for Humanity. It was an organization that had been around for ten years and focused on gender awareness training in workplaces, schools, and organizations.

As he clicked the button to send the article to press, Jack checked his watch.

Give it 24 hours, he thought.

Less than an hour after the paper hit the streets the next morning, Jack's phone rang. He looked to see who was calling and smiled.

"What's up, Ed?"

"Look, Jack, you know I'm as supportive as the next guy of all this women's rights stuff. And I can't ignore the fact that our circulation numbers have skyrocketed since you started writing these feature articles."

Jack heard him tapping his pen on his desk, searching for the next words.

"But we can't just focus on women here. We need to be balanced in our reporting."

"Who got to you, Ed?"

Silence.

"Ed?"

He waited. Finally, he heard a deep sigh through the phone.

"You know I can't tell you that, Jack. Let's just say that it has been suggested that we hear from some men's groups. Check your email. I'll send you a list shortly. And Jack? Don't shoot the messenger, okay? I'm just following orders."

Jack clicked open his email and found a list of four organizations. He recognized two as white supremacy groups. One was a Christian fundamentalist organization known for violent protests outside abortion clinics. He choked back a laugh when he saw the name of the fourth one: Men's Coalition for Humanity.

"I'm definitely starting with that one," he said as he typed the name into his search engine. He found few background details. The website was under construction; there was a social media page, but it had only been live for about 48 hours. There were just two posts: a photo of five men sitting around a table; and a short mission statement. Jack set up an interview with Matt Kowalsky, the spokesperson for the Men's Coalition.

"Tell me about this organization, Matt. How long has it been around and why was it formed?"

Matt explained that he and a group of friends from work were frustrated by all the focus on women and thought it was time their voices were included.

"For us, it's not men versus women," he said. "Believe it or not, there are men out there who support women's rights. We see what a tough ride it is for women, and we want to do something about it. But all the focus is on women's organizations and women's voices as if only women have the right to say anything about these issues."

Jack suppressed a groan. "So, help me understand, Matt, the goal of your organization is to promote *women's* rights. Even though you are all men?"

"Not exactly, Jack. We believe in human rights. Humans include all genders, not just men and women. The direction the government is going threatens everyone."

"Have you taken a look at the mission statement for the Women's Coalition for Humanity?" Jack asked. "Seems to me you might have a lot in common."

"Actually, that's why we chose the name for our organization. We want to get a discussion going with them; figure out how we can work together."

Lena and Shelley sat in Brian's kitchen, uploading posts to The Magdalen Club.

"Here's a good one," Lena said, turning her laptop toward Shelley.

I will not have my life narrowed down. ~ bell hooks

"I can do you one better," Shelley said, typing quickly.

They thought they could bury us; they did not know we were seeds. ~ Dinos Christianopolous

"Hang on, just one more," Lena said.

Revolutions, like trees, grow from the bottom up. ~ Gloria Steinem

They grinned and gave each other a high-five.

"Have you seen what's happening with the butterflies?" Shelley asked. "We've raised $1 million for the World Organization for Women in just two weeks."

"Go team!" Lena said, raising a fist in the air.

"So, what's next?" Shelley asked.

"Well, I haven't seen a lot of people our age involved in this. And we're the ones who will be most affected. Maybe we should start a youth movement."

With Brian's help, they spread word quietly through college student unions. Since students were already up in arms because their programs had been gutted, they were quick to join the broader protests by the thousands. Butterfly t-shirts with Magdalen slogans sold out in 24 hours.

Lena and Shelley shared their idea at the next meeting of the Cottage Lane Bookies. Audrey and Sam's granddaughter was the head of the student council at her high school. Her council shared the message with the national federation of student councils and the response was electrifying.

School councils brought in speakers on human rights, held workshops and seminars on racism, gender bias and oppression. When some school boards banned such activities from school property, students reconvened in public parks. On strike days and weekends, youth joined silent protests in the streets, wrote letters to politicians, and posted on The Magdalen Club.

Momentum continued to build around the country. *Walk and Talk*, a new meet-up group, spread through small towns and large cities like dandelion seeds in the summer breeze. Participants signed up and organizers matched them with someone from another cultural background. They shared their life stories as they explored different neighborhoods by foot.

The World Organization for Women set up a new website page, *"WOW ME"*, where people could inspire others by posting acts of kindness.

Count Me In! was the idea of a 15-year girl. One day, walking home from school, she saw a group of boys beating up a classmate.

"Normally, I would've just walked on by," she told Jack in an interview. "I mean, he's white, I'm Black. Different circles, right? But I knew that kid. I met him at the library when we did that *'What's Your Story?'* thing for school. He told me his story. I told him mine. And that changed everything. It was personal, see? So, when I saw those guys messing with him, I couldn't turn away. It's like they were hurting me."

She stood behind a building and videotaped the fight on her phone. When she yelled to a nearby adult to call the cops, the gang fled. The girl made sure the boy was okay before she left.

"I wanted to walk him home, but he said no. I kept thinking, 'What would have happened if I hadn't stepped in?' I guess I always thought that someone else would take care of things."

She started *Count Me In!* at her school and the idea quickly spread to other regions and states.

"That kid could've been killed if I'd walked away. That's when I realized we have to look after each other. We're one big family. The human family. I know it sounds lame. But really, we're all in this together, no matter where we come from. You grownups keep saying we're the future? Well, it's time to count us in."

A few weeks later, Lena and Shelley sat down with Madeline and Brian and gave them an update.

"Can you believe it?" Lena said. "Some students are producing a film about the movement and youth involvement."

"And the drama department at one school has found funding to stage a play," Shelley added.

"I think we have a pair of activists on our hands, Max. Whatever shall we do?" Brian said.

Madeline smiled.

"It was only a matter of time."

One-day work stoppages kept popping up across the country. The timing and location of walkouts seemed random, preventing employers from bringing in additional workers to fill the gaps. Large corporations began to lay off employees who went out on strike. The World Organization for Women responded with class action lawsuits against the corporations, and a financial support fund for those in need. Emails and phone calls inundated the offices of Congress members. Ryan was so busy screening the President's calls that he had to hire an assistant.

Business owners and union leaders demanded personal meetings with the President.

"You have to do something," the head of the national union of public employees shouted over the phone. "It's chaos out here."

"You're the head of the union. Do something yourself," the President said.

"It's out of our hands. You have to find out who's behind it."

Hospital CEOs clamored for back-to-work legislation. Nursing homes echoed the call. Factory owners threatened to shut down. At first, school boards brought in supply teachers to cover the gap on strike days. When most supply teachers walked out, school boards tried to combine classes under the supervision of guidance counsellors, principals, and superintendents. Teachers in one state returned for a week, only to have their colleagues refuse to show up for work in other states. School boards responded with lockouts.

Parents, faced with full-time childcare needs and reduced daycare spaces due to government cutbacks, turned to family and neighbors for support. Public transportation slowed; schedules became unpredictable. Restaurants and grocery stores opened and closed sporadically. Financial analysts predicted an economic depression worse than the 1930's if the government didn't take action soon.

The President sat behind his desk, facing a handful of business leaders.

"Something has to be done," one man said. The others nodded.

"They're trying to bully us," the President said. "They can't keep this up. We need to call their bluff."

"What do you propose?"

"Fire them all."

The group was silent.

"We can't do that," a corporate CEO said.

"Why the hell not? They're just a bunch of women. And if they're not working, they can stay home and make babies. Win-win for all of us."

"It's not just women. It's men too. They're cutting us off at the knees."

The President's Office issued warnings via social media.

@officeofthepresident We are not backing down

There was an immediate response.

@Magdalenknows Neither are we

@officeofthepresident We know who you are. We will take action

@Magdalenknows Make our day

Signs featuring *"United We Stand"* and *"Magdalen Is Watching"* sprang up around the country. Jack wrote a feature article with photos from some of the more spectacular locations: banners flying high above the Hollywood sign in Los Angeles, the Statue of Liberty in New York, spray-painted on the brick of the Freedom Trail in Boston, and along Pennsylvania Avenue in front of the White House.

The government didn't hesitate.

@theofficeofthepresident This is vandalism. Perpetrators will be arrested.

Chapter Forty-Two

In their weekly call, Joanna and her chapter leads decided it was time to pick up the pace.

"Keep in mind that there will be repercussions," she cautioned. "Please remind your staff and volunteers to keep all actions peaceful and positive. No matter what tactics the government and its supporters use, we will stick to our plan."

They expanded their phone and letter-writing campaign. State governors' offices stopped answering the phone. Letters to the editor in national newspapers spread across multiple pages. Radio and television call-in shows hit participation records.

In response, major corporations paid for full-page pro-government ads on billboards and in media. State governors appeared with their families at rallies, encouraging government supporters to take to the streets. Small groups gathered, huddling together, shouting slogans against abortion, immigration, and feminism.

The popularity of The Magdalen Club site skyrocketed. Articles like *"Five tips for activists"* and *"Trending Websites for Feminists"* went viral. The most popular hashtag on social media was #Magdalenknows.

Jack could barely keep up with the developments. He laughed out loud when he received a media release jointly issued by the Women's Coalition for Humanity and the Men's Coalition for Humanity.

"After several joint meetings and lengthy discussions, our two coalitions have decided to merge. We recognize that our basic goal is the same: raising gender awareness and promoting gender equality across all sectors.

Therefore, we are announcing that our two organizations will work together under the name 'People's Coalition for Humanity'. The directors of our existing coalitions will become co-directors of the new coalition.

We believe that the future lies in the ability of people of all genders to work together for the common cause of equality and freedom for humanity."

"Yes," Maggie exclaimed, pumping her fist in the air, when she read the news of the merger. "Finally, people are getting it. We can't keep acting in isolation. We have to work together."

Weeks turned to months. People filled the streets twenty-four hours a day. They surrounded the White House as well as every government building across the country.

Silent.

Staring.

Drones captured compelling video footage; posts went viral.

The President waved off suggestions from Senators.

"I know exactly what to do."

The President escalated his attacks on the World Organization for Women. He suggested that Black people like Jack Winthrup and Joanna Price were in secret meetings with Magdalen, plotting to take down the government.

Calling @allthepresidentsmen You know what to do

Full page ads appeared in newspapers across the country, offering rewards to anyone who could take out Jack and Joanna. An explosive device detonated in the parking garage of *The Nation Today*. A grenade was dropped into the main square of the World Organization for Women injuring several women and children.

@allthepresidentsmen Don't mess with us

The next morning, Maggie squealed when she saw the front page of the paper. She raced inside.

"Get down here, girl. You've gotta see this!"

Hannah came down the stairs, Evelyn in her arms, her blue robe flapping.

"What's up?" she asked, stifling a yawn.

Maggie danced an impromptu jig and handed her the paper.

Open Letter to The People
Momentum is building.
A new day is coming.
United, we stand.
Together, we are invincible.
Magdalen

Feet up on the desk, Jack shook his head. His well-researched article outlining the root causes of social inequality had been erased by Magdalen's latest front-page statement.

Meanwhile, in the Oval Office, the President pounded his desk.

"Ryan!" he yelled, "get in here."

Ryan poked his head inside the door.

"Have you seen the paper? There's another friggin' letter from that Magdalen. How dare she?"

The President stomped around the room, kicking everything in his way.

"Get Frank here," he shouted. "I want to know how I can reach all the people at the same time like she does."

After a brief discussion with Frank, the President made a surprise appearance on a national breakfast television show. He thanked the co-hosts for giving him airtime and turned to face the camera.

"I'm here today to speak to you, the citizens of our great country. I come on behalf of Congress and business leaders. We want to reassure all of you that we are working hard to ensure your safety and wellbeing during the current disruption. We recognize that it is in everyone's best interest to stabilize the situation and support citizens in returning to regular routines. Therefore, we are taking the initiative and inviting Magdalen to meet with us. We assure Magdalen in advance that, if she comes forward on her own, we will arrange for a safe, confidential meeting place."

The President narrowed his eyes as if focusing on one individual.

"Magdalen, I know you can hear me. I urge you to act in the best interest of the country and contact the Office of the President immediately."

The announcement caused confusion and chaos, as the President had intended. Messages on social media asked the same question as families around dinner tables, in pubs and grocery stores: will Magdalen meet with the President?

After a week of silence, a one-line post appeared on social media.

@therealMagdalen Come and get me, Mr. President

The country held its breath.

Chapter Forty-Three

The President shoved Ryan against the desk when he showed him the newest Magdalen message on social media.

"That goddamn bitch! Who does she think she's dealing with? I'll show her."

He scribbled notes on a pad of paper and threw the page at Ryan.

"Press release. Now."

Ryan hesitated.

"No, I do not need anyone's approval!"

Jack shook his head as he read the media release.

"Magdalen seems to think it's more important to play games than to resolve this situation. As you all know, the government wants what is best for you. We know we can count on your support to bring this situation to a close. Therefore, we have set up a confidential hotline where you can leave anonymous tips regarding the whereabouts of Magdalen.

"A reward of $10,000 is offered for information that leads us to her. If you have noticed any suspicious activity among your neighbors, your work colleagues or someone you know through social circles, call the hotline. The police will follow up on all tips and you will not be identified."

The hotline received hundreds of calls a day from people keen on claiming the reward. The police kept busy following up on tips. Jack's contacts inside the police force sent him data trends. Most callers pointed fingers at Black and Indigenous women, immigrants and undocumented workers. He ran an article on the "snitch line" as social media labelled it, showing a bar graph that highlighted the racist focus of the tips.

An Executive Order closed the door to immigration. The President claimed this would free up employment opportunities for American citizens and protect families from "the dangerous terrorist element".

He declared a State of Emergency and authorized a special police task force to round up undocumented men, women and children and hold them in protective custody until they could be deported.

Alicia was eating breakfast with the twins when a text message arrived.

Hello Magdalen. This is your President. I know who you are, and I know where you live. Turn yourself in to the police today, or I will call in the army and destroy your home.

She called Maggie in a panic.

"Mags, he thinks I'm Magdalen. What am I going to do?"

"Whoa, Ali, slow down. What are you talking about?"

"The President. I just got a text from the President," Alicia said.

Hannah stumbled into the kitchen, holding her phone up, as Maggie's phone pinged.

"Maggie, the President just texted me," Hannah said. "What's going on? I'm not Magdalen."

Maggie checked her messages. She started to laugh.

"Maggie, this isn't a laughing matter," Alicia said through the phone.

"Relax," Maggie said. "I bet he's texted everyone in the country with the same message. I knew he had the technology, but I never thought he'd stoop so low. He's getting desperate."

She put her phone to her ear. "You still there, Ali? Time to wake some sleeping giants. I'll take A to N; you do the rest."

Maggie slipped a disc into her CD player. The velvet tones of Carole King soared through the living room. She set her laptop on the dining room table. This is going to be fun, she thought.

Hannah listened to the music from the bedroom, tapping one foot nervously as Evelyn nursed.

Maggie opened file and highlighted a dozen names. She sent an identical message to each of them.

Hi,

I'm calling in a favor. You know why. I'll be following up the email with a phone call. Please let me know a time today or tomorrow that works for you.

Talk soon.

After putting Evelyn down for a nap, Hannah headed downstairs. Maggie was stretched out on the couch, making some notes.

"Maggie?"

"What's up, Hannah?"

"Do you think it would be okay if I sat out back for a bit this afternoon? I know Jack said I was to stay inside, but it's such a beautiful day and that text this morning really upset me. Being in the garden might help me relax."

Maggie nodded.

"Sure, Hannah. I don't think anyone can see anything in my yard. I might be on the phone a lot this aft, so if you want some peace and quiet, try sitting under the old pear tree in the far corner."

Hannah dozed in the afternoon sun. She was dreaming of her rose garden when a loud buzzing sound woke her. She glanced around and saw a drone hovering over her. She turned away, and covered her face, waiting until the machine flew away. She ran into the house.

"Maggie!"

Maggie jumped up and put her hands on Hannah's shoulders. Hannah was trembling.

"Whoa, child. Look at me. Everything's going to be okay. Do you hear me?"

Hannah nodded, tears streaming down her face.

"It's all my fault. I should have listened to Jack. He told me to stay inside. What if I've screwed everything up?" Hannah said.

"Slow down, and tell me what happened," Maggie said.

"A drone. In your yard. Do you think I've been spotted?" Hannah asked.

Upstairs, Evelyn began to whimper and then launched into a loud wail.

"Go get your daughter. She needs you right now. Bring her here and we'll figure out next steps."

Maggie texted Jack.

Trouble. Call me.

Jack called right away.

"What kind of trouble?" he asked.

"My houseguest may have been spotted by a drone today."

Jack felt his throat tighten. He forced his voice to stay light.

"Not good. But how could it have seen your guest through the windows?"

"That's the thing. Beautiful day, wanted some sun, rested in the shade of the tree…you get the picture."

Jack gritted his teeth, reminding himself that he was asking a lot of Hannah and Maggie.

"I did say they should stay inside for this exact reason."

"Comin' in loud and clear, commander," Maggie said. "but no use whining over spilt milk. It's done. If you need to yell at someone, take it out on me."

She paused and added, "What do we do now?"

Jack sat back in his chair, drumming his fingers on the desk.

"Did you see which way it went?"

"I saw nothing. But my guest said it seemed to head south."

Jack thought for a few moments.

"Okay, here's what we'll do. I'll get one of my contacts to check into it. In the meantime, keep them inside, and lock the doors. I'll double up security until we know more. Do not open the door for anyone you don't know, and if you see anything suspicious, call me, not the police. We don't know who's behind this."

Maggie hung up the phone and turned to Hannah.

"How did he take it?" she asked.

"We're under house arrest," Maggie said with a grin. "At least for now. Luckily, I got some groceries yesterday so we should be good for a while. I'll get some supper going while you feed the baby."

After supper, Hannah gave Evelyn a quick bath while Maggie tidied up the kitchen. When Hannah came back downstairs, Maggie was sitting on the couch, chewing on the end of a pencil, reading her notes.

"Baby sleeping?"

Hannah yawned.

"Yes, finally. She seemed really alert and busy tonight. I do miss having Jack at home. He always seems to know when I need a break. How much longer do you think this is going to go on?"

Maggie turned the notepad over and set it on the coffee table. She tucked the pencil behind her ear.

"Who knows? Listen, I'm making a cup of tea; do you want some?"

She hesitated in the doorway and turned back to Hannah.

"I don't know anything about babies, but is there something I can do to give you a hand with Evelyn?"

"That would be great," Hannah said. "Sometimes it just helps to have someone else hold her for a while, you know? I start to feel like I'm nothing more than a feeding station and an amusement park."

After Hannah went to bed, Maggie decided to sit on the front steps and watch the sun set. She could hear children shouting and laughing in the nearby playground. A neighbor drove by, honked and waved. She raised her hand in response.

Suddenly she heard a loud buzzing. She looked around, expecting to see a swarm of angry hornets. She couldn't see anything, but the sound was growing louder. She looked above her neighbor's roof and saw it – a small drone, hovering. She stood up and watched. The drone zigzagged around the neighbor's yard, following a small dog. Back and forth the dog raced, yipping with excitement.

"Oh, bugger off!" she yelled, waving her arms above her head as if swatting a large mosquito.

The drone changed direction and zipped away, coming down in front of a house four doors down the street. A teenager in low-slung jeans and a baggy t-shirt waved at her. Maggie headed for him.

Ten minutes later, Jack's phone pinged with a text.

Call me.

Jack picked up the phone.

"Maggie? What's up?

"Good news," Maggie said. "I just saw my neighbor's son flying a drone. He said he's had it for about a week. He's been flying it all around the neighborhood just to get the hang of it. Maybe it's the one that came into my backyard."

"Let's hope so."

Chapter Forty-Four

Joanna's phone had been ringing non-stop for two days. She was getting calls and messages from organizations she hadn't worked with actively for several years: The Indigenous Alliance, Immigrant Women's Association, Coalition for Refugees, Latinas for Change, among others.

She kept hearing the same message from all the callers.

"Our two organizations have worked side by side on issues before, Joanna, but this time it's different. We need to be a united front. Otherwise, we'll be easy targets, and those bastards will skewer us like chunks of meat."

She agreed to convene a meeting at her headquarters within the week. At the end of the day, Joanna sat back, wondering at the sudden show of interest in a formal coalition. She smiled and picked up the phone one more time.

"Maggie? Joanna here. Just wanted to say thank you."

A few days later, Joanna closed the door to the meeting room and turned to face the women gathered there. She walked slowly around the group, resting a hand on each woman's shoulder as she passed. She sat down in the empty chair on one side of the circle and nodded to the group.

"Thank you for coming. I think you all know each other, but let's start by going around the room, sharing your name, organization and why you want to form this coalition."

It was a diverse group, representing a range of issues affecting women and children. Regardless of background, their message was clear: we each have our own battles, but we all have the same war.

"It's time to bring down the patriarchy," one woman said. "And we can only do that by uniting our organizations under one umbrella."

"What's that quote by Maya Angelou?" asked another.

"'I come as one, but I stand as ten thousand.'"

"That's it. We need to remember that each one of us represents all the generations of women who came before us, and those who will come after us – our daughters, granddaughters and great-granddaughters."

"And this is not a fight against men," said Nikka from Proud to Be Me. "The government will try to dismiss us as men-haters. We've heard it all before, and we have to be prepared for the worst possible slurs."

Nikka glanced around the table. "One more thing. No offense, but this can't be just another white feminist movement that only wants our numbers. This coalition has to stand for the needs of all our members, no matter our background, identity or race."

"You're right, Nikka," said Joanna. "We need to be clear and inclusive about our purpose and priorities. And that we work as one coalition. Preferably with one spokesperson in terms of the media. We can't give the government any opening to divide us."

"Divided we fall," said Marta, from Pro-Choice.

"But together, we are unstoppable," added the director of Muslim Women for Change.

Over the next two hours, the twenty participants debated the purpose and the name of the new coalition. They agreed unanimously that Joanna would be the spokesperson.

"For any public communications, I will be clear that I am speaking on behalf of the coalition," said Joanna, "not the World Organization for Women. How do we ensure there is no confusion?"

"Maybe we could all be present with you for any televised or public presentation," Maya suggested. "The Organization for Immigrants and Refugees will be proud to stand beside you, showing solidarity."

They agreed that all media releases would be approved by the coalition members prior to publication, as would statements and speeches. Before the meeting ended, they agreed on a name for the new coalition, drafted a press release and decided to hold weekly teleconferences and monthly face-to-face meetings for as long as required.

"It's also important that we share regular updates with members of our own organizations," Nikka added.

"And when there is a call for wide-scale action, we can encourage our members to participate," said Sara, from the Poverty Action Group. "The larger the numbers, the louder our voice, and the more leverage we have."

"Before we wrap up," Joanna said, "there is one more important item to discuss."

She looked at the women around the table.

"I think Nikka said something interesting when she pointed out that this isn't a fight *against* men. It got me wondering: what are we fighting *for*? It seems to me that we are fighting for a society in which we all have equal opportunities and equal respect. The focus is on humanity, not just women. Humanity includes men."

She raised a hand to calm the muttering.

"I can anticipate what you are going to say. Please hear me out first. There have been many movements, organizations and actions over past generations in support of women's rights. And they have all been successful…to a point.

"The government started this war by putting an end to women's reproductive choices, but they haven't stopped there. The reason many of you are here today is that the President has gone further: restrictions against Blacks, immigrants, and refugees. This is on top of existing legislation banning same-sex marriage and parenting. The government is attacking all of us.

"And so, I am suggesting that this has become a fight *for* humanity. And for that reason, I'm wondering if we should be inviting men to join our coalition as allies."

The women sat in silence for a few minutes. Joanna read the struggle on their faces.

Sara spoke first.

"In the Poverty Action Group, we have quite a few men. Poverty affects everyone, regardless of gender, race, or religion. If we are to be part of this new coalition, I would have a hard time excluding some of my membership."

"It's harder for us," Marta said. "But I have to say that we do have a lot of men in the pro-choice movement, just as there are women in the anti-abortion campaign."

"For many women," Susan added, "men are the problem. For generations, men have abused us. They have always held the power. And that's true in many cultures. It will be hard for some women to see men as allies. While I agree with you, Joanna, how can we involve truly supportive men and be sure the women we represent are safe and heard?"

Mariana, who had been quiet for most of the meeting, finally spoke up.

"I'm really glad you raised this, Joanna. I wanted to, but I wasn't sure how to go about it. I think I may have the start of a solution.

"As you may have heard, our organization, the Women's Coalition for Humanity, has recently decided to merge with the Men's Coalition for Humanity. The new organization has two co-directors: me and Matt Kowalsky, the current director of the men's organization. Maybe he could join us here at the table.

"The men in his organization are proving to be solid allies, and since we want to focus on human rights, not just gender- or race-based rights, this could be a good opportunity. What do you think?"

A few women nodded.

"Could you send us a summary of the mission statement and goals for the Coalition for Humanity, Mariana?" Joanna asked. "That might help us feel more comfortable. Safety for the women we represent is key for all of us."

"Sir?" Ryan's voice trembled.

"What now?"

"This media release just came through. I printed off a copy for you. I, uh, think it might be important?"

He handed a sheet of paper to the President and stepped out of arm's reach. The President took a quick look, crumpled the page, and tossed it in the waste bin.

"God damn them! They think they can pressure us into backing down by ganging up in a stupid coalition?"

He flung a pen across the room. Ryan ducked.

"Voice of The People? What kind of a name is that? The government is the voice of the people."

Frank tapped on the door frame to the President's office. The President beckoned him in.

"Figure out what to do about that press release," he ordered Ryan, running his fingers across his bald spot. He turned to Frank.

"Give me some good news."

Frank handed him a thick binder.

"This is a list of all the women named Magdalen across the country. We also included variations on the name. I should point out that one of them is your wife, sir. Her full name is Magdalena Irina, although she goes by Magda."

The President snorted.

"We did narrow it down to about fifty women, based on full name, educational background, and life history. According to the psychological assessment, it has to be a woman who hates men, so we checked their personal history for things like rape, abuse, alcoholic parents, incest."

The President ran his finger down the list.

"Good work. Arrest them."

"All of them? On what grounds, sir?"

"We don't need grounds. Can't you bring them in on suspicion of treason or something?"

"I'll figure something out."

He didn't move. The President rolled his eyes.

"Is there something else?"

Frank nodded.

"I think we have located the journalist's wife."

The President clapped his hands together.

"Finally, something's going our way. So? Where is she, and what are you going to do about it?"

"She's staying at a house on the outskirts of the city, sir. With an old lady. No sign of the baby though. We're going to try and draw them out of the house."

"Well done, Frank. Once that reporter knows I have his wife and child, he'll dance to whatever tune I want to play. Keep me posted."

Chapter Forty-Five

Maggie was dozing in the shade on the front veranda. Her reading glasses hung around her neck on a turquoise band; a half-read book overturned on her lap. She was snoring lightly as a man walked up the steps.

"Excuse me, ma'am," he said.

Maggie sat up; eyes wide.

"Who the hell are you?"

"Sorry, ma'am, I didn't mean to disturb you."

"Well then ya shoulda' walked away," Maggie muttered, rubbing her eyes, and setting her book on the table. She glared at him.

"Well? What do you want? I don't have all day."

"I'm looking for Mrs. Winthrup," he said. "I have reason to believe she's staying with you?"

"Who?"

"Hannah Winthrup."

"There's no one here by that name. You must have the wrong address."

"No, ma'am. I have a package here from her husband."

"Show me," Maggie said, putting on her glasses and reaching out her hand.

She looked closely at the brown envelope.

"Right address," she said. "Wrong name. Now leave me alone."

She leaned back in her chair, took off her glasses and closed her eyes. When the man didn't move, she flicked her fingers and gestured for him to go.

"Leave, or I will have you arrested for trespassing," she said.

"Sorry to bother you, ma'am," the man said, turning to leave.

"And for fuck's sake, stop calling me ma'am!" Maggie roared. "Makes me feel like an old lady."

She watched him walk down the path and get into a dark blue truck. She picked up a pen and jotted the license plate number on the inside of her palm. Round one to the old lady, she thought with a grin.

Maggie pretended to go back to sleep. Twenty minutes later, she stretched and yawned and slowly stood up. She looked out at the street, picked up her book and headed inside.

Hannah was in the living room, feeding the baby, a light blanket loosely draped over her shoulder and the baby's head.

"We had company," Maggie said in a low voice.

Hannah's eyes opened wide.

"It's okay," she said. "I handled it. But I need to let a certain person know so we can prepare for next steps."

Jack was not impressed when Maggie told him what had happened. He insisted on having a security officer move in with them. Maggie refused.

"You have no idea who you're dealing with, Maggie. Be reasonable."

She laughed.

"Jack, my boy, you have no idea who *you're* dealing with."

"Maggie, this could be dangerous. The government is determined to silence me. They've already sent death threats. They even shot at me. Twice. I can't put my family, and that includes you, at risk. If you won't let me beef up security, then we have to get you all out of there and to a safe place."

"Jack, I've been dealing with death threats since before you were born. Stop being such a baby. I have a plan. If you want to increase security, go right ahead. But we have to make sure that everything appears the same on the outside."

"Do you know how to use a gun?"

"The only weapon I need is one I was born with, Jack. I'm a woman. An old woman now. And that gives me a huge advantage in situations like this. People see what they want to see. I know how to work those assumptions. Trust me on this one."

Before she hung up, Maggie agreed to have a security system installed in the house.

"But you have to make it look like it's the cable company fixing my connection, Jack. Old ladies don't need security systems; but we sure as hell need a working tv."

"She's just an old woman," the agent told Frank. "She was sound asleep on the porch when I got there, snoring away. She probably naps every afternoon, so all we need to do is watch her for a few days, pick a time she's napping and sneak in through the back door. Even if she wakes up, what can she do? By the time she calls the cops, we'll have the woman and baby and be long gone."

Frank frowned.

"Maybe," he said. "But she didn't admit that they were there, so all we have to go on is the drone footage. It wasn't the clearest image. We can't make a mistake."

He thought for a moment.

"Okay, watch the house day and night. Figure out her routines. Try and see inside the windows, especially the upstairs where the bedrooms must be. If she's outside and there's movement inside, we know there's someone else. Oh, and check records. Find out who that old woman is."

Maggie peered through the half-opened curtains on her living room window. Her neighbor was taking out his recycling bin. A black truck had just pulled up across the street.

She grabbed her father's old wooden walking stick and opened the front door. Showtime, she thought as she pretended to hobble across the front veranda. She kicked the newspaper down the stairs so that she would have to navigate the steps. Clutching the railing, she took the stairs one at a time, leaning heavily on her cane.

When she reached the bottom, she bent forward and pretended the paper was out of reach. She stumbled, managed to grasp the newspaper, and stood up, hugging the paper to her chest.

"Maggie!" her neighbor called as he walked back up his driveway.

She limped toward him, waving the paper in the air.

"Oh hello, Martin," she said. "Haven't seen you in a while. How are the grandkids?"

"Couldn't be better, Maggie. But what's happened to you?"

She managed a smile.

"Old age must be catching up to me," she said, raising her voice as if she was hard of hearing. "Sciatica. Flares up more often than not lately. Whatcha' gonna do?"

They chatted for a while and Maggie returned, slowly and painfully, to the house. Before she went inside, she turned to check the flowers in the planter box on the railing. As she did, she glanced quickly at the black truck. She saw the glint of binoculars aimed at an upper window.

Nice try, she thought, shuffling inside, and closing the door behind her. She had already moved Hannah and Evelyn into the back bedroom.

She set the cane in the umbrella stand, straightened her back, and raised a fist in the air. Round two to the old lady.

Frank read through the report one more time. The old woman, Margaret Carpenter, had not left the house for the past week except to pick up her paper and yell at the neighbor's dog. Photos showed her walking with a cane.

A conversation with a neighbor suggested that she had mobility issues. The only movement in the front bedroom was her getting ready for bed at night – not a pretty sight.

The agent had tried to get images from the back of the house, but all the windows were blocked by big trees. A trellis with some sort of flowering vine masked the kitchen window. Old biddies and their flowers, he thought.

He set the file down on his desk. Someone rapped on the door.

"Come in."

"I've done the background check on Ms. Carpenter, sir. Looks like she's one of those feminists from way back. You know the burn-the-bra kind from the seventies? Turned up quite a bit of info – newspaper clippings, interviews. I made photocopies of everything for you. No kids or siblings though. Parents dead, but I guess you'd figure that, she's 75."

"Keep watching the house until further notice," Frank said. "I'll be in touch."

He picked up the folder and began to look through it. The agent was right: she had been an activist in her younger days. He glanced at a photo in one of the clippings. Quite a looker too. He read the caption under the photo and caught his breath.

"No way."

He studied the grainy photograph more closely.

"Fuck!"

Frank stood with his hands clasped behind his back, staring at the carpet. The President waited by the window.

"Sir, we have a complication," Frank said.

The President frowned.

"What do you mean?" he asked.

Frank hesitated. "The journalist's wife? She's staying with Margaret Carpenter."

"Who?" the President asked.

Frank swallowed noisily.

"Meg. Meg Charbonneau."

Frank watched the President stumble backward, clutching the edge of the desk. He sat down heavily in his chair. His face was the color of drifting snow.

Frank said nothing.

The President stared blankly at the wall. After a few minutes of silence, Frank shifted his feet and cleared his throat.

"What's your plan, Frank?" The President's voice was barely audible.

"I thought perhaps we should get Daniel here for a meeting."

"Good idea. And beyond that?"

Frank shook his head.

"I don't know," he said. "I was hoping the three of us could figure something out."

Chapter Forty-Six

Daniel had moved into his penthouse apartment downtown. He couldn't stand the growing stench and clutter in the house. From the floor to ceiling windows in the apartment, he had a view over the whole city. When he looked out the bedroom window, he could see the White House.

He tossed the keys on the table by the door. His mistress still refused to see him, so he had hired a hooker for later. He glanced at the clock in the kitchen. He still had a few hours to finish up some paperwork.

As the sun set, he noticed an unusual glow in the streets. He walked over to the windows and looked down. The streets were filled with people holding candles. He went into the bedroom. Candlelight shone around the White House. People stood at the fence surrounding the gardens, leaving just enough room at the gates for cars to enter and leave.

His phone rang.

"C'mon up," he growled.

"Daniel?"

"Mr. President?"

"Are you expecting someone?" the President asked.

"Oh, ah, just the pizza delivery," Daniel said.

"Bring it with you. We need to talk."

The President hung up the phone and glanced out the window.

"What's with the candles?" he asked Frank.

Frank stepped forward. People filled the streets in all directions. They were holding candles, swaying back and forth.

"And what's that sound?"

Frank listened.

"Humming, I think," Frank said.

They listened.

"I think it's '*We Are the Champions*'," Frank whispered.

Daniel picked up a pizza on the way to the White House. When he arrived at the President's office, he tossed the box on the desk. The President glanced at it and turned to Frank.

"Tell him."

"I've been trying to find that journalist's family," Frank said to Daniel. "His parents have vanished, and I thought his wife and kid had too. But the drone I've had scouting the city got some photos of his wife in a backyard on the outskirts of the city near Columbia Heights."

"So that's good news, right?" Daniel said.

"That part is, sure. But the house belongs to Margaret Carpenter," Frank said.

Daniel looked at him blankly.

"We knew her as Meg Charbonneau." Frank paused. "See the problem?"

Daniel's eyes bulged. His right cheek twitched, and he thrust his hands in his pockets. He took a step back and began to pace.

"Danny boy," the President said softly, "the photos are secure, right?"

Daniel stopped and faced him.

"Of course. I keep them in my safe and no one knows the code but me."

The President walked around to the other side of his desk and sat down. He picked up a letter opener and twirled it between his fingers.

Frank and Daniel glanced at each other.

"It's time, Daniel," the President said. "Destroy them."

Daniel nodded.

"And Frank? Make those arrests. We need Magdalen under lock and key."

Frank hesitated. "What about Meg," he asked in a low voice.

"Not our problem, boys. She clearly doesn't know about us. If she did, she would have acted long ago. We'll deal with her later. Right now, we have to stay focused on our end game."

The President slammed the letter opener on his desk and picked up the remote control. As Daniel and Frank left the office, the evening news was blaring with stories about the candlelight protests in the streets.

Daniel grabbed Frank's arm as they got to their cars.

"Frank, you still know where Lena is?"

Frank nodded.

"Do me a favor. Arrest her."

"She's a kid, Daniel."

"Look, her name could be short for Magdalen, right?" Daniel said.

"Is it?" Frank asked.

"No, of course not," Daniel said, "but that doesn't matter. It just gives you a reason to arrest her along with all the others. When Madeline finds out, she'll come running to save her little girl. She'll do anything to get Lena back. Anything I want."

Chapter Forty-Seven

When Daniel left the White House, he had the driver take him straight to his house. The air inside the mansion was pungent. The place had been closed up since he moved out. Empty pizza boxes littered the kitchen counter; dirty glasses and dishes filled the sink. The contents of the garbage bin sprawled across the floor. The cat had disappeared.

Daniel headed upstairs. He sniffed the air as he reached the top landing. It smelled like a men's locker room – sweat-drenched clothes and testosterone. He sprinted into his office. He was panting by the time he pulled the oil painting off the wall. He reached up and turned the dial back and forth on the combination lock – his birth date. With a confident click, the door unlocked. He shoved it open.

Everything was there.

Or so it seemed.

He pulled the top five envelopes off the pile and tossed them on the desk. He reached for a black metal box at the back of the safe that had been hidden by the envelopes. He lifted out the box and set it down on the desk.

Sitting back in his black leather armchair, he opened the side drawer of the desk and reached for the bourbon. He took a swig and placed the bottle on a side table. As he pressed lightly on a small panel at the back of the drawer, it popped open to reveal a small gold key.

Holding his breath now, he held the black box in one hand and jiggled the key in the lock. He lifted the lid slowly and let out a sigh. A large manila envelope lay there, "PRIVATE" scrawled across the front in black marker. He pulled the envelope out and pushed the box away.

Within a few minutes, twenty black and white photos covered the surface of his desk. Virgins, all of them. Big brother made sure of that.

"Nothing but the best for you, kid," he used to say.

He admired the angles of the shots. Damn, I'm good, he thought. The lighting, positioning, and even the way he arranged their hair – as if they were in the throes of ecstasy.

He snickered. Ecstasy. Good one. Drugged out of their minds.

He grabbed another envelope from the box. One by one, he matched a second photo to each one on the desk. Before and after shots.

There were no names on the backs of the photos, just initials and dates, but he recognized who they were on sight. He scanned the group for Meg. There, that one. He smiled at the memory. He nodded to himself, poured another drink and raised the glass in a toast.

"Teamwork."

We learned a lot that night, he thought. He sat back in his chair, holding his empty glass up to the light. He had known the President would ask him to get rid of the photos at some point. He had duplicates stored at a warehouse in Rome for this exact reason.

He texted his security team to confirm there had been no unusual activity at the warehouse. The response was immediate.

All good. Security cam checked daily

He rocked back in his chair. He didn't have to destroy the originals. He could just say he had. They'd never know.

Daniel tucked the photos back in the envelope and locked them in the safe. He stretched out, the couch squeaking under his weight. He kicked off his shoes and poured another glass, placing the half-empty bottle within reach on the floor.

His eyes felt heavy, as he downed the drink and tossed the glass on the rug. Just a quick nap, he thought, and then I'll go back to the condo.

Husky snoring soon rumbled through the room.

Jumbled images bounced and twisted through his mind. Tommy, grinning at him, calling him by his nickname – Bud … grabbing a smoke behind the gym … Jimmy's bedroom, the latest Playboy magazine … driving, windows down, The Rolling Stones blasting … going to class drunk … the soft plop of pennies whipped at popcorn ceilings while the teacher's back was turned … jacking off in the bathroom …

Daniel sighed and turned over, settling into a deeper sleep, images dissolving into a kaleidoscope of color, and then … nothing.

He heard her voice, and his eyes shifted. He zoomed in on her face. There she was, graduation night, sitting on Tom's lap, laughing, tossing her head back, running her fingers through her long black hair. She was cool; different from any girl he'd ever met. Dark eyes that flashed when she was angry; so smart – she had the top marks in the school; she made him think of a cat when she walked – alert, ready to pounce or dart away, more wild than tame. And he wanted to tame her. She was the one he picked when they shared their plan with Jimmy.

"Anything for my lil' brother," Tom said, punching him in the arm. "Your first time needs to be special. Whatever you want."

Jimmy was cautious. He had already had a few run-ins with the local cops. He knew them on a first-name basis.

"We have to think this through," he said. "I can't afford to get caught again. Pete warned me that I'd be behind bars next time."

"No problem, man," Tommy said. "Gotcha' covered. I'll slip something in her drink; she won't remember a thing. We'll take her to that abandoned barn in the back forty, and no one will ever know."

"We can't leave her in the barn," Jimmy said.

"No, that's your job, kid," Tom said. "You know the back alleys. You find the spot. We'll drop her there and cover our tracks. Piece of cake."

Someone hit the fast-forward button in his mind. Suddenly, they were in the barn. Tom and Jimmy ripped off her clothes and stuffed them in a garbage bag while he got his camera set up. He pushed them out of away so he could arrange the shot.

"C'mon guys, this is my night. And I want a good photo. So, back off. You'll get your chance."

He got everyone posed, stripped down, pressed the timer, and joined them for the photo.

Tom and Jimmy held back, so he could have the first go. When he was done, he sprawled on his back, gulping air. He felt huge, powerful, and drunk. He craved something more. He stood up and watched Tommy fuck her. When Jimmy hesitated, Daniel growled and shoved him away. He bent down and slapped her across the face. Her head bounced. No response from her but it turned him on.

"What the fuck, Bud?"

Jimmy grabbed his arm and pulled him off. He pushed back.

"You said you'd let me do it my way," he hissed. "And this is what I want. If you can't handle it, go wait in the car."

Jimmy said no one would find her down by the wharf.

"Not even the addicts go there," he said.

It was 3 a.m. They left her body behind a dumpster.

"Time to move on," Tommy said, clapping his hands together as if slamming a door shut. "Happy birthday, kid. Even if she wakes up, she won't remember a thing, so we don't need to worry about being fingered for this."

He asked for a copy of the photos.

"You, Jimbo?"

Jimmy shook his head.

As the images blurred, Daniel rolled over on the couch, his mind doing cartwheels. When the dizziness passed, the videotape in his head sped forward. Jimmy in a suit … Tom's stag night … he could hear Tom's voice.

"She's a virgin, bro. Just the way you like them. See you at the church in the morning. Don't forget the ring."

Another wave of dizziness as he pictured the naked body of the unconscious girl on the bed. Daniel sucked in cool air, turned, and threw up on the carpet. He pushed himself to a sitting position and held his head in his hands. A drum solo worthy of Nick Mason hammered his skull as random scenes of girls, sex and blood flashed behind his closed eyes. Years of teamwork and pleasure. Every year on his birthday and a few in between. The girls remembered nothing.

Tommy made sure of that. Jimmy found the drop-off spots. Jimmy was the one who insisted they stop once DNA testing came in.

"Too easy to trace," he said. He was on the police force by then, working his way up.

It had also been Jimmy's idea to dump their first names and use their middle names when they went away to college.

"It'll be harder to track us," he said. "They're not the names we used in high school, so no one can find us in the yearbooks. I'll get us new ID."

Tom smiled. "Good idea. So, I'll be Andrew. What's your middle name, Jimbo?"

Jimmy frowned. "Francis but call me Frank. Sounds like a real man, not a monk."

"And of course, you'll be Danny boy," Tom said, punching him in the arm.

"No way! It's Daniel or nothing," he glared.

"Oh, and one more thing," Tom added. "From this moment on, you and I? We're not related. We have different fathers and different last names anyway. No one will know."

"What's the big deal?"

"I have plans, Danny boy. Big plans. One day, it might make all the difference in the world."

His stepbrother always had an angle, Daniel thought.

He grabbed his chest and tried to sit up, a sharp pain stabbing his left side. The room shifted, his eyes blurred, as he gulped air in small breaths. When the throbbing eased, he pushed himself onto his feet and staggered out the door.

Chapter Forty-Eight

The President turned off the news and tossed the remote onto a side table. The arrests would definitely stir things up. Push-pull, he thought. The basics of a good golf swing...and political strategy.

He strolled down the hallway from the office to his bedroom, stopping periodically to admire the immense portraits of the founding fathers along the walls. Tall, strong white men just like him who knew what was best for the country. For the world.

He sat down in the armchair in the corner of his dressing room and shook off his shoes. He thought about the conversation with Frank and Daniel.

"Beware the weak link," he muttered, rubbing his chin.

Daniel had seemed suitably scared. He had skittled out of the room like his feet were on fire. Frank seemed … hesitant. The President had seen his eyes flicker as he brought Daniel up to date.

The President drummed his fingers on the desk. I've known him for years, he thought. He doesn't have secrets from me. He stretched out in the chair and closed his eyes, remembering their adventures. It had started the night of their high school graduation, Daniel's 18th birthday. And it became an annual tradition.

He sat up and frowned. Daniel and his damn photos. The President strode over to where his suits hung and pushed them out of the way. He touched a button in the center of the back wall. A small section lifted up and a drawer appeared. He scanned the contents and closed the drawer, halfheartedly shoving some suits back in place. His copies of the photos were still there, if he needed to put some pressure on either of the men.

He sat on the edge of the bed and started to take off his tie. His hands paused; his mind raced.

He was there every time, but he never fucked one. He closed his eyes and pictured the moment Frank straddled Meg's body, hesitating.

"Guys, she's totally out of it. I can't do this if she's not even moving."

They shoved him onto her, and he went through the motions.

He was in all the photos. But he never did it. He became the driver. He knew the best places to stash the bodies.

The President rested his hands on his knees.

Frank's hiding something, he thought.

Frank pounded his fist on the steering wheel.

"Fuck this train!"

The freight train which had been crawling past the intersection had now stopped, blocking traffic in both directions.

He thought about wheeling around and trying another route but realized that, given the length of the train, it was probably blocking the next two crossings.

He reached over and turned up the radio, slapping his hands on his thighs in time with the heavy metal bass. The train reversed, inching across the road. He picked up his phone and sent a text.

Back in 10

Frank turned off his car and gazed into the night. A crescent moon peered above the horizon, casting an eerie light on the distant trees.

He leaned forward, drumming his fingers on the dashboard.

"C'mon, c'mon," he snarled. He picked up his phone and typed in another message.

Make it 20

He could see the three engines again. He heard the squeal of metal against metal as the train ground to a halt. A dull throbbing growl echoed through the valley. The train snaked forward, gradually picking up speed. He counted the cars and quit at two hundred. He rested his forehead on the steering wheel.

"Longest train in the world," he groaned. If he could just get home, everything would be okay. All he had to do was keep things under control for six more months. Then he could retire and live life on his own terms.

Bells clanged in the crisp air as the crossing arms lifted. He turned the key and revved the engine. He allowed the car in front of him a bit of lead room and pressed his foot to the floor. The Corvette leaped forward, like a racehorse from the starting gate. He pulled into the underground parking garage of his condo ten minutes later.

He took the elevator to his penthouse suite. The apartment was dark, illuminated only by the glow of the moon through the floor-to-ceiling plate-glass windows. The lights of the city sparkled below.

Flicking his eyes appreciatively at the white leather couch, he strode into the bedroom.

Alessandro stretched his long legs and stood up, dropping the white chenille blanket on the floor. His naked body glistened in the moonlight. He followed Frank into the bedroom and softly closed the door.

Chapter Forty-Nine

Over a twenty-four-hour period, fifty women from across the country were taken into custody and charged with treason. According to Executive Order signed during the night under the Emergency Measures Act, treasonable offences were punishable by death.

"Daniel, I want you to preside over this case," the President said.

"But it needs to go through the lower court first," Daniel said.

The President stood in front of Daniel and placed his hands on his stepbrother's shoulders.

"I'm sure you can figure out a way," the President said, holding Daniel's gaze.

"Well, of course, if a case is considered to be of imperative public importance," Daniel said dropping his eyes to the floor, "we could justify moving it directly to the Supreme Court. But it's highly unusual."

"Make it so, Danny boy."

The President strode out of the room.

Daniel called an emergency conference of the Supreme Court Justices. After a brief discussion, he emerged and called the President.

"It's a go."

The President issued a press release announcing that Magdalen had been arrested and would be tried for treason.

"In the interest of public safety, it is imperative that this case be dealt with immediately. Therefore, the Supreme Court will hear the case on Wednesday."

Jack was trying to pull together the details when he got a text from his father marked urgent. He called him right away.

"What's going on?"

"We went back to the house to pick up the mail. I know you told us not to, but you know what your mother's like. She gets an idea into her head and won't give up."

"Get to the point, Dad."

"Anyway, as soon as we walked back to the car, a police officer came over and asked your mother for her full name. She told him and he arrested her. He wouldn't give me any explanation, just snapped handcuffs on her and pushed her into the patrol car. I followed them to the station but still couldn't get any answers. What do we do?"

"Where are you now?"

"Outside the station. The cops shoved me out the door and threatened to arrest me, but I won't leave your mother here alone."

"Okay, I'm going to make a few more calls and see what I can find out. I'll get back to you as soon as I can."

He checked in with his contacts and called his father back within ten minutes.

"Looks like the President is rounding up anyone with the name "Magdalen". Mum has done nothing wrong so I'm sure she'll be released on bail, but she may have to stay there overnight."

"Our lawyer just arrived. And he's talking to the officer now. I'll let you know what comes of it."

Jack turned back to his laptop and checked his messages. He called his editor. Then he placed a call to the President's Office.

Madeline dropped the grocery bags on the table.

"Lena? I'm back. Wanna go for a swim?"

No response.

She walked quickly down the hall and checked the bedroom. Lena's laptop was on the bed, along with her headphones. She wasn't in the bathroom or on the porch. Madeline ran to the water and looked up and down the beach. No sign of her.

As she turned back, she saw Brian and Shelley racing toward her.

"Max!"

Madeline froze, afraid to ask the obvious question.

"Lena's been arrested."

Shelley put away the groceries while Brian explained what had happened. Madeline sat on the edge of the bench, tossing her keys back and forth in her hands. With each toss, the jangling grew louder.

"Lena said she was coming over to our place," Brian said. "When she didn't show up, I decided to check. As I came out the door, there was a cop pushing her into the backseat of his car. She yelled that she was being arrested and to find you. I tried to talk to the guy, but he elbowed me in the chest and drove off. We've been watching for you to come back."

She threw her keys on the table and exploded.

"This has gone too far. He will pay for this."

She stormed into her bedroom and slammed the door.

Brian and Shelley looked at each other. Brian walked quietly down the hall and knocked on the door.

"Max? Is there something we can do?"

Her voice was calm, but he could hear rage howling behind every syllable.

"No. Thank you. There is nothing you can do. But I know exactly what *I* need to do. Please go home. I will be in touch."

Brian turned and gestured to Shelley. He wrapped his arm around her shoulders as they walked back across the lane.

Madeline sat on the edge of the bed, scratching her head. She still wasn't used to the haircut; all bristles on one side, and so short on the other. Damn you, Daniel! Our daughter? How could you?

She paced around the room, staring at the pine floorboards. She noticed dust bunnies clinging to the legs of the old blue dresser. She leaned against the window frame and watched the waves crash on the shore. Children darted back and forth as if playing tag with the water. A mix of shrieks and laughter tumbled on the wind.

Her eyes slid to the photo of Lena and Max on the desk. It seemed like yesterday – Lena was seven, a tangle of arms and legs and a goofy grin; Max looked like she had just stepped out of a fashion magazine, as always. She had her arm around Lena, heads touching, joy sparkling all around them.

Max wouldn't hesitate, Madeline thought. She always played to win. No matter the risk.

Madeline remembered huddling over the chess board with her sister on long winter evenings at the cottage when they were kids. Their grandmother pulled the game table close to the woodstove and wrapped them up in matching handmade quilts.

Max played quickly and easily, a satisfied smile lurking at the edges of her mouth, confident of the outcome. Madeline felt more like the elephant in the room, plodding along, reaching out to make a move and then pulling her hand back.

"Mad, you can't do that," Max would complain. "Make up your mind and go for it. There is no other way."

Okay, Max, Madeline thought. If you say so.

She sat down at the desk and drafted an email with just two words: *Go girl.*

She pressed Send.

"Your mother wouldn't hurt a fly," Hannah said when Jack called and told her the news.

"I know. This may be a ploy to bring me out of hiding. Stay inside with Evy, please. I can't have you in danger too. I've told Maggie not to answer the door for anyone."

Maggie took the phone and cautioned him to be patient.

"Patient? That's my mother he's got in jail. This is personal."

"It's all personal, Jack. Haven't you figured that out yet? Everything that's said or not said, done or left undone is personal to someone. A lot of damage has been done to a lot of people for many, many years. If we keep stirring the pot, all that rage will boil over and those in power will finally have to answer for their actions."

"But what can I do, Maggie?"

"Check your email."

Jack skimmed through the photos and profiles Maggie had sent. Fifty women, ranging in age from 21 to 76, as different as can be, but all bearing some variation of the name "Magdalen".

He caught his breath when he saw his mother's photo. There was nothing in her profile that was new to him. Except maybe…he reread the last paragraph and let out his breath. She had been a journalist when she was in her twenties. She gave up her career the year he was born.

No wonder she's so proud of me, he thought.

He checked with his editor. They couldn't use the names and photos of those arrested without permission from their families, but he got the green light for a feature.

By afternoon, media across the country led with the arrests and related stories. Lawyers stepped forward, volunteering their services to represent the women since many were unemployed or on a fixed income. The World Organization for Women sent teams of counsellors to the jails and communities to provide trauma support. Community centers opened doors to meet the needs of the women's families. Neighbors brought hot meals, offered to take in the children, and set up online fundraising.

The Voice of the People called for a mass gathering in the streets, around government buildings, the homes of members of Congress, corporations that financially supported the government, and all major transportation networks across the country: highways, railways and airports.

The Speaker of the House called the President on his private line.

"I can't even get out my driveway this morning. The street is full of people. Men, women, children. And they're marching. In place. Staring at my house. My wife and kids are terrified. They're holed up in the basement. You've got to do something."

Chapter Fifty

At a small outdoor café in Italy, Max heard her phone buzz. She grinned when she saw the text from Madeline.

"It's about time, Sis," she whispered.

She took one more sip of her wine, set the glass on the table and paid for her meal. Her red heels clicked a steady beat on the cobblestones as she crossed the crowded piazza. By the time she reached her apartment on the top floor of an old stone building, her plan was ready.

She changed into black yoga pants and a hoodie, took off her glasses and popped in her contacts. She tucked her red-framed reading glasses into the pocket of her jacket. On her way out the door, she slipped her feet into black shoes with no tread. She drove into Rome, her white Opel Corsa-e purring like a contented kitten, and parked on a quiet side street in the warehouse district.

Madeline had sent her the address a month ago as a precaution so that she could stake out the building. The single-story concrete box was surrounded by bushes and a six-foot high mesh fence in poor repair. At first glance, it looked abandoned. Max had spent a week exploring the area, timing the movements of the security guard, and confirming there was only one entrance, one camera and no alarm system.

She crept in through a broken spot in the fence and settled into the bushes to wait. The moon was in its dark phase, so the only light came from a streetlamp on the far side of the building. As she waited for the security guard to complete his rounds, she thought of her father.

She remembered sitting on his knee one evening when she was six. He pointed at the chess board on the table in front of him and whispered in her ear, "Play to win, child. Play as if the lives of strangers depend on your next three moves."

If he could see me now, I wonder what he would think.

After the guard disappeared around the corner, she turned off the camera over the entrance using an app on her phone. She pressed a code into the keypad and stepped inside, closing the door softly behind her. As her eyes adjusted to the dim light through the single grimy window, she checked her watch. It was 11:30 p.m. Ten minutes to find the one photo that would tip the balance.

No pressure, she thought.

Rows of metal shelves stretched before her into the void. She glided forward, pulling out her reading glasses.

M. C., 1967.

She reached for the cardboard box and set it on the desk under the window. A dust tornado spiraled upward, captured in the dim light shining through the cracked blind. She grabbed the bridge of her nose to avert a sneeze. No need to alert the security guard to her presence.

With gloved fingers, she sorted through brittle newspaper clippings and … gotcha! She glanced at the black and white photos and shook her head. She tucked two pictures into a thin leather pouch and stuffed it into the pocket of her hoodie. Out of the corner of her eye, she saw the worn brown boots of the guard as he strolled past the window. She checked her watch: four minutes left. She placed the lid on the box, returned it to the shelf and took a photo of the label.

She pulled the black hood up over her head, took off her glasses and slid them back into her pocket. Slipping quietly out the door, she pressed in the lock code and disappeared into the shrubbery. Before ducking through the opening in the fence, she paused to reset the security camera from her phone.

The camera clicked back into operation as the guard rounded the far end of the building.

Madeline caught her breath when her phone pinged with a message from Max.

Photos attached. Warning: graphic content

Your move, Mad…Make it count.

Madeline braced her shoulders and printed out the black and white photos. She stuffed one inside an envelope. She sat back and typed a short note with a date and three names and taped it to the outside of the envelope. She tucked everything into a brown padded package, scribbled an address on the front and added a small handwritten note on the back corner.

"Either she'll know how to use this to advantage…or she'll shatter, and I'll never forgive myself."

She grabbed her car keys, drove into town, and dropped the package off with a local courier.

Maggie closed the curtains in the living room and turned on the television. Images of huge crowds flooded the screen. She watched carefully, scanning the faces. She sat back in her armchair and smiled.

"That's more like it."

She turned to Hannah.

"See? It's not 'just' a women's issue now. Arrest fifty innocent people and you're going to get a reaction. What you're seeing here is the beginning of the end for the President and his gang of thugs."

There was a knock at the door. Hannah got up, but Maggie put a hand on her shoulder.

"No," she whispered. "You stay here where no one can see you. I'll deal with it."

She glanced through a crack in the curtains. A delivery van was idling in her driveway.

"Why don't they turn the damn thing off?" she muttered.

She peered through the peephole in the door. A young man in a brown uniform shuffled his feet, whistling to himself as he listened to music on his earbuds. He held a padded envelope in his hands.

She opened the door.

"Margaret Carpenter?" he asked.

She crossed her arms and nodded.

He handed her the package.

"Sign here."

As he turned and headed back to the van, she glanced down at the return address. She didn't recognize it. She flipped the package over and noticed a small handwritten note in the bottom right corner: *Open in privacy.* She set it aside to look at later.

When Hannah woke up from her afternoon nap, Evy was still asleep. Yawning, she went downstairs to the kitchen. Maggie wasn't there. She checked the office and the living room. Then she climbed the stairs to Maggie's bedroom. The door was shut. As she raised her hand to knock, she saw the note stuck to the door.

Migraine. Make yourself supper. See you in the morning.

Chapter Fifty-One

Maggie sat with her back to the wall, the comforter tucked like a cocoon around her body. She glanced down at the contents of the package – a letter with three names, a date, and a warning about a photo that now lay face down on the bed. She felt like a deer trapped by the headlights of an oncoming car. The image in the photo had seared into her pupils, blurring her vision, and flooding her mind with terror and shame.

Daylight was fading. She shivered and tugged the comforter closer. Oblivious to everything but the accelerating drumbeat in her head, she stared out the window.

Soft footsteps in the hallway broke her trance. Hannah. Maggie held her breath until she heard the footsteps moving away.

She turned the photo over with the tip of her baby finger. It was like touching a poisonous snake. She stifled the wild cry that threatened to crack open her chest and forced the anguish back into the box where she had locked it away so many years ago. No, not now. Not ever. No, no no no no…. a voice howled inside her head.

Her mind skidded sideways, careening over the edge, splintering like shale on a mountainside.

The room grew dark.

She was shaking. Cold. Reaching out, she felt a smooth icy surface. She tried to sit up and slipped, cracking her head on something unmoving. She lay still, waiting for her eyes to adjust to the darkness.

Where…am…I?

She rolled onto her side and pushed herself up slowly. She could see a white outline now, a cold box encasing her body. She blinked. Dark and light squares emerged from the blackness.

And a putrid smell.

She pulled one knee underneath her and leaned forward. As she reached out, she realized she was sitting in her bathtub. But that made no sense. Grabbing the faucet and the side of the tub, she heaved herself to her feet. She leaned on the towel bar, stretched out and flicked on a switch with the edge of a finger. A blinding flash.

"Oh … my … god …"

Orange and yellow blobs floated in the toilet bowl, mingled with brown crusty splotches of…blood? She stepped on the bathmat and looked in the mirror. A jagged line sliced the upper edge of her cheek, shooting up toward her left eye like a bolt of lightning. Her eyes felt fuzzy, and the room started to move. She sank to her knees and stretched out on the cold tile, wrapping the bathmat around her trembling shoulders.

Hannah stretched and looked at the clock. It was 5 a.m. Dawn shimmered on the windowpane. She put on her slippers and padded down the hall to the guest bathroom. There was a light on in Maggie's room and she could hear the pounding of fingers on the keyboard.

She fed Evelyn and put her down for a sleep. When she went down to the kitchen to make breakfast, she was surprised to find Maggie at the table, gulping down coffee and skimming the morning paper. She had dark circles under her eyes, her hair was matted, and she had a bandage on her cheek.

"Maggie, what happened? Are you okay?"

"Rough night," Maggie said, as she stood up and poured herself another cup of coffee. "Gotta go. Things to do."

She headed to her bedroom.

Chapter Fifty-Two

In the streets, everyone was talking about the mass arrests and the upcoming trial. Headlines screamed: *Magdalen Tried for Treason!* Lineups for courtroom seats stretched for blocks from the Front Plaza near the Supreme Court. Media outlets scrambled to get a spot. Social media went wild.

@Magdalenknows You got the wrong girl

@iamMagdalen I am Magdalen

@onguardforMagdalen Convict at your peril

@theMagdalenclub Blood on your hands, Power

@therealMagdalen Catch me if you can

"This one," the President said, pointing to a photo of a young woman with dark hair. "That's the one we'll start with."

"But we don't have any proof that it's her," Daniel said.

"Doesn't matter. She's the bait. Whoever Magdalen is, she'll come forward. She won't sacrifice a young girl for the cause."

"Are you sure this will work?" Daniel asked.

"Have I ever been wrong? Of course, it will work. If another letter shows up from Magdalen, we know we haven't got her in jail. And then? We'll change our tactics. Gotta keep those bitches guessing."

He punched Daniel's shoulder.

"Make it memorable, Danny boy. I'm counting on you."

By the day of the trial, the country was buzzing with rumors. City cafes and country kitchens hummed as people declared an unofficial holiday, and sat glued to their devices, waiting for the live audio from the Supreme Court.

Daniel arrived at his office early. He needed a police escort to get through the growing crowds. He gulped down a few shots of bourbon before putting on his black robe. Pacing around his chambers, he glanced at his notes, anticipating the Marshal's call.

Maggie sat in the back corner of the courtroom. She wrapped a red shawl across her chest and clasped her hands in her lap. Alicia came in, gave her a little wave, and found a seat near the door. She had a long red scarf around her neck.

Brian, Shelley, and the rest of their book club sat together, wearing white t-shirts and a touch of red. Maggie's book club members sat near the front. Hannah had begged to come but Maggie insisted she stay home with the baby.

"We don't know what they're up to. It could be a trap. You need to be safe. Keep the doors locked."

She was startled to see Jack walk in. He looked around the room and when he spotted her, he gestured that he wanted to talk to her.

Later, she mouthed.

"All rise," the Marshal called.

"The Honorable, the Chief Justice and the Associate Justices of the Supreme Court of the United States. Oyez! Oyez! Oyez! All persons having business before the Honorable, the Supreme Court of the United States, are admonished to draw near and give their attention, for the Court is now sitting. God save the United States and this Honorable Court!"

Daniel entered the courtroom and took the center seat behind the bench, flanked by the other Justices. He adjusted his glasses and looked up into a sea of white and red. Mostly women. A scattering of men. He frowned and examined the faces. His wife wasn't there. Madeline will come, he thought. I know her.

"The Supreme Court of the United States in now in session. Please be seated."

There was a murmur as the spectators took their seats.

"Calling the case of the United States versus Maria Magdalena Alvarez."

A middle-aged woman near the front of the courtroom sobbed. The man beside her wrapped his arm around her shoulder and whispered in her ear. The parents, Daniel thought, raising a hand to his mouth to hide a grin.

The Solicitor General stood and began his opening statement.

"Mr. Chief Justice, and may it please the Court…"

A deep voice resonated from the back of the courtroom interrupting him.

"I…am Magdalen, Your Honor."

Daniel stared at the woman. Wrapped in a red shawl, eyes blazing, her face framed by gray curls, she glared at him. She tossed off her shawl to reveal the words written in bold print across her white shirt: **I AM MAGDALEN**

The entire courtroom turned in her direction.

"Arrest her!" the Marshal shouted.

Two court officers moved toward Maggie. Another woman with gray hair stood, took off her red scarf and pointed to the words on her shirt.

"I am Magdalen," she announced.

The officers stopped and looked back to the Marshal for guidance.

"Arrest them both."

One by one, women around the courtroom stood, displayed their shirts and announced that they were Magdalen. The Marshal grabbed the gavel and pounded the desk.

"Order!" he shouted. "Order in the court!"

Additional officers arrived to make the arrests. The Marshal glanced out a window and approached the bench.

"Mr. Chief Justice? The streets are filled with them. All wearing those shirts. We can't arrest them all. We don't have the manpower."

Daniel held a quiet conversation with the Associate Justices.

"The court will adjourn for one hour," the Marshal announced over the clamor.

Daniel strode out of the courtroom and into his chambers, locking the door behind him.

He collapsed in his leather chair, head in his hands.

"Get a grip," he muttered. "This was supposed to be open and shut. Think, man, think."

He reached in the side drawer for his bourbon and noticed a black and white photo taped to the bottle.

It was a photo from his safe. The one of Meg.

He dropped it on the desk, like it was on fire. He glanced around, expecting to see someone standing in the shadows. The office was empty.

Then he saw the note under his glass.

Five words. Typed in bold.

We are coming for you.

He crumpled the note and filled the shot glass to the brim.

As he finished a third glass, he heard a key turning in the lock. His left hand shot under the desk, ready to press the alarm.

A tall slim grey-haired woman stalked into the room. He took a long look: silver-studded black leather boots, tight black leather pants, a white t-shirt knotted at the waist, short black leather jacket and large, red-framed glasses. Daniel's right hand dropped to his crotch.

The woman tossed her head back with a chuckle.

"Checking the 'crown jewels'? I see you haven't changed a bit, Danny boy."

Daniel froze. He examined her face more closely.

"Madeline?"

"In the flesh, my darling. Have you missed me?"

She blew him a kiss. He jerked back.

"Where the hell have you been? And how did you get in?"

Madeline held up her hand, keys dangling.

"You gave me a key, years ago, don't you remember, dearest? In the hope that I might visit for a little afternoon delight."

She took a few steps forward. He launched himself out of his chair.

"You think you're so smart, don't you?" he growled. "You've played right into my hands. I knew you'd come out of hiding for your darling girl, you bitch."

Madeline crossed her arms, planting her feet firmly on the floor. Her eyes narrowed; her voice grew hard.

"Shut up, Daniel. Sit down. I see you found the photo."

She paused, watching his face. She pulled another photo out of her leather briefcase. A photo of a dusty box, labeled 'M.C. 1968'.

"How the hell did you get that?" he shouted. "I'll have you arrested. That's private property."

He lunged for the photo. She dangled it above her head and shoved him back with a boot to the knee. He fell against the desk, breathing hard.

"Not so fast, sweetheart. Here's what you're going to do for me."

She handed him a piece of paper.

He scanned the paper and dumped it into the waste basket.

"No way."

"Oh yes, Daniel. This photo is just one of many. Forty photos, from your little collection. Twenty women, wasn't it? Before and after you and your buddies had your fun. Packages are ready to go to the police and all the major media outlets in the next 30 minutes. Your choice."

He crossed his arms and stared at her.

"You're bluffing."

"Maybe, maybe not."

She placed her hands on her hips.

"Some of those girls died, Daniel. Did you know that? You could face murder charges. How long do you think you would last in prison? All those men whose appeals you denied over the years might enjoy getting to know you better, if you catch my drift."

She watched him squirm. As the silence grew, she smiled.

"It might be time to give Big Brother a call," Madeline said. She put the photo back in her briefcase and checked the gold clock on the wall.

"Although, if you wait ten minutes, I have the feeling he's going to call you. He's also entertaining a guest, right about now."

She strolled toward the door.

"Oh wait, one more thing."

She dug a legal-sized envelope out of her briefcase and tossed it on the desk.

"Open and sign, Daniel."

He tore open the envelope. Divorce papers.

"No way," he said. "You can't get away with this."

"Watch me," Madeline said, pulling the photo out of her briefcase again and waving it in the air.

Daniel signed. She picked up the papers.

"Ciao, amore."

Madeline walked out the door, wiggling her fingers in a final goodbye before locking the door behind her.

Daniel shredded the note and the photo. He poured another drink.

A few minutes later, he heard a knock on the door.

"Come in."

The Marshal unlocked the door and poked his head inside.

"Sir? We have a problem."

"Ya think?"

"We checked all the women in the courtroom like you asked. Their names really are Magdalen. It's on their ID."

Daniel shook his head.

"All of them?"

"Yes, sir."

"It just gets better and better, doesn't it?"

"Sir?"

"Call the Justices to a conference, and then call the court to order. We'll be there shortly."

He pulled Madeline's list out of the garbage and drank straight from the bottle.

After a brief conference behind closed doors, the Supreme Court Justices returned to the courtroom.

"All rise."

Daniel took his seat and raised his eyes to the ceiling. Everyone followed his gaze.

He closed his eyes and said in a low voice.

"The case is dismissed."

Shocked silence filled the room, fractured by sudden cheering that spread like a tidal wave through the hallways, spilling out into the streets. Daniel slumped in his chair, head in his hands. The Marshal pounded the gavel and called for order. No one paid attention.

Maggie and Alicia hugged. Book club members did high-fives. Jack grinned as he made his way through the crowd to Maggie.

"How's it feel?"

"You don't need me to tell you, Jack. Look around. And this is just the beginning."

He studied her face.

"What else do you have planned?"

"Who me? Nothing."

She winked.

Chapter Fifty-Three

The President stared at the woman in the doorway.

"You've got a lot of nerve coming here," he said to his wife, taking off his tie and pushing up his shirtsleeves.

"Oh, don't I though?" Magda laughed.

"Where are my daughters?" he asked. He stood up and came around to the other side of the desk.

"You already know the answer to that one, Andrew. Or should I say…Tommy?"

She watched his eyes. Fear flickered and vanished. He shifted his feet and assumed a wider stance.

"You don't even know you're doing it," she said.

"What?"

"Sizing up the threat, checking the exits, preparing to fight to the death if needed. Still the Finger Lakes high school boxing champ."

"I don't know what you're talking about."

Magda smiled and handed him a sheet of paper.

"These are your instructions, *Mister* President. I suggest you follow them to the letter."

"Is that a threat?"

He stepped toward her. She held her spot and shrugged her shoulders.

"Just an observation. Think about it. If I know your real name is Tom, what else do I know?"

She paused and added, "Better question – who else knows?"

She sauntered toward the door and turned back.

"I understand that murder is an impeachable offense. I can see the headlines now. Can't you? Your glory days are over. Oh, and your stepbrother is expecting your call."

She gave him a one-finger salute as she left, her laughter bouncing off the walls.

Maggie stood in the shade of a large oak tree across from the DC Jail. She watched the women come out, one by one, and disappear in a sea of hugs from family and friends. As Jack pulled up on his motorcycle, she stepped back behind the tree so he wouldn't see her.

He joined the group of people at the gate, standing beside a tall man with short dark hair and a beard speckled with white. The man turned and wrapped an arm around Jack.

A woman with curly brown hair walked out and paused in the center of the sidewalk. She looked around, searching. Jack ran forward.

"Mum!"

The older man followed, grinning widely.

As the three embraced, Maggie turned and walked briskly through the park. She swiped at a stray tear.

Madeline threw her arms around Lena as soon as she appeared.

"You're squishing me," Lena protested.

"I'm never letting go."

Lena pulled her head back.

"Can we get something to eat? I'm starving."

Madeline laughed.

"That's my girl. Shelley and Brian are waiting for us. We can pick up food on the way."

Brian and Shelley headed back across the lane after a celebration over beer and burgers. Madeline and Lena cleaned up the kitchen, giving each other hugs every few minutes. Lena hung up the dish towel and slumped into a chair by the window.

"I'm beat," she said.

Madeline sat down across from her.

"How did they treat you in jail?"

Lena shrugged.

"There were so many of us that they had to group some of us together. It was a bit of a party, really. We knew they didn't have anything on us, so we weren't worried. But we had no idea what was going on. I figured it would just be a matter of time and you'd find a way to get me out."

Madeline reached over to touch her knee.

"I've never been so worried in my life."

"After all the things you've done, Mo…Auntie Max?"

"This was you. And that makes all the difference."

She got up and turned on the radio. She leaned close to Lena and whispered in her ear.

Brian was surprised to see them packing up the car the next morning. Lena rushed through his front door looking for Shelley.

"Hey, girls," he said, "leaving already? What's the rush?"

Madeline smiled and reached out to give him a quick hug.

"Lena and I are going on a little road trip," she said. "It would do us good to get away for a while."

"Good plan," said Brian. "Where are you heading?"

"Not sure yet. We'll play it by ear."

"Well, if there's anything I can do…"

"Actually, there is something, Brian. Can you handle the book club next month? We might be back for the following one. I'll let you know."

"No problem. Happy to help. Safe travels."

Lena and Shelley came out to the porch, arms around each other's waists. They hugged and Lena got into the car.

"C'mon, Auntie Max. Time's a wastin'!"

After driving for an hour, Madeline pulled into a roadside motel. They registered in the office and took their bags to an upstairs room.

Lena kicked off her shoes and collapsed face-down on the bed.

"I am exhausted," she moaned, her voice muffled by the pillow.

"Have a nap, if you want," Madeline said. She picked up her backpack and went into the bathroom.

Lena pulled her phone out of her back pocket and rolled over. She scrolled through social media sites and fell asleep.

Madeline emptied her bag and set a few things on the counter. She looked in the mirror.

"Goodbye, Max. It's been real," she said taking off the red-framed glasses and putting in her contacts.

Lena stretched and yawned. She opened her eyes and blinked rapidly.

"What did you do with my Auntie Max?" she whispered to the blonde woman sitting on the edge of the bed.

"She needed to go back home," Madeline replied with a wink. "You get to travel with your Mom now."

Lena sat up and gave her a big hug.

"So, can I call you Mom again?" she asked quietly.

Madeline laughed.

"Yep, and you can stop whispering."

Lena reached up and touched the shaved side of Madeline's hair.

"I seem to remember my Mom wore her hair in a ponytail. But, you know, this is a good look. You might want to keep it."

"We'll see how my sister feels about that," Madeline said.

Chapter Fifty-Four

The story hit global media as a triumph for women's rights. Talk show hosts wanted to interview the women who had been arrested but they all refused. Reporters approached Joanna and Magda for their perspective, but they were reticent. Social media blazed with comments and opinions.

Victory, like chocolate, can be addicting. As soon as word of the case dismissal hit the streets, millions of protestors thronged into city parks, spilled across roads, and engulfed legislative buildings. The police were outnumbered. The crowds anticipated the President would call in the army. Their mood grew jubilant as hours passed and nothing happened.

Music blared from apartment buildings; impromptu street parties sprang up; neighbors danced, cheered, and hugged. By the next morning, media drones transmitted images of a massive sit-in across the country – roads closed, businesses shut down. It was as if the nation was in a holding pattern.

No one could get in or out of the legislative buildings. The President and Daniel had spent the night at the White House, trapped by the groundswell of activity in the streets. Ryan and the President's other aides had been on phones and computers, trying to monitor movements and anticipate the protestors' next steps.

Ryan set up an emergency teleconference with as many members of Congress as he could reach.

"Some aren't answering," he told the President. "A few are stuck in their cars on the highway. Nothing's moving. If they don't have good network coverage where they are, they won't be on the call. All they've said is that you have to do something. And fast."

The President looked at Daniel.

"Get Frank here," the President said.

"But how?" Ryan said. "Everything's closed.

"He'll find a way," Daniel said. "Tell him it's urgent."

When Frank arrived, he was wearing sunglasses, a ballcap and faded jeans with a black t-shirt.

"Quite the disguise," the President said. "Glad you could make it."

"It's a mob scene out there," Frank said. "Like a big block party. Wasn't sure I'd get through but your assistant said it was urgent. What's up?"

The President glanced at Daniel, who cleared his throat, refusing to look at Frank.

"We've run out of options," he said.

"What do you mean?" Frank said.

"Our wives have got us by the balls," the President said.

"How?"

"Madeline found the photos," Daniel mumbled.

"Why you goddamn son of a bitch," Frank yelled, lunging for Daniel. He grabbed him by the throat, held him against the wall and landed several punches before the President intervened.

"Back off, Frank," he ordered. "This gets us nowhere. We have to move into damage control now and that's why you're here."

"No," Frank said.

"What do you mean, no? We're a team, remember. To the end."

"No," he repeated. "After all I've done for you. You had one job, Daniel. Destroy the photos, remember?"

He shook his head. "You two are on your own now. I'm outta here."

The door slammed behind him.

Daniel looked at the President.

"I don't think we have a choice. Where's the list?"

Ryan came back into the office just as the President was wrapping up his teleconference with Congress members.

"Look, I don't like it any more than you do," the President said. "But this is the only way we can restore order. We appear to give in, give them what they want, and in a few months, we try again. Deal?"

He scribbled a few notes on a piece of paper and handed it to Ryan.

Ryan skimmed the notes and headed to his office.

Jack read the media release in disbelief.

The government was committed to repealing all anti-abortion and anti-contraceptive legislation in the coming weeks. The President announced an immediate increase in daycare spaces and related funding. New legislation equalized salaries regardless of gender. The borders reopened to immigration and a family reunification program was established. The only explanation was a vague quote from the President.

"Congress recognizes that we may have moved too quickly toward the future. Therefore, we plan to give Americans time to learn more about our vision. Change is hard to accept but we believe citizens will ultimately support the direction we are heading."

Joanna was delighted when funding was restored to all human rights organizations across the country. It was also increased for social programs such as low-income housing and food banks.

"I guess you can head back to the newspaper office now, Jack," she said. "The tide has turned."

Daniel Power announced his retirement. When pressed by Jack in a phone interview, he said it was time for a change and ended the call.

The President submitted his letter of resignation to the Secretary of State and refused to speak with the press. The Speaker of the House agreed to become Acting President for the remainder of the term since the vice-president was still in a coma.

Jack couldn't understand the sudden change. He called Maggie.

"I'm coming over. Put the coffee on. Oh, and tell Hannah to pack her bag. We're going home."

"I keep waiting for the ball to drop," Jack said when he met with Maggie. "There's a piece of the puzzle missing. I can't figure it out."

Maggie sat back in her chair and watched him like a cat toying with a mouse.

"Do you need to know?" Maggie said.

"I suppose not, but I feel like something happened right under my nose and I missed it."

"Let it go, Jack."

"You know what it is, don't you?"

Maggie shrugged and sipped her coffee.

Chapter Fifty-Five

A week later, a media release from an anonymous source announced that Magdalen would appear at a press conference in Lafayette Square.

Media around the world collaborated to broadcast the event. Screens appeared in parks, stadiums, and concert halls. Crowds flooded into venues, singing songs, and wearing Magdalen t-shirts. As the designated time approached, people began to chant, "Magdalen, Magdalen, Magdalen." Families gathered in Lafayette Square called out, "Magdalen for President!"

At exactly 3 p.m., the crowds grew quiet. All eyes focused on the stage in the center of the park. Jack leaned against the back of the camera truck, watching and waiting.

A short woman with gray curly hair bounced up the steps to the stage. She was wearing jeans and a blue denim jacket over a white t-shirt emblazoned with a butterfly.

The crowd roared and applauded.

The woman raised her hands and signaled for people to be quiet.

She stepped up to the microphone and adjusted it to her height.

"I am…not Magdalen."

Confused muttering tumbled through the audience. She raised her voice, commanding attention.

"I have been asked to introduce Magdalen."

A group of women, men and children began to climb the stairs, gradually filling the stage. Maggie, Alicia, Joanna and five other women stood in the front row.

Maggie stepped up to the microphone again.

"As I said earlier, I am not Magdalen."

She paused as frustration swept across the faces in the square. She spread her arms wide and indicated the people behind her on the stage.

"*We* are Magdalen."

She turned her hands palms up and gestured at the cameras and the throngs of people in front of the stage.

"And so are you," she added.

People turned and looked at each other.

"Yes, take a good look at the person standing next to you. Who do you see? Do you notice what's different or what's the same?"

Her deep chuckle danced through the air.

"You see, we're the same in so many ways. We all have stories; we know what it is to be hurt, and to be held; to be loved and to be hated; to be believed and to be ignored. We have fears and dreams, secrets and challenges. We want to be respected and appreciated, but sometimes we forget how to respect and appreciate each other."

Jack was struck by the silence – thousands of people looking at each other with curiosity. The wind was cool, but the air felt warm. He couldn't find the right word, but he knew when he had felt like this before. In the delivery room right after Evy was born. As if time had stopped.

Alicia stepped up to the mike, her voice strong and compelling.

"The events of the last six months are the result of years, generations, centuries of struggle and hard work by those who came before us. Each time people pushed back against injustice, ground was gained. This time was different though, wasn't it? We learned to set aside differences and work together. The message is simple: together, we are strong. Using our combined talents and abilities, we can right any wrong and fix any problem. Divided - by gender, race, economics, education, religion, sexual orientation – we will fail."

Joanna spoke up.

"Who is Magdalen? Each one of us. People of all ages, genders and backgrounds. And it is our responsibility to work together to make our world a safe, welcoming, healthy, and sustainable home for all. Not just for you and your family. For the greater human family."

Maggie stepped forward again.

"This is just the beginning. There is much work ahead. Whenever you feel afraid, lost, or confused, remember today, and ask yourself one question: What would Magdalen do?"

Chapter Fifty-Six

Maggie straightened the tablecloth for the tenth time. The coffee was ready, and the muffins were cooling on the stove. She paced between the kitchen and the living room, peering out the bay window, looking for the car.

She glanced at the clock on the mantel. As she put the muffins on a plate, she heard car doors slam followed by the low tone of voices. She took off her apron and walked slowly to the front door, arriving just as her guests knocked.

She counted to five and opened the door.

Jack stood on the step with his mother. My daughter, Maggie thought. The two women stared at each other, neither one moving.

"Is this as s-s-strange for you as it is for me?" Maggie stammered.

Mary nodded.

Maggie swallowed hard and stepped back.

"Please come in," she said. "Make yourselves at home."

As Jack passed, he gave her a wink. Hannah gave her a big hug.

"I knew there was something special about you," she whispered.

I will not cry, I will not cry, Maggie told herself, as tears filled her eyes. She followed the others into the living room. Once they were all seated, she passed the muffins and poured coffee. No one spoke.

Maggie closed her eyes briefly and stepped into the silence.

"Thank you for coming," she said. "It feels unreal and awkward, but I want you to know how much I appreciate this moment."

Tears began to escape. She shook her head and sniffed.

"I promised myself this wouldn't happen. So much for willpower."

She noticed her daughter was smiling.

"You have a strong will, I take it," she said to Maggie.

"You betcha," Maggie said. "My claim to fame."

Her daughter reached out her hand.

"I'm Mary," she said, "and it's good to meet you."

Maggie took the outstretched hand in hers and cleared her throat.

"I'm Maggie, and I never thought I'd meet you."

Jack watched the two women closely. He glanced at Evelyn and back at his mother and grandmother.

"You know," he said, "I can see a resemblance. It's in the eyes, and the way you tip your head when you're talking."

"I do not," exclaimed Maggie, exaggerating the tilt of her head. Everyone laughed.

"Do you talk with your hands?" she asked Mary.

"All the time. The only reason I'm not is because I'm holding this cup."

"Better put it down before you spill," Jack said. "Remember what happened last night when you were talking to Hannah."

Mary set the cup on the table.

"I spilled my tea everywhere," she said. "Hannah told me she and Evelyn had been staying with you all that time, not knowing. My hands started to shake."

Maggie cleared her throat.

"I'm not sure how to proceed," she said, "but there are a few things I want to say. And you probably have questions."

She clasped her hands in her lap.

"I had a whole thing prepared in my mind, but it's all gone out the window. I just want you to know that I have always loved you," she said, looking at Mary.

"When I was pregnant, I talked to you all the time. I shared my dreams with you. You meant everything to me. In fact, there was a song I used to sing to you at night. Not really a lullaby, but I knew I would have to let you go when you were born, and I didn't want you to forget me. It goes like this."

Maggie began to hum and then sang, eyes closed, hands on her belly, rocking gently.

"You are my sunshine, my only sunshine…"

She stopped and opened her eyes. Mary, Hannah, and Jack were staring at her. Evelyn was awake, watching her closely.

"What?" she asked.

"That song," Mary said in a soft voice. "I used to sing it to my boys when they were babies."

"And I sing it to Evy," Jack added.

"Oh my," Maggie said.

They sat in silence until Evelyn began to gurgle and squawk.

"I need to feed her soon, so can I just go up to my room? I mean the guest room?" Hannah asked. "Do you want to hold her for a moment first?"

Maggie reached out her arms for the tiny bundle. Evelyn looked up at her, eyes deep and dark.

"Such a miracle babies are. I'd never held one until Hannah and Evelyn came to stay."

"You didn't get to hold me?" Mary asked.

Maggie shook her head, eyes focused on Evelyn.

"No, they wouldn't let me. They said it was better that way."

She looked at Mary.

"They didn't even tell me if you were a girl or a boy. I didn't know until Jack came to see me."

"Oh my God," Mary said. "I can't imagine."

Maggie gazed at Evelyn, caressing her cheek.

"None of that matters now," she said.

Chapter Fifty-Seven

Two weeks after his resignation, the former President left the White House unannounced and sped off into the countryside in his red sportscar.

At least I can arrive in style, he thought as he pulled into the long gravel driveway past the wrought-iron fence.

He grabbed his bags from the trunk and set them on the front porch of the two-story brick house. He rapped the brass knocker three times. With authority, he thought, straightening his shoulders.

Daniel opened the door.

"Andrew? What are you doing here?"

He glanced at the suitcases. "Are you moving in?"

"Can I come in? It's a bit chilly out here."

"Sure, be my guest."

Daniel stepped back and gestured for his stepbrother to come into the living room.

"Danny boy, it's good to see you. Sure could use a drink. Got anything handy?"

Daniel's face fell. He sat down in an armchair and held his head in his hands.

"Part of the deal," he muttered. "You know she divorced me. Not allowed to drink. Have to attend AA for three years or she will take this house too."

"You've got to be kidding. Have you got any money?"

Daniel nodded.

"She got the proceeds of the house in the city, but she did leave me one bank account, and she gives me a monthly allowance as long as I stay sober."

"That sucks. Those frickin' witches."

Daniel glanced up. "You too?"

His stepbrother nodded.

"You know how the prenup said I couldn't divorce her? Well, you didn't tell me she could divorce me. And she took it all. I've got nothing but my car. And the clothes in these bags."

"At least you've got wheels," Daniel said. "I'm not allowed off the property. She has a car pick me up for the AA meetings. The driver goes in with me, stands by the door, and brings me straight back after. Like I'm a kid. It's embarrassing."

"I've got a car," Andrew said. "Where you want to go?"

Daniel shook his head.

"Not a chance. She's got someone watching the house. One day I tried to sneak out the back gate, but as soon as I got close to the fence, an alarm sounded. Nearly shit my pants at the sound. I'm not doing that again."

Andrew rubbed the back of his neck.

"Any chance you can put me up for a bit until I can get my feet on the ground again?" he said. "It would be like the old days. You know, when we were kids. Only we wouldn't have to share a room."

Daniel stood up and shrugged.

"We'll see. So far the only person she's allowed inside the gate is the driver for my meetings. He brings me groceries once a week too. And it's all healthy crap. Vegetables and stuff. I hate cooking."

He went into the kitchen and poured two cups of coffee.

"Still take it black?"

"Yep. Thanks."

When he returned to the living room, his stepbrother was pacing back and forth in front of the window, hands clasped behind his back, eyes focused on the floor. Daniel set the cups on the table.

"I've been thinking about it, and I've got a plan," Andrew said. He turned toward Daniel, a grin spreading across his face like the sun coming out from behind a cloud.

"We'll call their bluff. It's been weeks, and nothing was sent to the media. They can't prove anything. And there's a statute of limitations, right? Look, you draw up the legal papers. We'll find Frank and get him to dig up something juicy that we can use as blackmail. We just have to show them who's boss and take back what's ours. What do you think, Danny boy?"

Daniel started to speak but was interrupted by a knock at the door.

A young man in a brown uniform handed Daniel an envelope.

"Daniel Power? Sign here."

Daniel signed and closed the door. He tore open the envelope and found two smaller ones inside.

"One for me, one for you," he said, handing one to Andrew.

They ripped them open and pulled out a single piece of paper with one typewritten line.

Their eyes met.

"We need Frank," they said in unison.

Chapter Fifty-Eight

Maggie studied her reflection in the floor-length mirror. She turned her head from side to side and shrugged.

"I think this looks better on you," she said, handing the red hat to Max.

"You're in Italy now, *cara mia*," Max said, setting the hat on her own head. "Maybe it's time to try something new. Besides, Lena and Madeline get in tonight. We need to celebrate."

"We'll celebrate when it's all over," Maggie said. She stepped back and took a long look at Max.

"You and your sister are so alike. I don't think I could tell you apart even standing side by side." She glanced at her watch. "It's time. Go get 'em, girl."

"You'll want these," Max said, smiling. She handed Maggie a small pair of binoculars.

As Max strolled out of the apartment, Maggie put on her sunglasses and opened the floor-to-ceiling glass doors. She stepped out onto the balcony, setting the binoculars on the patio table. She grasped the warm stone balustrade and looked out over the Piazza del Popolo.

Students, office workers and parents pushing buggies wandered by, chatting on cell phones. She couldn't hear the conversations, but it didn't matter. She didn't understand Italian. She was only interested in two well-dressed men at a small table in front of the coffee bar at the far end of the piazza.

Perching on a wrought-iron chair, she raised the binoculars for a better view. The gray-haired man rearranged his raincoat over the chair beside him and then gently tapped the other man's hand. She wished she were a fly on the table.

"You know, I could get used to this," Frank said.

Alessandro smiled. "My sister says we can keep the apartment as long as we want. Her contract in Florence has been extended so she's not coming back for a while."

Frank studied the gray-hued stone buildings that flanked the piazza. If those walls could talk, he thought, the stories they could tell – centuries of invasions, revolutions, power and influence. It was the ideal spot for a man with secrets – a town nestled among mountain ranges, tucked away in the heart of a foreign country where no one knew his face.

"We'll have to do something about my visa," he said.

Alessandro shrugged. "My cousin will take care of it."

He nudged Frank's arm and pointed across the piazza. Frank turned and watched a tall fashionista approach, her red leather boots clipping the cobblestones with attitude.

"I thought you liked men," Frank whispered.

"Oh, you know I do," Alessandro said, "but I also appreciate a woman with style."

As she came closer, Frank noticed she was wearing a red wide-brimmed hat, large sunglasses with red frames, and a fitted cream coat that brushed the top of her boots. Her gray hair was cropped on one side and shoulder-length on the other.

All eyes turned as she passed by. She seemed oblivious, but Frank gasped as if he'd been shot.

The woman walked into the bar, paid for a coffee, and leaned against the counter, twirling her sunglasses in her hand. As she sipped her drink, she half-turned and gazed around the piazza. He saw her dark eyes focus as they crossed his face.

She set her cup down on the counter and took a small envelope out of her large red shoulder bag. Readjusting her sunglasses, she walked out into the piazza.

As she passed them, her heel caught, and she tripped. She fell forward, bracing herself with one hand on their table. Alessandro reached out to help her.

"*Stai bene signora?* Are you okay?"

She waved him off.

"*Tutto bene, tutto bene, grazie.*"

Straightening up, she brushed her coat with one hand. They watched her stroll across the piazza and disappear around a corner. Frank stared after her, mind racing, barely breathing.

Alessandro glanced at him.

"What's wrong?"

He noticed a small envelope wedged between their coffee cups and picked it up.

"Who's Jimmy?"

Frank snatched the envelope with trembling fingers.

Inside, he found a piece of paper. A single typewritten line.

Magdalen is always watching.

Alessandro watched Frank's lips move as he read the note, the color draining from his face.

Maggie lowered the binoculars and set them on the table.

That's it, she thought. That's the moment right there. When life, as he knows it, ends.

And mine begins.

Acknowledgements

Six years after I typed the first word of *Make No Mistake* on my tablet, here we are. I may have been alone with Maggie and her friends initially, but no book is ever published without a wide circle of support.

Special thanks to Ralph Morgan, my first and final reader always.

And to Mary Burbidge, the "Diana" to my "Anne", who saw potential in my manifesto and insisted that I write Maggie's story.

I wrote the first chapters in 2019, at a writing retreat led by author Jean E. Pendziwol on Porphyry Island, Lake Superior, in northern Ontario. The combination of beauty, inspiration, and her encouragement was the catalyst I needed to begin this project. Her belief in me as a writer kept me writing.

My early beta readers – Dr. Jo-Anne Muise Lawless, Mary Burbidge, Bruce Madole and Ralph Morgan – and the participants in Brian Henry's Creative Writing Intensive helped me shift and shape the story into what is contained in these pages.

During long walks and talks, Debbra Mikaelsen nudged me toward releasing the chapters as serial fiction on Substack. It was the members of the Penticton Writing Circle, in particular Angela Douglas, Faye Arcand and Gordon Dawson, who insisted that *Make No Mistake* leap from the pages of Substack into the paperback you now hold in your hands.

And so, to all my readers, thank you for being part of Maggie's journey.

Bonus Section For Readers

1. About the author
2. Discussion questions for book clubs
3. Suggested reading
4. Author Q & A

About the Author

Julie Wise is a writer from British Columbia, Canada. Her poetry, fiction and nonfiction have appeared in multiple publications and in two anthologies. Her writing focuses on the connections that define our lives, shape our perspectives and form our memories.

Make No Mistake is her debut novel.

Discussion Questions For Book clubs

1. As you read the book, which character did you most identify with? What made that character feel real to you?

2. There are many twists and turns in the story. Which one surprised or affected you the most? Why?

3. If you could sit down with Maggie over coffee, what would you like to ask her, or share with her?

4. What is your biggest takeaway from the story? Is there anything in the story that changed your perspective, or inspired you in some way?

5. Maggie and Alicia talk about being invisible as older women. If this is part of your experience, share some examples of when you have felt invisible and how you handled it.

6. The book clubs in *Make No Mistake* mention a wide range of books for their discussions. Which books surprised you? Are there other books you think should be included?

7. How did you feel about the ending? Did you want more or were you satisfied with the outcome?

8. If you had written this book, what would you have done differently?

9. What do you feel is the main message of the book?

10. When you look at the world around you today, after reading *Make No Mistake*, do you feel change is possible? What are some steps you can take to make a difference, within your book club, and within your community?

Suggested Reading

Adichie, C.N. (2017). *Dear Ijeawele or A Feminist Manifesto in Fifteen Suggestions.* Knopf Canada.

Alcott, L.M. (1868, 1869). *Little Women.* Roberts Brothers.

Armstrong, S. (2019) *Power Shift: The Longest Revolution.* House of Anansi Press.

Bennet, B. (2020). *The Vanishing Half.* Riverhead Books.

Eltahawy, M. (2019). *The Seven Necessary Sins for Women and Girls.* Beacon Press.

Evaristo, B. (2019). *Girl, Woman, Other.* Grove Atlantic.

Kendall, M. (2020). *Hood Feminism: Notes From The Women That A Movement Forgot.* Viking.

Kendi, I.X. (2017). *Stamped From The Beginning.* Bold Type Books.

Kimmel, M. (2013). *Angry White Men.* Nation Books.

Klein, N. (2017). *No Is Not Enough.* Knopf Canada.

Lamb, C. and Yousafzai, M. (2013). *I Am Malala.* Little, Brown and Company.

Landsberg, M. (2011). *Writing The Revolution.* Second Story Press.

Lloyd-Roberts, S. and Morris, S. (2016). *The War on Women and the Brave Ones Who Fight Back.* Simon & Schuster.

Maracle, L. (1990) *Bobbi Lee, Indian Rebel.* Women's Press Literary.

Mitchell, M. (1936). *Gone With The Wind.* Macmillan.

Montgomery, L.M. (1908). *Anne of Green Gables.* L.C. Page & Co.

Munsch, R. (1980). *The Paper Bag Princess.* Annick Press.

Rand, A. (1957). *Atlas Shrugged.* Random House.

Steinem, G. (2019). *The Truth Will Set You Free, But First It Will Piss You Off.* Random House.

Traister, R. (2018). *Good and Mad: The Revolutionary Power of Women's Anger.* Simon & Schuster.

Woolf, V. (1929) *A Room of One's Own.* Hogarth Press.

Author Q & A

How did you come up with the idea for *Make No Mistake*?

In 2022, the U.S. Supreme Court officially overturned Roe v Wade, eliminating women's constitutional rights to abortion. As early as 2018, however, the writing was on the wall as individual states began to rule that abortion was illegal. I was shocked that fifty years of progress could be so easily overruled. By 2019, I was outraged at the way women's choices, and control over their own bodies and lives, were being deliberately eroded by men in power. I wrote what became the manifesto in the middle of the book.

At the time, I thought the manifesto was a stand-alone piece, but characters and a storyline quickly emerged. Maggie arrived first, full of rage and experience, soon followed by the other characters who feature in her life. They insisted I write their story. I obliged.

Given that you wrote the novel in 2019, how do you explain the parallels between your fictional story and recent political events in the United States?

As I wrote the draft of *Make No Mistake*, I did a lot of reading and research. I began to see the potential fallout of existing changes to women's rights, and I understood how easily that could shift to human rights in general. There is a quote in the book about how women's empowerment is intertwined with respect for human rights (Mahnaz Afkhami). It wasn't hard to imagine a future where everything we take for granted in a democracy could be dismantled and destroyed. At the time of writing, I was speculating, never imagining how easily fiction could become reality.

After January 2025, many events that I had written about six years earlier suddenly became headline news. Congress meeting in the dead of night, baby bonus to increase the birth rate (as daycare funding was cut to ensure the woman stayed home), extreme fines and prison sentences for doctors performing abortions, investigations into miscarriages, a snitch line and deportations of immigrants and American-born citizens, separation of children from parents, and on it went. Each day, I saw more parallels between what I had written as fiction and what was quickly becoming the new "normal". That's when I decided to release chapters of *Make No Mistake* on Substack. I thought Maggie's story could inspire readers to work together for the change they wanted.

What kind of research did you do for this novel?

I did a lot of reading and research while I was writing. Most of the resistance approaches Maggie uses in the story have been implemented with success elsewhere in the world. For example, in 1975, Icelandic women declared a one-day strike. They did not work outside the home, do any housework, or childcare. They gathered in the centre of Reykjavik for a day-long rally where they listened to speakers, sang and talked to each other about how to achieve gender equality.

Iceland's Parliament passed a law guaranteeing equal rights the following year. In 1980, the first female president in the world was democratically elected in Iceland.

In *Make No Mistake*, butterflies become a symbol of the resistance movement. In the 1960's, three sisters in the Dominican Republic joined other activists to resist the dictatorship of Rafael Trujillo. They were known as *Las Mariposas* (butterflies). This is where the idea came from for the design that Shelley and Lena use for the movement.

And as recently as May 2025, I discovered that people were connecting in an online book club to read banned books and books about resistance. Just like the book clubs that Maggie and Madeline establish in *Make No Mistake*.

Which character do you most identify with?

That's like asking a parent which child is their favorite. All of the characters in *Make No Mistake* are vivid and real for me. I could see them as I was writing and hear their voices. Each one had a story to tell, and it was my role to put that story to paper. I hope I did them justice.

Did you plot out the whole story before writing? Did you know what would happen to the characters or how the story would end?

Since I began with the manifesto, I did not know the beginning or the ending of the story. I knew the manifesto would be central to the novel, but the rest evolved as the characters came forward. In fact, the beginning changed multiple times in later drafts. So did the ending.

What is your writing process like?

In a first draft, as the story is unfolding, I try to commit to writing about 1500 words a day on average. I find I do my best writing in the morning. If I can put in about four hours of writing, I consider it a good day. But writing for me also takes the form of gardening, walking, spending time in nature, doodling and daydreaming. Everyday life is part of my writing process because I think a writer's brain is always trying to untangle the knots in a story, even while washing dishes or sleeping (especially when sleeping).

What are you working on next?

I have another novel that is close to final edits. It focuses on nature and environmental issues, and like *Make No Mistake*, has a message of hope. I also have a novella nearly ready to share, and it is a magical thriller (if there is such a category).

And as always, poems scattered like petals here and there.